A Sip
of
Absinthe

A Sip of Absinthe
Copyright © 2019 by T.F. Feldman

This is a work of fiction. Names, characters, places and incidents are the products of the author's imagination or are used fictitiously. Any resemblance to actual events, locales, or persons, living or dead, is entirely coincidental.

All rights reserved. No part of this book may be used or reproduced in any form, electronic or mechanical, including photocopying, recording, or scanning into any information storage and retrieval system, without written permission from the author except in the case of brief quotation embodied in critical articles and reviews.

Cover art: *Café Table with Absinthe*, Vincent van Gogh (1853 - 1890), Paris, 1887; marked as public domain, more details on Wikimedia Commons: https://commons.wikimedia.org/wiki/File:Caf%C3%A9tafel_met_absint_-_s0186V1962_-_Van_Gogh_Museum.jpg

Book design by The Troy Book Makers
Printed in the United States of America
The Troy Book Makers • Troy, New York • thetroybookmakers.com

To order additional copies of this title,
contact your favorite local bookstore
or visit www.shoptbmbooks.com

ISBN: 978-1-61468-501-2

A Sip of Absinthe

T. F. FELDMAN

PROLOGUE

Her father was sorry she saw it, it's not something you want your four-year-old to witness. He was driving back with her on icy roads and she was strapped into a child's safety seat in the back with her birthday cake on her lap. The cake had her favorite green mint ice cream, and he wanted to get home quickly before it melted. The January sky was already dark at 5:00 p.m. when the street lights went on, all of them except for the one on the corner by the United Methodist Church of Resurrection leaving it in the dark. No one could possibly see the black ice on the macadam by the Church. An oncoming car slid over the ice into his lane and he reflexively jammed his brakes but still couldn't avoid the crash. The left front end of his car got crushed like a tin can and he spun around in a three-sixty. Even though they were severely jolted, neither he nor Adrianna were hurt, and miraculously, they weren't killed. Looking out the window from her safety seat, Adrianna stared wide-eyed at the body of the woman who had been thrown from the oncoming car, not more than ten feet away. She was face up in a full length green dress, barefoot. Her shoes somehow got lost during her fateful end. She looked up at Adrianna with a Mona Lisa smile but Adrianna was never sure it was a smile.

Looking for something?

Knowing what to look for can be hard.

If you knew, you could recognize it.

But if you don't know what to look for, even when you encounter it unwittingly, how would you know you found it?

CHAPTER ONE

A Midwest University Campus, 2015

He must have suffered with a facial disorder and severe case of acne. Looking at him was uncomfortable, his distorted, discolored face, and the left side of his upper lip which twitched spasmodically. You pitied him and felt ashamed you had to look away. He sat in the lecture hall in the far right section of the amphitheater—never the larger middle section where everyone else sat—with his head down out of a habit he learned to avoid incredulous and pitiable stares. He kept himself private; he was in his seat before anyone came, he was the last to leave.

He was drawing in his sketch pad even after the class in Psychology 202 began, and as usual, no one noticed him. The young professor sporting his new reddish goatee in his sweater and corduroys, took his position behind the small polished lectern in front, carefully laid his notes on it, and welcomed the undergraduates back after the Thanksgiving holiday. He was disappointed more students had not signed up for his course: at least half the seats in the small amphitheater were empty. He began with, "Any questions about Maslow's hierarchy of needs before we move on to humanistic psychology?"

Someone asked what was the difference between self-actualizing and self-image actualizing.

"Who can answer that?"

In the second row, an international student who looked like he might be from India, raised his hand.

"Yes," the professor acknowledged him.

In a strong foreign accent, the international student stood up and began, "Well, I would like to say in the very first place . . . ." He continued on in smug self satisfaction, and although he answered the question, it was clear he only wanted to demonstrate how smart he was. But he made his brownie points by needlessly and excessively demeaning the girl who had asked the question who now shrunk into her seat shamefaced. He finished and took his seat with a smirk.

"Good, we can move on to see how that became a foundation for humanistic psychology," the prof said looking down at his notes. At that moment, the one with the face stopped sketching and spoke out, keeping his face partially hidden.

"Professor, I'd like to answer that question too."

"Certainly." The prof studied his notes. He didn't want to forget to cover something this time.

In voice and manner, the sketcher made a parody of the international student. "And I too would like to say in the very first place . . ." intentionally mimicking the other's way of starting. He tore the answer apart as well as the international student. He launched into a diatribe about being true to one's self and not another's ideal of what you should be, the timeless quest to truly know one's metamorphosing self, the dangers of conflating the virtue of self-actualization and the reality of self-actualization, and then ended with a comparison to Confucian jen and yi and a Buddhist's view of karma, all with detailed citations. He was academic and impressive but no one in the lecture hall understood a word of what he said. The young professor couldn't either but pretended he did. By the end, the international student had been so surgically eviscerated and thoroughly emasculated, he wasn't going to answer a question that way again—not in that class at least.

The pretentious professor perked up. "Very interesting! Those comparisons and parallels were not in the assigned readings. Where did you get all that?"

"Some extra reading," the sketcher replied not looking at anyone and barely hiding his ennui. He said what he wanted to say and wasn't about to help the professor.

"Well, maybe we can talk about it later," the professor replied thinking it might be something he could use for his first book if he understood it better.

When the hour was up, everyone began to close their laptops and gather their things. The sixty or so undergraduates started to file out and move up the two raked aisles that flanked the middle section of the amphitheater toward the rear exit doors at the top. An overweight girl with a constant chip on her shoulder and ready to confront anyone about anything, glanced over at the sketcher as she passed his row and thanked him. She said that other guy, the international student, was mean spirited and has a reputation for answering questions like that—at other people's expense—and had to be put in his place. "The power to us, the invisible ones!" she exhorted and raised her clenched hand in salute. He didn't look up but allowed himself a private smile, nodded slightly and kept sketching, flipping back and forth to a different sheet in his sketch pad, adding, erasing, absorbed in his work.

Behind the overweight girl and paying her no attention, was pretty Adrianna donning a pink headband over her blond hair. She slowed her pace and hesitated for a moment as she passed by his row and her demeanor subtly changed from one of confidence to something more tentative and cautious. Whatever was on her mind passed and she continued to walk up the aisle to the exit doors and left. Outside, she met some fraternity boys, each trying to outdo the other and vie for her attention, and she responded flirtatiously, enjoying all the attention and nonsense, and she put aside, for the moment at least, whatever had affected her when she passed by the sketcher's row.

That was Tuesday. Classes meet on Tuesdays, Thursdays and Fridays, and Adrianna couldn't stop thinking about that class. She was a bit anxious at Thursday's class. She turned in her seat for a furtive look to see if he sat where he was the last time. She hadn't noticed him before. With twenty thousand students sprawled over acres and acres of this Midwest university campus, anyone could stay hidden. Besides, she wouldn't have noticed him even if it were a small college. Not that she didn't care about others, she did, or needed to be the center of attention, which she often was, but rather she was uncertain of herself in a way that sometimes held her back.

At the end of class, she walked up the aisle but when she reached the exit doors, she stopped and moved aside to let those behind her get out. She continued to stand there mumbling to herself even after they had all gone. She nodded her head to herself and turned around. In measured steps, she walked down to his row and stood in the aisle while he kept sketching in his worn sketch pad, the kind with spiral rings on top, absorbed in his work, apparently oblivious to this very pretty girl standing close by and looking in his direction.

She waited a few moments for him to look up, feeling more uncomfortable the longer she waited. She didn't know what to expect. She waited in the aisle and felt like others before they stand up and make a speech in front of a room full of people. Despite her anxiety, she had decided to speak to him, it would be the right thing for her to do. But as she stood there, she thought more about it. Maybe this wasn't such a good idea. He was so engrossed in his sketching he didn't even know she was standing there and she'd really have to interrupt him to get his attention. She was about to turn around and leave, when without any conscious thought, words sprung up on their own volition.

"Excuse me . . . excuse me," she had to repeat it and clear her dry throat. "I wanted to thank you," she said as loudly as she could muster in order to gain his attention. He stopped sketching and deliberately took his time to look up from his work, and slowly . . . very slowly . . . turned toward her—Oh that face!—turned toward her so she saw it fully face on. He looked at her and assessed his intruder. He then granted her a moment of his now-interrupted time and attention, which made her feel inconsequential and even more insecure.

"I . . . I . . . I wanted to thank you," she managed to get out.

She never saw his face so clearly and closely as she did standing there in the aisle and it affected her like it did everyone else. No one expects to see something so abnormal in a normal setting, something so unnatural.

"For what you said I mean. I was the one who asked the question about self-actualizing and self-image actualizing last time, you know, with the international student."

She had trouble coming up with the words. She was repulsed to look at him and wished she hadn't stopped. It was too late now and she didn't want to be rude so she concentrated on looking at his eyes.

"I had a legitimate question and he made it seem like I was stupid. I'm not stupid and he shouldn't have made it seem like I was. He was very selfish and nasty. I just wasn't sure of the difference between them. I don't think he was so right either but he said it so confidently I was afraid to say anything. I shouldn't have been so insecure and he really hurt me. But then you started to talk and somehow you . . . I don't know how to describe it and I have to confess I couldn't follow a word of what you said. But you cut him down to size and put him in his place for putting me down and being so cruel. So thank you. That's what I wanted to tell you. Thank you."

She looked at his eyes so she wouldn't have to look at his face. He knew she was uncomfortable. He looked back at her, but not just her eyes. He took her in, breathed her in, all of her: her voice and the words she used, her demeanor standing in the aisle, what she wore, and the large, irregularly shaped, fawn colored freckle on the right side of her neck. He made a mental note and took his time before he said anything. She stood waiting uncomfortably and disoriented in the aisle. He finally spoke.

"Don't thank me for it. He created a disturbance. I fixed it. That's all it was. He shouldn't have done that to you, and he shouldn't do that to anyone."

She apparently had interrupted him with an inconsequential or needless triviality which took him away from his work, and now regretted she disturbed him.

"Well I only wanted . . . ." She started to say more but didn't realize he wasn't finished since he had paused so long before he went on.

"Things aren't what they seem. What I said was part true and part made up. I mixed phony facts with fallacious arguments and no one listened carefully. Besides, they couldn't recognize what was right from what wasn't anyway . . . a common human failing."

He paused again and she looked down at his sketch pad. She was sorry for him. It must be hard for him to talk to someone close up, especially a good looking girl. She was glad she turned back to thank him and be kind to someone so pitiable. She was about to leave with that good feeling when he again continued after another long pause.

"I am trusting you with that small confession about my making some of it up. I'd appreciate your not telling anyone. Not your suitemates or family, or anyone. Do you think you can do that?" He dared her to keep it secret and then added, "I shouldn't have told you any of that."

She didn't answer but moved her laptop as if it might slip from her grasp. He was breathing her in. It wasn't supposed to work this way she thought. She braved herself to do the right thing and give her thanks to a stranger who turned out to be horrendous looking and must be socially inept. He ought to accept her thanks humbly and not make demands on her. Who does he think he is? She was talking like this to herself without saying anything, mumbling almost, and then she nodded. "Okay . . . yes. I guess I can keep your secret."

She left thinking she just spoke to someone who under any other circumstances she never would have spoken to, only to be kind and thank him for something that didn't really require any thanks—and do a good deed on her part! Instead of getting a quick shy or humble "you're welcome", he confronted her very unexpectedly which she neither anticipated nor appreciated. Boys have always craved her attention but this ugly one didn't care at all; he completely and unpleasantly rebuffed her proudly given gratitude. He wasn't obsequious as he should have been nor was he impressed with her looks, at least as far as she could tell. Maybe that's because she was so obviously out of his reach she thought. Anyway, she wanted to thank him and did what she knew was right and that's the end of it, no reason to speak to him nor look at that face again.

But inwardly, something began to stir.

The next class was Friday and when it was over, she started up for the doors. Though she had determined not to speak to him, she peremptorily blurted out from the aisle even while he was absorbed in his drawing.

"Why did you tell me you made up part of your answer last time? You don't know me and even so you told me a secret you made me promise to keep. I said I would but now I think it wasn't very nice of you to ask that of me, to obligate me that way to keep a secret. I was being nice to you to thank you for what you did. And, I might add, you weren't very appreciative of my doing that!"

She said exactly what she was thinking with a rush of courage which even took her by surprise, and she boastfully congratulated herself for saying the right thing at the right time, instead of later realizing what she should have said but didn't. She continued to stand there feeling good for having spoken out but didn't know whether the episode was over or was she expected to wait for his response.

He again took his time to look up and the left side of his upper lip began to twitch spasmodically. She didn't know what got into her! She was suddenly deflated and wished she hadn't said anything at all. Now she was looking at that face again, and a lip that twitched even more than last time, trying to avert her eyes and not look at it in that long moment before he finally spoke. Her discomfort grew the longer it took him to say something as if he did it on purpose, knowing it made her more uneasy the more he kept her waiting.

"You seem somewhat upset," he finally said haughtily, "as if you did something—noble?—and I didn't acknowledge it the way you expected. Is that it?"

It was only then, when he realized just how uncomfortable she had become, that he looked down to spare her having to see his face.

Wait a minute, she thought, I'm in the right here, not he! Why is he making me feel like I did something wrong? When was the last time a girl, a pretty girl, stopped to talk to him? She didn't answer but turned and marched off without realizing he touched something lurking inside her. He's weird, an ingrate and rude so she's not going to talk to him again!

She avoided him at the next class which was a clear sign of "Dead End" ahead. However, at the class after that, undaunted, or just without acknowledging any road signs, he looked up from his drawing when she passed his row and asked for her opinion about his sketch.

"Excuse me?" She could have ignored his request, kept walking and thrown up another sign, i.e., "Road Ends", but she didn't.

"I want to show you something and I'd like your opinion as a girl, as a young woman. That's someone I'm not, in case you haven't noticed." He was cordial today and hardly as arrogant as he was the first two times though a little nervous around her.

"Thank you, but no thank you," she curtly replied and continued up the aisle. She could have said nothing, not even the "no thank you", but she was brought up to be polite and always respond to or at least acknowledge someone when they spoke to her and not totally ignore them. That would have been bad manners on her part even if they didn't deserve the courtesy of her reply.

"Please . . . wait," he said.

He stood up facing her and noticed she wore a mint green headband holding her hair back, a green that matched the color of her eyes. She stopped and turned around to listen which her upbringing mandated. It wasn't in her makeup to snub anyone.

"Look, this is hard for me, very hard. I'm a very private person." He paused before resuming. "I don't have any female friends. But since it looks like we're going to be friends, we have to be brutally honest with each other. I'll start. You're pretty... you're very pretty. You know that and I know that. Lots of people know that. Me, I am not pretty. My face is grotesque and hard to look at. I know that... you know that. Lots of people know that. If I say you're good looking or pretty, that's not a compliment. I'm not about to ask you out. It's merely a statement of fact. That's all. You are pretty. If you say my face is repulsive, it's not an insult and it doesn't make me feel bad. It's a fact. My looks don't define me. I know what I look like whether you say it or not. It's not like you'd be reminding me of something I forgot. So, be brutally honest with yourself and with me. Always. It's the only way. And another thing, you don't have to look at my face when we talk, it's okay, I know. That'll make it easier for you. Okay?"

She was surprised and unsettled by his punch to her equilibrium. How can he talk so freely about his face? She was uncomfortable with it even if he wasn't. Be friends with this ugly, arrogant loner? She can't bear to look at him. She wanted to extricate herself, turn around and escape, but she couldn't bring herself to say no, nor could she permit herself to ignore him either. At a total loss of what to say or what to do, and just to have an exit line, she said, "Sure, fine, okay," and turned and left. She didn't look at his sketch.

CHAPTER TWO

Since she was a little girl, her mother drilled into Adrianna, *ad nauseum,* the importance of good looks and Adrianna was lucky to be pretty and had to take advantage of it. It was who she was and the most important thing for her in finding the right young man. If she heard it once, she heard it a thousand times: the good looking girl gets the good looking guy. Adrianna didn't want to disappoint her mother so she tolerated and embraced her mother's neurotic insistence and even got the nose job her mother demanded and strove to emulate the look of a model. She kept herself up to date with fashion magazines and adorned herself with funky or colorful headbands—her signature statement which said she was indeed model-like. She was flawless in complexion, blond, green eyed and trim, an avid jogger with a statuesque figure, a top student and liked by her friends.

Bright enough to know something was amiss. That's not who she really was but it was what she was taught to show. There was something she hadn't figured out and it troubled her like she was standing in front of a thin curtain but couldn't see through it to make out what was there, something tied to her fears.

The friendly girl-next-door persona masked those hidden fears and occasional nightmares. Only her family knew; not even her best friend and suitemate Samantha suspected. Her father thought it was because of the car accident when she was four and he blamed himself for that. Adrianna could never understand why he blamed himself when it was clear to everyone it wasn't his fault; a guilt, she thought, which pushed him from her and drove him closer to her sister Charlotte.

Everyone in the family knew about Adrianna's visions of the dead woman in a green dress lying on the road looking straight up at Adrianna, her shoes scattered to the side. But Adrianna told only Charlotte about her fear that the dead woman was always nearby, about to grab her.

When she was young, everyone else had gone out for the evening and Charlotte came back late. Adrianna had been left alone in the house. She was scared to look into any room because the dead woman would be standing there... waiting... slowly approaching Adrianna, her arms reaching out for her. So she spent the night until Charlotte came home, in her pajamas sitting on a big club chair which she pulled up to the livingroom window, her cheek pressed to the window to be sure she wouldn't see into the house, counting the seconds out loud until Charlotte came home. She was terrified. She couldn't turn around, the barefoot woman would be there. When Charlotte finally came home, Adrianna ran to the bathroom; she had held herself in waiting for someone to come home, afraid to walk through the house alone.

And there was the fear of climbing the stairs to go to her bedroom at night. She told Charlotte she was scared to look behind her on the stairs. The dead woman was only a few steps below, climbing up and gaining, about to grab her leg, and when she did, something terrible would happen. So she ran up the stairs—fast. She kept her head down and she stared only at the few steps in front so she wouldn't accidentally catch a glimpse of what was behind her. Above all, she made absolutely certain she didn't look in the oval hallway mirror in case she might inadvertently see a reflection of the dead woman there.

The Bittfields, her parents, knew most but not all of this. They had been high school sweethearts and married a few years before Charlotte was born; Adrianna was born five years later. Mrs. Bittfield had been a beautiful young woman whose good looks Adrianna inherited and was her mother's favorite; Charlotte took after her not so good looking father and was his favorite.

Charlotte was the opposite of Adrianna: humdrum and uninspired in both looks and life. She lived at home with the Bittfields and worked in a boring, entry level job at an accounting firm right out of college while doing the bookkeeping for her father's small plumbing supply business. No expert on the subject of sex, she slept with one guy one time, and he then broke up with her. Alas, they both knew her love life was to be lived vicariously through Adrianna, and so they talked about Adrianna's boyfriends freely and often. Charlotte asked Adrianna about her current boyfriend Julian.

"You've been seeing Julian pretty regularly but you don't talk that much about him. What does that mean?"

"I don't know. Any advice?" Adrianna asked.

"I wish had some, but I don't. What is it?"

"I'm not sure," Adrianna said, "I'm not sure. I'd like to be closer to him, but I just don't know. I don't feel any chemistry. I don't know if it feels right. I don't know what it should feel like."

"Well, I know you," Charlotte said. "You never want to hurt anyone's feelings but that's no reason to stay with him, if that's the only reason. He isn't one of your stray dogs or cats you take in."

"Well, until I figure it out, I'm not going to drop Julian or make a commitment either."

Afterward and unsatisfied she couldn't come to a decision about Julian, the ugly guy from class came to mind even though she didn't want to think about him. He annoyed her, she knew that, but why? That wasn't so clear. He's nervy, arrogant and self assured, and not humble which he ought to be. Yet her experience with boys also told her he was a little awkward or nervous around her. How incongruous. Is this the first time for him to have anything to do with a girl? At his age? Did she want to become friends with him? He seemed to think so. Did she do anything that encouraged him? She thought she ought to be careful and not encourage him, that wouldn't be right. She didn't want to hurt him, he must be hurting enough underneath that face even if he doesn't show it. But if you disregard his face, what he said was ... well ... different, honest, and he was polite even if way too forthright. He was at home in his skin while she was not.

How odd she thought: he was arrogant but not so much with her. She decided she should talk to him next time. It would be kind of her to talk to someone when no one else did, and she could spare a few minutes after class as long as no one else was around to see them. And something else attracted her. She thought it might be some sort of fascination, or just someone who didn't fawn over her, or whatever. She didn't know what it was that drew her to this strange one but there was an unseen, unrecognizable connection that she never experienced before.

CHAPTER THREE

Adrianna was in her seat readying herself for today's class amidst the chatter of others killing time getting in a little conversation or catching up on texts, emails and the current vogue of social media before class started. She looked over to where he sat and studied him. There he was—drawing. What was he doing? No one sat near him; he didn't talk to anyone; and other than that one time, he didn't participate in class. He was invisible unless you got up close and caught sight of him when he looked up from his sketching.

The class started and it seemed longer than usual to Adrianna. When it was finally over, she purposely took a long time getting her things together so she could be the last one to leave. Everyone was in the aisles nearing the exit doors except for the young professor who also stayed behind and made his way over to him. She couldn't hear what they said until she got closer when she heard him talking to the professor.

"It would be better for you if I didn't write it down," the sketcher said. "You may want to take notes, otherwise you might be accused of plagiarism," and then he added, "you know, plagiarism—copying someone else's work and passing it off as your own?"

"You're right, yes, of course, thank you, thank you," the young professor said and jotted down a few notes. "The way how you show more meaning to some of these things, it's really quite remarkable. It's so plain the way you lay it out. I can't take things for granted anymore. One more minute, please. I want to see if I wrote this down right."

He opened up his notepad and read what he had just written, "You said experiential knowledge, even when supported by trusted criteria, is always—what was that?"

"Always temporal."

"Right, always temporal," and the professor corrected his notes, "always temporal and should not necessarily be taken as fact. If we accessed avenues of inquiry beyond our perceived abilities or norms, and paid more attention to details—even seemingly unimportant or incongruous details—explanations of behavior and our experiences would stand out and emerge, altering our preconceptions? Right?"

"Close enough," he said, wanting the professor to simply leave, thinking he misunderstood half of it, and the other half was baloney he made up for his own amusement.

The prof turned around and walked up to the doors and added another note while Adrianna went over to the sketcher's row. She was unsure if he saw her standing in the aisle as he began to work on a sketch. She fought off her nervousness, took a breath and spoke up to get his attention.

"What are you drawing? Is that what you wanted me to see last time?" she said innocently, clearly making a friendly overture and putting up a "Road Open" sign.

As if he had hoped—or perhaps knew?—she would stop, he said, "Yes, I can show you if you like," and he motioned for her to come closer. She continued to stand in the aisle and didn't take either of the two empty seats between them although she moved a little nearer. She avoided his face by looking at the sketch pad he was reaching for. He put it on the writing arm of the seat to his left and opened it to the page with the sketch. It was a pencil drawing of a woman's evening dress. She looked at it from the aisle, inched a bit closer and leaned over to get a better look.

"You did that? It's quite professional, really good, I mean it." She had no idea what she had expected to see but certainly not a sketch of a woman's evening dress.

"Do you like it? Would you wear that? Remember, it's not finished yet." He spoke as if they had known each other for a long time, not like the way he spoke to her before and obviously not with the arrogance he just showed the professor. He's changed, she thought, what made him change? He's friendly and more assured with me, and I like that.

"Yes and yes," she said. "It doesn't show the color. I'd like to see it in color. I think a pale green bodice would be nice with a cream or white skirt."

"Like the color of the headband you wore last time?"

He noticed that. Is he gay? "Yes, like that green. Is this what you do? Draw? Is that your design? Where did you learn that?" She was genuinely intrigued.

"We can talk about that some other time," he answered, evidencing a polite end to that last particular inquiry.

"What are those over there?" she pointed to loose sheets tucked in a flap on the inside cover of his sketchbook, aged brittle sheets which had been torn from another sketchbook.

"Someone sent them to me. They're sketches of dresses drawn twenty five years ago. I refer to them from time to time. A good idea is a good idea even if it's an old one."

He took one out to show her. She looked at it but quickly closed her eyes and grabbed hold of the top of the seat nearest her for support. She was dizzy and queasy.

"Are you alright?"

"Yes, pretty much." It was an unsure-of-herself answer. "I think I got dizzy or something for a second leaning over to look at that. I hope I don't develop migraines. My sister gets migraines and that's how it started, getting dizzy."

She left out she had one of her unsettling visions of the dead woman lying on the street. He thought he detected something more troubling than her just getting dizzy.

"Are you sure you're okay? You seem worried or something. Is there something I can do? I'm pretty good at helping people, hard as that it is to believe."

She didn't answer and he decided to let it pass. She wondered how he saw that, no one does when she has those demonic visions. Suddenly, the freckle on her neck began to itch and she rubbed it making it redder. Her freckle had never itched her before.

"I brought lunch," he said.

He took out a brown paper bag from a backpack on the other side of his seat, a paper bag that had been used before. He opened it and took out two wrapped sandwiches. One was in brown paper like the bag it came out of and had grease marks, the kind butter might leave behind. The other was wrapped in neat, crisp, white glossy paper artistically folded. He put them in front of him.

"Please, sit down. We can share this. Actually, I had some of it before so you can eat what's left here. There is a half left of each of these two sandwiches. I have an apple." He took out a Granny Smith apple from the bag.

"No. No thank you," and she began to move back to the aisle. She found herself a little lightheaded and spoke more slowly, thinking about her words more.

"You know in Nigeria," he said, "it's a sign of rudeness not to accept someone's offer to share a meal in their home. There are other cultures too where it would be a real slap in the face. I don't think you were ever rude to anyone in your life, at least not knowingly. Were you?" He paused as if to let her answer what was obviously a rhetorical question. "You don't want to start now, do you?" Another pause.

Adrianna didn't respond; she stood quietly in the aisle waiting for something. Whether it was his face, or the lead he took, or something else, she held herself back now even though she was the one who initiated the conversation.

"Please," he implored her gently. "Hardly anyone stops to talk to me after they see me the first time. I've learned to expect that so I usually turn my back on them and don't give them a chance to prove me wrong. But in spite of my doing that, you're stopping to talk to me again now."

It wasn't clear to her what she should do with this very sincere and pleasant invitation from this very unpleasant looking someone.

"Please. Sit down and have a little lunch with me. It's funny, I feel like this isn't the first time we're eating together though we both know it is."

Without waiting, he picked up his sketch pad and put it on the seat with his backpack. He moved the sandwiches to the seat next to his and then looked up with a little smile that said, "come on, sit down." This time, his lip wasn't quivering.

She saw his smile and reflexively smiled back a small one of resignation accompanied with a slight nod. She didn't want to leave. She sat down in the aisle seat, leaving one empty seat between them, not wanting to get any closer to him but close enough for him to notice that the freckle on her neck was a little darker and larger than he first thought.

"Which one do you want, I'll be 'the other half'?" Adrianna finally asked. She was more formal sounding than he was.

"I guess you can be 'the other half' for either or both, I'm not having any more. I already ate. There's this one in shiny white paper and this other in brown paper."

"This one looks good," she said.

She took the white origami one and opened it carefully since it was wrapped so delicately. Inside was a half sandwich which could have been featured on the cover of an *Epicurious* magazine. It was beautiful and geometrically perfect, garnished with cut and curled red and orange slivers and rinds of some unrecognizable sort which added an accent of bright color. She picked it up and bit into it.

"What do you think?" he asked.

"Very nice. Different," she said very politely but obviously it didn't meet her expectations.

"Really? Remember, if we're to be friends, you have to be brutally honest with yourself and with me. I'll ask you again, what do you think of that?"

She pursed her mouth and shook her head while she thought of what to say. "It has no taste. It looked good but it doesn't taste like anything. It's okay, I'm not hungry."

"Try the other one."

"No, really, it's okay." She didn't want to touch the other sandwich, let alone eat it

"Please, try it. It won't bite you—even if you bite it!"

She smiled involuntarily at his pleasantry and cajoling. He was gentler than the first couple of times they spoke, engaging her with a give and take in a gracious way.

"Go on, try it. Tell me what you think."

She shook her head saying to herself, "I don't want to do this but against my better judgment, here I go." Tentatively, she put the origami sandwich aside and moved the other one closer. It was hard to separate the bread from the paper holding it. The half sandwich fell apart and pieces of it fell onto the stained and wrinkled brown paper.

"It's okay. I think I'll pass on this. Thank you anyway. I think I have to go."

"I have a napkin here," and he handed her a napkin to help with the mess.

She didn't want to eat that miserable looking excuse for a sandwich but she felt obliged to. She picked it up as best she could. More parts of the sandwich fell apart and onto the paper when she took a small bite and began to eat. She concentrated on the half sandwich so she wouldn't have to look at him as much.

"Mmm." She finished that bite and took another and began to eat with gusto. With her hands full of the disintegrating sandwich and her mouth full of food, she gave him a little smile without stopping. She hadn't thought about smiling at him, it was a reflex. When she finished the half sandwich, she picked up the fallen pieces with her fingers and ate them too. He picked up the napkin and again handed it to her.

"You liked that."

"I guess you can say that. What was that?"

"The second one in brown paper was better than the first in white." It was a statement, not a question.

"That wasn't hard to see," she said.

"No, not to me either."

He changed the subject by pulling out a book from his knapsack.

"You know the question you asked in class about the Maslow reading when we came back from Thanksgiving? You might want to read the sections I marked. It explains the difference between living by, or up to, someone else's ideas of who you are, and choosing which ones to live by yourself. I believe it means we can and should decide what we want to make a part of ourselves, and what not. You know, try something out, keep it awhile, or not, see how you like it, and not just do or be what we think we're supposed to. You can give it back whenever. And here's a poem I wrote. It's not directly related but it ... well ... tell me what you think first. Don't read it now but if you do read it, read it three times just before you go to bed but the last time out loud. Don't read it during the day, and then do it again for one or two more nights until you don't want to, or it's enough. Then we can talk about it, if you want to, of course."

"Thank you." He's trying to be nice and was thinking about me, she thought, and that's sweet but I hope he doesn't think this is going anywhere. Maybe I should tell him I have a steady boyfriend? She took the book and piece of paper with the poem and put it inside the book. She didn't mention Julian.

"I don't know your name. What do you go by?" she asked.

"Tee ay oh." He pronounced it oddly. "Teo, they call me Teo."

"Teo. That's unusual."

"But I'd like it if you called me René. Most don't but when we talk by ourselves, please call me René. When you talk to others, then it's Teo."

"Sure. I don't know why but that's up to you."

This seemed odd but she didn't feel comfortable questioning him about it. Besides, she's not going to be talking to him that much, in or out of class.

"And your name is Adrianna."

"How did you know that?"

"I must have overheard it. But, and I hope you don't mind, when we talk, I'm going to call you Aimée."

"Aimée? I like that but it's not my name. It's French, right? Can't you call me by my name? What's wrong with Adrianna?"

"Nothing wrong with Adrianna. It's a nice name and it suits you too. Aimée, *ça c'est bonne aussi, n'est-ce pas?*"

"We're speaking French now? Did you know I'm in the French Honors Program?" she asked thinking he must have known somehow. He didn't answer. "I guess it doesn't matter to me, the names I mean. We only speak to each other here in class. Thank you for the book, and the poem too."

She relaxed a bit but what's with using different names? Is he unstable? Today he seemed almost normal, and despite his face, she actually liked talking to him. What a weird one. He was not someone she ever would have spoken to back in her middle class, homogeneous hometown of Bellevue.

"And don't forget to read the poem. *Au revoir. À bientôt,* until next class!"

She chuckled in a minimal way, and said "*mais oui, au revoir,*" and thought he had a terrific natural French accent, much better than hers even with her top grades.

When she got up, she saw his face which brought back searing reality. Instantly, she tensed and walled herself in. A cold shiver came over her—a sad and foreboding ripple—ominous, inexplicably confusing and bittersweet, though somehow distantly familiar in a way she couldn't fathom.

CHAPTER FOUR

Adrianna put on the pale green headband which reminded her of Teo and his sketch of the dress, and she again debated whether or not to talk to him. She figured she could stop without an explanation but it wasn't in her nature to be thoughtless like that. She could stop with an explanation but what would she say, you're so disgusting I can't bear to look at you? On the other hand, he was interesting and thoughtful. He gave her a poem he wrote and a book which he highlighted about the question he remembered that she had asked in class. In the end, she figured so long as it's only after class so no one else would see them, she would keep it up. After all, she was doing a good deed and liked herself for that. She must be getting something out of it, even if unsure what it might be. Why else would she question herself and continue on with him? She stopped by his row at the end of the next class to talk to him.

"Hi. I read your poem. The way you asked. I thought I was through with it the first night but I read it for a couple more nights, each time before I went to bed, like you said."

"And? I thought and hoped you might."

"Well, it was okay but nothing to write home about! The images of a visored knight in shiny metal armor jousting with one in black who got knocked off his horse, and people running to rescue him, were rather prosaic, sorry to say. So, as a poem, I don't give it high marks. You better think of another career!" she said with a little laugh.

"However, it gave me weird dreams. By the third night, I couldn't get it out of my mind. It was imprinted in me, running through my mind, over and over. Things got repeated out of order, you know how things don't make sense in a dream. I was back in the Middle Ages on a journey. I had no map and I didn't know where I was. There were a lot of people crowded all around me on this narrow trail, pushing and shoving. They tried to help me but I wasn't sure I could trust them. We came to this barricade blocking the path. There were shards of broken glass, concrete and sharp twisted metal. It was so dark and hard to see. Some climbed up and over the broken glass and metal, others just stopped, and a few slipped and fell into a deep black abyss right at the side of the path. To reach those who fell in, a bunch of them made themselves into a human chain grabbing each other, a hand grabbing someone else's hand, arm or a leg. Several bodies were upside down, their arms and legs hooked onto someone else's, going down deep into the blackness. Suddenly, someone bumped into me. It was pitch black so I really couldn't see, and he or she pulled me up where this cart—oh, I fell into the black hole too, I forgot to tell you, something pushed me off the path and I was falling too—where this old cart with wooden wheels and a driver in a monk's habit was waiting. A small horse moved around nervously and nickered, and a man held its mane to quiet it. Another old man in the cart was rubbing the back of his hand and he helped me up. Then we left."

"That was a lot more than I wrote. I think you should be writing poems! Did it frighten you?"

"I don't know about my writing poems, I've never written one in my life but parts of yours made me scared and also sad, while other parts made me feel, I don't know, hopeful that maybe I was on the right path. Does that make any sense?"

"You know reading or writing poems touches people differently, it depends on who you are inside, where you've been, where you're going. Let's talk about something else—eating! Look, I have some lunch here and teas too. Please share them with me and don't be rude by saying no."

He wanted to face her to make his case but knew he'd be better off if she didn't have to look at him directly, so he turned away to pick up the lunch bag as he spoke to her. He dropped any talk of poems and her dream. He was wearing an olive cashmere sweater and as he reached over for the lunch he had prepared, she noticed the musculature of a strong torso and back.

"Even though we're not in Nigeria, I don't want to be rude," she said in a friendly, singsong sort of way. She sat next to him without any hesitation but still didn't look directly at his face. They ate veggie filled pitas, cut up pickled carrots, cornichons and Morbier cheese, and he asked about her suitemates and family. He questioned her politely with a sincere interest to paint a picture for himself of her life, her whole being, not just the pretty face.

Well, she told him, there were three suitemates, all seniors too. They got along well except for Erika, the exchange student from South America, and they get together once a month for a meeting to go over things. (She didn't mention she hadn't told any of them about him. She was embarrassed to tell them, and now with Teo, she was even more embarrassed to admit that to him.) She has an older sister Charlotte who lives with their parents and he cautiously inquired further and asked questions which she freely and openly answered.

"Here is a photo of my father holding Charlotte, and that's me next to her, and that's my mother holding me and making me sit up tall. You can see how she always fusses over me to be sure I look good. And here's another of my father and Charlotte, and one of me and my mother straightening my dress."

He noticed Adrianna took after her mother who must have been a good looking young woman but seemed defeated to Teo and more aged than she should have been. Her father seemed ordinary enough and out of the family flow which Adrianna said was a good observation because her father was surrounded by women and constant female talk which he said he couldn't and didn't want to penetrate.

"It seems your mother is very proud of you and the way you keep yourself looking so nice. That's important to her, right?"

"Oh, definitely, for sure."

"And you do too, care about it I mean . . . I think," and then added, "and your father, doesn't he care about that?"

"Not at all. If anything, I can tell my mother gets on his nerves when she starts in on that."

"Does your mother know that, that it irritates him when she talks to you about the way you look?"

"Not really. I know they love each other and us, but they have their blind spots."

"Well, if she starts in on that a lot, your father must know why she does it. I suppose he knows how to handle those blind spots?"

When Adrianna didn't react to that, Teo dropped it and continued on to something else.

"Do you have a boyfriend?"

Talking about her boyfriend touched a nerve, and she abruptly withdrew from the camaraderie that had barely begun.

"I'm not sure that's any of your business!"

She knew immediately she overreacted. Before she could backtrack, he motioned with both hands held up, palms facing her. It was a gesture of okay, calm down, I won't go there.

"It was an innocent question. To me, it was getting to know you like knowing about your family. None of anything is any of my business. Sorry, I didn't mean to offend."

He couldn't have been more sincere or apologetic. He had assumed she wanted to talk about herself. He didn't realize she might also have places that were private. He saw in her more than just her pretty mask, something else, something familiar he couldn't put his finger on.

"No, you didn't offend. I just didn't feel right to talk to you about it." She was embarrassed. Why shouldn't I be able to talk to him about Julian? Am I ashamed of Julian or that Julian is my boyfriend? Is there something wrong with my having a boyfriend?

"Rule one was to be brutally honest with ourselves and each other. I know—that you know—you would never be my girlfriend. You don't have to spare my feelings. You can talk to me about anything, boyfriends, whatever. You can't and won't hurt my feelings as long as you're brutally honest. And if you don't talk about yourself, that's okay too."

Adrianna was not used to such self confidence in someone like Teo, or, for that matter, in any of those guys who try to impress her and be someone they're not. Even Julian was a lot like that. It was usually superficial, she didn't take them seriously and they didn't learn much about her, nor *vice versa*. But could she and Teo talk to each other without a subscript, and without pitying him, in a straight forward and direct way? Part of her wanted to but she wasn't sure if that was possible.

She continued, "Well, I dated a lot and now I guess you can say I'm kind of seeing someone from Alpha Sigma Phi. His name is Julian."

"Is it serious?"

"I don't know if I would call it serious. We date. I don't know what will happen. He's nice." She really didn't want to talk about this. How does he get me to talk like he does?

"Is he good looking?"

"Yes, he's good looking." I don't believe this, she thought, he's asking me the same thing my mother does! Is that the first or only thing everyone thinks about! Whether someone is good looking or not? Is that all there is?

She needed to change directions and try to exercise some control.

"I've told you about me but you haven't told me anything about you. It's your turn Teo."

"Sure. Have some tea, and it's René to you."

He reached into his knapsack and took out a small thermos and two cups which he had packed in anticipation of this. He poured the tea which was still fairly hot. She was happy not to talk about Julian and what kind of relationship she may or may not have with him, and she forgot to follow up about Teo's life.

"I like this. Is it green tea? I like green tea."

"It's a special blend. I have a collection from all over the world and I use different teas or combinations of them to make a thermos of hot tea, depending on what I want. This particular one helps digestion and keeps me alert for a while. It doesn't have any caffeine but it does help me focus. See how it affects you and tell me about it next time."

He casually slipped in "next time."

"What are those books?" pointing to the books which stuck out of his knapsack. She drank the tea, it tasted funny but not unpleasant.

"Glad you asked." He had anticipated this too. "They're storybooks, for children. I volunteer at a children's ward in the University hospital. When we finish eating I'll be walking over there."

"You volunteer there? Isn't it far to walk? What do you do?"

"Yes and no and I help out. If you go out the main entrance of the campus and along the roads, it's long. But I found a shortcut when I was around the government research building. I go by the fraternity quad, then along Stadium Road past the football field and then behind the sports stadium and over the railroad tracks. There you can find a path past the research center which takes you through the cemetery and then to the back of the hospital."

"I didn't know you could do that," she said. "No one I know ever goes over there, it's so out of the way. The research center, it's the small grey cinderblock building, right? They say the military is working with some European countries on something like mind expanding drugs over there."

"Yeah, I know that."

"And then the cemetery? It's pretty lonely and desolate. I've seen it but never went in," she said with a small degree of apprehension.

"Sure the cemetery is obviously quiet and desolate but I like that. It takes about twenty five to thirty minutes with the shortcut. There isn't a direct path through the cemetery so you take some paths but also have to walk over and around graves, but there's never anyone around to spot you. Besides, I've seen you jogging in the mornings with Phi Beta Kappa when you stop and talk—or should I say flirt?—with the fraternity guys. This should be a piece of cake for you."

(Phi Beta Kappa was a street mutt, part German shepherd and the other part or parts was anyone's guess. Adrianna rescued him in her first winter at the University and now he was a campus pet who belonged to no one. The frat boys fed him but he always looks for Adrianna and joins her when she goes jogging. She always has a dog treat for him.)

He's seen me jogging and flirting with the fraternity boys? How is that? And the cemetery? I'd have to walk over dead people? He's just full of surprises but why should anything he says surprise me. After all, I really don't know him at all. She drank more of the tea which affected her in a way she couldn't identify.

"Why don't you come? No experience needed. You can read them a story. If you come, I think you'll be glad you came. It's 12:30 now and we can be back here by 3:00 or 4:00. Finish your tea and we can leave."

"I don't know... the cemetery... and besides, I don't like being or speaking in front of people, I get too nervous with all that. I don't know. I wouldn't know what to do. What could I do?"

He laughed. "They're kids. Just kids. If you don't want to stand up in front of anyone, then read one or two of them a story or talk to them. Play with them. Don't overthink it, just do what feels right. If you do what feels right, you can't go wrong and will actually go right. You're thinking it through too much."

"I don't know," which sounded like "there's a part of me that wants to go so please coax me some more." She felt a little off, maybe the tea or lunch didn't agree with her.

They were alone in the amphitheater after the class had ended. Suddenly, Teo became somber and looked intensely at her in a mystical way, a way that took control of her. Up to now, she could look away from his terrible face if she wanted, but not now. A fog enveloped her and drew her to him at a level she didn't understand. As if she were a lovely Monarch butterfly he caught in its multi-generational migration, he pinned her to a hidden scrim and kept her vulnerable and immobilized. She stood there pretty and still, hardly breathing, waiting for him, exposed, magnetized. She stared into his eyes, eyes which compelled her attention and beckoned her. He spoke slowly, monotonously, in a faint, far off voice—almost inhuman—a strange voice she hadn't heard before.

"Aimée, listen to me. This is important. I think inside you, you have an internal compass." He let that stay in the air for a moment. "There is a compass. I sense it. You should find it . . . and use it. Let yourself see where it points, to who you are, don't be afraid of it. You have the power to see." He let this soak in before he spoke again in that strange, unsettling voice. "I'm beginning to feel it even though I know you don't. It won't be easy for you, and one more thing, you will have no control over it and you won't be able to stop it."

She was mystified as if hypnotized. He eased off and waited. After a moment, she was breathing normally and was herself again.

She thought that as soon as she might actually spend some time with him outside of class, he upended her with a sucker punch which knocked the wind out of her. She wished he wouldn't spring things like that on her. It throws her off balance. She didn't know what she was feeling but she was definitely feeling something.

"René, you're scaring me. I don't know if it's your face or what you said or the tea but you're scaring me. Where did that come from? It didn't even sound like you. That was creepie."

"I really don't know myself. It's a puzzle to me when that happens," he answered. "Sometimes I hear myself say things like that. I don't think they're my words or my thoughts."

"That's happened before? It's not even a normal voice."

Teo nodded and broke off his hypnotic gaze. She now recognized that face of his, the face you didn't want to see. Oddly, looking at his awful face was a relief from the piercing arrow he just shot threw her about her "internal compass" and how she couldn't avoid something difficult lying ahead of her.

"I think you really want to come to the hospital and see the kids. Don't you? Really? Come on, we'll take the shortcut and, as a bonus, I'll tell you a little about me on the way, which is something I rarely do." He spoke to her in his familiar, reassuring voice that said I am your friend, don't worry, I won't hurt you. She now felt behind the face and her first impression of him, was someone she could trust in spite of his being so different and private, yet not so very foreign either.

"Yes, I do want to go. Let's go but only because you promise to tell me about yourself on the way!"

They started out for the University hospital through the campus and the shortcut through the cemetery. They walked side by side, in a graceful gait in sync: she with a model like posture, and he with an athletic strength.

CHAPTER FIVE

New York City and Paris, 1952

Samuel was an only child, thirty one, and never married. After high school, his father had insisted he work in the fur business which his father had started when he came to the U. S. from a small village outside of Minsk. When his parents both died at an early age, he was left alone and had to continue the business, otherwise he would have been forced to close it. That would have put all the workers out of work, and it also would have ended the income it amply generated for him. While it meant his plans for a college education ended too, he did suddenly take control of a thriving business. But instead of working as an apprentice furrier, he was now in charge. His father was proud to have made a small business to support his family where he could work with his own hands on the oily, foul smelling animal skins and turn them into furs. Samuel never liked that dirty work, so he let others do it. It freed him to manage, market and expand out of New York into other major cities. He was methodical and combined an adroit entrepreneurial ability to take risks while at the same time exercise caution. He took that small business and created the foundation of what years later would be a very successful empire.

He was a quiet young gentleman, refined, immaculately dressed and groomed, with an aquiline shaped nose, and generous to and well respected by his workers, all Russian immigrants. He hired Russian immigrants like his father did, and spoke to them in their native Russian, and helped them whenever he could. He shrewdly knew that helping them in their personal lives would be good for him as well. When he was a boy, they called him Sasha, the pet name his father used when he started to help in the factory. He liked it then, but not now, now that he was in charge. But he allowed it anyway; it was the price he paid to hear them tell those stories he enjoyed about his father getting married in the shtetl in the old country.

He worked hard—a good business model which would, and did, motivate his workers to work hard too. He buried himself in his work and it covered up his barren emotional life with the satisfaction of making money.

His large apartment in a 1930's pre-war building on West 77th Street shared the fourth floor with one other apartment, a family with three children who treated him in a small way as an adopted uncle. Other than that, he had no relatives and no close friends, neither male nor female. He generously showered the children with presents and recently took them to the circus where an old hag of a fortune teller sitting in a green tent held each one by the hand and predicted their futures—the children's and Samuel's, impressing on Samuel he was soon to begin a long journey. Soon after the beldam of a fortune teller said that, he began to feel something, like there was a hole or something missing in his life, something that eluded him. He wondered if he would ever find someone and perhaps have his own family, like the family next door.

In the Spring of that year they were going on a vacation and invited Samuel. No, he thanked them, but it occurred to him that he should take a vacation, it would be his first. His managers could handle things and there was no reason not to go away for a month. It was a fateful decision which changed destinies more than most decisions do.

He chose Paris. He had never been anywhere outside the States and he liked big cities, cities that had good restaurants, where you could take long walks, like New York. He found a small hotel on the left bank by Saint-Germain-des-Prés and spent the first two weeks in Paris walking. He relished the French cuisine, went to the Louvre, the Jeu de Paume, saw the sights and walked.

Today, after walking all morning, he ended up at the Place de La République and then walked over to the Canal St. Martin in the Tenth Arrondissement where he stopped at a small café. The café had a few tables outside overlooking one of the quaint iron bridges that crossed over the canal locks, a room inside with several more tables to sit at, and a bar made of a dark glossy wood. Behind the bar was a large gleaming commercial espresso maker which could make three cups at a time. On the wall behind it was a mirror with shelves where the bottles of liquor were displayed. The bartender was reaching up to the rack above the bar to hang the wine glasses she just cleaned. Three patrons stood at the bar drinking a café or a pastis and looked at the canal bridge reflected in the mirror as they chatted with the bartender while she cleaned two more glasses.

Samuel sat outside at one of the small round metal bistro tables with a marble top to rest and enjoy the early Spring weather and canal view, and tried to order a café and a *croque madame* from the waiter who bristled at Samuel's attempt at French. This bistro was off the beaten tourist track and the waiter had no desire to ingratiate himself with an obviously American tourist. Another man sitting at the next bistro table couldn't help but see and interceded and ordered the café and *croque madame* for Samuel. They started to talk across the small round tables. He was an older French gentlemen, white haired and mustached, well dressed with a vest and bow tie, and spoke English fairly well; almost a dandy but too jovial to be one.

"Thank you for helping me. I think the waiter actually understood my order but you made it simpler," Samuel said.

"*Pas de quoi*, I mean, don't mention it. French waiters take getting used to. They should know better than to be rude to tourists, but you know they are rude to the French as well! It must be part of their training!" he said in a friendly laugh. "My name is Didier, Didier Hermus. You are a traveler here, yes? May I join you?"

"Hermus, an interesting old name," Samuel said.

"Yes, I like it, it suits me, my name," Didier said.

"Please, please join me. My name is Samuel Zeelyoni," and he extended his hand. "I haven't had a conversation with anyone but waiters and the like for two weeks, and you see the extent of the conversation! I would like to learn French but it's surprising how easy it is to get around not knowing it, so at least for now, there is no great need to learn French but one should speak the language of the country they are in. It's easier for you here in Europe to speak other languages. You are surrounded by so many other countries. Back home, everyone speaks English. There is neither the need nor opportunity to speak a foreign language. One of my regrets for not having gone to college is I didn't learn to speak foreign languages although I did learn Russian from my parents which is useful in my business."

"*Mais oui, bien sûr*. Your name, Zeelyoni, that's Russian, *n'est-ce pas?*" Didier said.

"Yes, it is Russian. I am falling in love with your Paris, I could love it almost as much as I love my city, New York I mean. Paris is much prettier than New York and excellent for walking, but New York has the energy."

Samuel was starved for conversation and welcomed this vignette of a travel moment. He moved a chair back from his small bistro table so Didier could sit next to him.

"I would like to go to your New York City one day. So much energy, so many people. You could get lost there if you don't know where you are going."

"It's only a plane ride away. If you came, I could help you order a BLT and a side of fries!" Samuel joked.

"What is that?"

"A kind of sandwich and not as good as a *croque madame*."

"Isn't it expensive to fly here?"

"I don't know, it's all relative. I fly from time to time to visit my businesses which are all over the country." He didn't want to assume this older gentleman could afford to fly although he looked well off.

"Ah, yes, you said you are a businessman. I too am a businessman. What do you do?"

"I started off in my father's business of making fur coats but expanded into clothes and textiles and have contracts with governments to make military uniforms and such. What about you?"

"I do import and export between Europe and the Far East. You should expand your business here and I can expand to America!" he said jokingly.

They continued to talk about their businesses, and whether it was fate or just coincidence, what at first was chit chat, later became serious talk of how they could actually benefit each other. As their pleasantries grew serious, they delved into more details, and after an hour or so, they agreed they needed to continue exploring the idea of working together. Didier ordered more coffee for Samuel and a pastis for himself and they took a break from talking about business.

"I come to this café because according to Camille, my housekeeper, and her daughter Jeanne-Marie, they have the best *pain au chocolat* in Paris. They live near here so they know. Have you had any *pain au chocolat*?"

"No, I don't think so. What is it?"

"Better than telling you, you have to taste one. But you already had lunch. So I propose that you come to my home for dinner. *Pain au chocolat* is usually for breakfast but you can try it after dinner."

"That's very kind, but I don't want to impose."

"*Pas de tout*. I insist. I will ask Camille to make us a supper of lamb pie and we can talk business. Who knows? My home is near Park Monceau but come a little early and walk through the park, it is most agreeable and historic. Here is my card and the address. I propose, say, seven thirty?"

Samuel took the card and agreed to meet Didier at his home. He was alone in Paris and this was an opportunity to spend an evening with someone rather than a book again. He also took his advice and arrived early to stroll through Park Monceau which he pleasantly discovered contained elegant gardens, statues, a large pond, and a few scaled-down architectural follies like an Egyptian pyramid in an area dotted with sumptuous mansions from another era.

* * * * * *

While Samuel was enjoying the park, Camille was finishing up the supper which Didier would serve Samuel. She asked him where she should set the table, in the dining room or at the small table by the window in the kitchen.

"I think the dining room would be better even though less cozy," Didier answered. "Besides, it has all that nice artwork on the walls not like the kitchen with all those copper pots and pans hanging down from racks waiting to crack your head! And all those aromas of the cooking!" But when he realized he might have seemed ungrateful, he added, "Which I mean smells very, very good, thanks to you, my dear Camille. The kitchen would be nice but the dining room perhaps better for tonight."

"Some of the art in the dining room, you bought it after the War. Do you know where the art came from?" she asked.

"Does it matter where it came from?"

"Yes, to me, if you are asking me. If it's Jew art, the art stolen from the Jews by the Nazis during the War and the ones they kept in our Jeu de Paume, then I don't approve. Of course, you are free to do what you wish."

"Well, I didn't steal it, and the gallery I bought it from didn't steal it either," Didier said.

"But, if you thought it was Jew art, would it matter whether or not the gallery stole it, if someone else had stolen it?" She pressed on. Camille spoke her mind when given a proper opportunity.

"How can one ever know where something came from?"

"Well, did you pay a fair price, or did you, like you always do, bargain for a very low price for them?"

"In between a low price and a fair price. Does that make me a criminal, a bad person? If it is Jew art, perhaps the owners needed money desperately and sold their art at very, very low prices in order to get money quickly so they could escape from Germany or Austria. If so, the buyers helped them escape and at the same time, preserved the art and got a good deal too. No?"

"A convenient answer," Camille said, "though it does have merit, but also only works if you had nothing to do with their plight and desperate need to escape the concentration camps."

"I didn't cause any of that horrific inhuman treatment," he said. "I wasn't the messenger who brought that down on them."

"But did you try to do anything to stop it?" She continued to press him.

"Did I have an obligation to do something from here? Remember, with the Vichy regime, I would have put myself at risk. It was better to do business with them and not antagonize them. Anyway, I think I bought only two paintings that might possibly qualify as Jew art, and it would be hard to find out the true provenance now. What would you have me do?"

"I don't know. You are a good man no matter what. I won't take that away from you. Even if you bought two paintings stolen by the Nazis or someone else, I suppose there are degrees of culpability and one can live openly and blamelessly with the lowest degrees of complicity.... I'm not so sure about the Church though." She then added, "I hope I didn't overstep my bounds to talk like this."

"No, not at all. One of the many things I love about you is your intellect and our far ranging conversations. Never hold back on me and teach young Jeanne-Marie the same."

At that, Camille went to set the large dining room table for two places and wondered which two paintings might be Jew art, perhaps the one with the caduceus in it which Didier was fond of. She imagined a large festive room in another elegant house where it might have hung on a parlor wall, or maybe in a dining room where a family had their dinner, chatting lovingly about their day's accomplishments and challenges, oblivious to the unthinkable genocidal end of their world. She put the lamb pie in the oven to warm, and asked Didier if there was anything else he needed before she left.

"No, dear Camille, you always think of everything and I am lucky to have you. Thank you, my dearest Camille," he said with a tender smile.

"Ah no, I am the lucky one to have your love and kindness," she quickly answered. "I wish I could have it all to myself, but I know that cannot be. You love and enjoy life so very much . . . and perhaps you have loved and still love a great many . . . and a great variety . . . of people too, isn't that so?"

She sighed and reached over to examine a button on his shirt.

"This needs to be mended. Leave it for me and I will sew it for you tomorrow. Maybe one day, if I had a good sewing machine like the ones made in the United States, I could make clothes and mend things even better. Even though you are generous in your love and money—and I mean it when I say I appreciate your sharing a part of yourself with Jeanne-Marie and me, I am grateful for even the small part—I need to be careful and plan for the future for me and for Jeanne-Marie. I cannot rely on that husband of mine whose manhood suffers and cannot see me. If I could sew and teach that to Jeanne-Marie, we might not be so dependent upon you or other men. In the next life, if God be willing," and she made the sign of the cross with her right hand, "I'd like to come back as a man. It's hard to be a woman and I ask, 'why did God do that to us?' I was taught to follow God's commandments and the Church's teachings," she paused and looked down at her hands which she had now clenched tightly and spoke without looking at Didier, embarrassed and pained, "and as a young girl, I was given special, private—very private—individual attention in the Church. But even so . . . even so," she sighed and looked up at him, "but even so, I still maintain my trust and have faith that God has reasons, and will provide for us too. But one needs to be practical and resigned to living within the world we see, not the one we are told to hope for. I want Jeanne-Marie to learn to accept her own circumstances and depend on herself, not others—nor prayers—to help make a good life and to decide what is right and what is not, what is acceptable and what is not. Don't you agree? For her?"

She got up and moved toward the kitchen. "Well, I must go now. Tell me more about *monsieur* Samuel tomorrow. Until tomorrow then." She left by the service entrance.

* * * * * *

Samuel finished his walk through the park and made his way over to the address Didier had given him. It wasn't an apartment which he had expected but one of those grand yet small mansions close to Park Monceau. Didier greeted Samuel at the door with his hands on Samuel's arms and kissed him on each cheek, three times in all.

"In Paris, we do the cheek kiss three times. I think we do it to be different from the others! You found this street without trouble?"

"Yes, I have a map and guide book, and in New York we use subways all the time so your Métro wasn't too bad for me. I found the Monceau station at the park's main entrance on Boulevard de Courcelles and went through the tall black wrought iron gates, the ones embellished with gold. They were impressive."

"Fantastic! You Americans are good at following a map, and look where it takes you! Please, come in, come in."

Didier ushered Samuel through the foyer to a sitting anteroom which had high ceilings and tall windows that stretched nearly from floor to ceiling, European window latches and door handles from a former time, old wooden floors, and a view of the park. It reeked of a genteel Parisian mansion.

Both shrewd businessmen, and careful when embarking on a venture with someone new, they spent time talking about something other than their businesses, trying to get the measure of the other. They sat in the sitting room, one of many rooms with furniture befitting such a mansion. At Didier's urging, Samuel agreed to drink some absinthe which Samuel had never tasted.

"Absinthe was banned here in 1914 and in many countries including your own. In fact, you banned it before we did," Didier said while he prepared the drinks in the traditional French way. "It is called the 'green fairy' because it has psychoactive effects and is thought to be an hallucinogen. It isn't a cordial or liqueur because no sugar is added, so it is a spirit. I hope you like it. It's not easy to find since it's illegal to sell. I drink it all the time, probably too much so be careful you don't become addicted like me! But if you see the Degas painting of the woman who drank it, called *L'Absinthe*, or Picasso's *The Absinthe Drinker*, you may decide not to drink it at all! I like to buy art, it is a passion of mine. It not only is a pleasure to behold and own but is usually an excellent investment, and with no upkeep! As much as I would love to have a Degas, his *L'Absinthe* would cost so much and is probably not even for sale. Maybe a colorful Chagall instead."

Didier slowly poured cold water over the sugar cube he had placed on the split spoon and balanced over the glass with the absinthe.

"You see what I do here, the sugar on the split spoon over the glass? Picasso made a series of six small sculptures of this called *Glass of Absinthe*. I don't think you can see them in any museums though. Ah, forgive me, I can bore anyone when I talk about art! Oh, and Van Gogh painted just a glass of absinthe on a table, and guess what he called it—*Café Table with Absinthe*! I could have come up with a name better than that! Names are important, they tell you things. Ah, I can't help myself, forgive me. I have trouble stopping once I start in on art."

With their drinks in hand, he brought Samuel into the large dining room to sit on a red silk covered chair at the far end of an enormous antique oak table and excused himself to serve the meal Camille had prepared, a simple meal by French standards. For dessert, in addition to other pastries, Didier served Samuel a *pain au chocolat* which certainly was not what the French would have had for dessert but Samuel wasn't French and devoured it with gusto savoring every bit of the flaky, buttery pastry and hint of chocolate. He wiped his fingers on the white damask napkin Camille had set for him, leaving buttery oils and smears of chocolate on it.

After dinner they went back to the sitting room and though there was ample seating, they sat next to each other on a small French provincial sofa with a curved back covered in a cream and white striped silk.

"You are alone here?" Didier asked.

"Here and everywhere. This is my first vacation."

"Ah, *mais oui*, you are looking for something then?"

"Funny you say it that way. I mean, not funny, but coincidental. Do you know what I mean?"

"I think so. Not 'ha ha', *mais je ne sais pas*, to another point?"

"Exactly."

"What are you looking for here in Paris? You know painters come here to paint, writers to write, they come to find themselves or each other, and *je ne sais pas*—I don't know—but something."

"I don't know either," Samuel said. "Something to fill a hole? Something that I don't know what but I think I will know it when I find it. Does this make any sense to you?"

"*Bien sûr mon ami*! You are not alone!"

"You know what I mean? No, I don't think so. I know everyone looks for something but what I am looking for is not like that. Excuse me if I say this, but I don't think you really understand what I mean. I think I am alone in this. I am not a writer nor an artist like you say. They know what they seek, I don't."

Didier put his hand momentarily on top of Samuel's in a paternal and comforting way. "True, we only met today but still it is enough time for me to recognize something. Let me tell you what I recognize, what you are looking for, and then you tell me if it is not so." He finished with an inimitable French "*oui?*" that sounded like "mwheh."

They sat close to each other on the sofa while Didier spoke at length and Samuel listened. Didier put his hand on Samuel's briefly from time to time to convey a more earnest, heartfelt explanation. When Didier finished, they nodded their heads in mutual understanding having found a common thread.

"So, dear friend, you see I know. I too have been looking and would like to give up. I am tired of looking but cannot." Didier sighed.

"Did you ever have a wife, or family?" Samuel asked.

"No, I live alone, probably like you. Have you ever been in love?"

"No. Have you?" Samuel asked.

"*Oui*, Yes."

"Well, isn't that it?"

"No, *monsieur* Samuel, I don't think so, not exactly. I found a kind of love and it is *magnifique*. Even though she still works for me, I can tell you secretly I love my Camille and she loves me, and I will explain it all to you one day, but even so, it was never enough for me. I want my Camille but I needed another thing also, something more. It is late for me, too late.

But you *monsieur* Samuel, you are young. You must not give up looking. Believe me, don't give up!" Didier was excited to find someone to share and pass on his longing.

"Have you ever known anyone else like this?"

"Ah, *monsieur* Samuel, perhaps you are afflicted like me. When I was a young salesman, I met a woman who ruined my life. I didn't understand everything she said, and now, it has been so long, I cannot even remember it well! Eh, well, you see I was traveling through a country village by a small stream late in the afternoon, and I stopped at a café where a frail woman dressed in black sat at the bar. She looked like someone Toulouse-Lautrec would have drawn with a craggy nose and face. Do you know Toulouse-Lautrec? No matter. Ah, *mon Dieu*, she was the saddest woman. She had come from a funeral and sat at the bar, a black veil covered her face. She said the young woman who died, had died on her wedding day, and she, the old woman, didn't have the strength—or she might have said the power—and wouldn't live long enough to do it again and asked for help. I wasn't sure what she meant. Her hand was shaking as she tried to pour some absinthe into a glass. She stared at me from beneath her veil and looked at me with an eerie intensity. I reached to steady her glass, and as she kept staring into my eyes, she poured the absinthe, spilling it on my hand. I didn't know then, but I know now, it was no accident—she meant to spill it on me. She picked up her veil, bent over and licked the absinthe from my hand. Can you imagine that, she licked my hand with her dry rough tongue! She asked me to drink some so I took a sip of absinthe. I never should have done that! She put her pale hand on mine, right where she had licked off the absinthe. I asked her if I could help and she nodded yet kept staring at me. And while her thin cold hand was on mine, she squeezed it tightly and studied me. She drilled her eyes into mine. I saw a green spot or mole or birthmark on her hand. It was disgusting! She took my hand and pressed it hard on top of that green skin of hers. She pressed so hard I thought for sure my hand would turn green too! She did it like this."

He spilled a drop of absinthe from his glass onto Samuel's hand and pressed it hard, very hard, for ten seconds onto his own.

"I understand, I understand," Samuel said, urging Didier to stop. Didier released Samuel's hand and continued.

"Then with an inner sense of relief, she said yes, she'll let me help and asked me to do *La Louche*, the louche ritual. I took another glass and poured ice water over the sugar cube and slotted spoon and we watched the absinthe turn to murky shades of green. She sighed and said she was old, too old to go through this, find them or do it again and I was kind to help. She was relieved. What must I do? I asked. She said look for 'it' and never give up—ever. She said I had to find something or someone to make me or it complete, and so I have been doing that for many years. Too many years. Although I am too tired to keep looking, I still cannot stop. She cast a spell on me and I cannot shake it loose."

"So you spent all these years looking for this something?" Samuel asked.

"Yes, and I never understood how she did it but she assuredly did. I have no peace, and that's when I started to drink the green fairy, the absinthe, that spirit. I wish I never met her and her damned green spot! She said I might find others like me, either searching or helping, and today, I think I have."

"It seems I may end up like you," Samuel said.

Didier groaned audibly. "Oh Didier, excuse me, I didn't mean that the way it sounded." Now Samuel put his hand on top of Didier's. "That wasn't nice of me and I like you, and you have been kind. Please forgive me for saying that. I only meant I may spend many years looking in vain for what, I don't even know. Why bother?"

"I understand," Didier assured Samuel, "but don't pity me. I have a love, my Camille. I confess to you now when I bought this house fifteen years ago, I was looking for someone to clean and cook and she was looking for work. She was, and still is, married to a man who doesn't love her and behaves badly even now. During the first few years we talked and shared our secrets, and then over the years, a deep trust and respect grew between us, and we fell into a kind of love. It has to be secret because she is married and has a little girl. I love her and Jeanne-Marie, and she loves me but that has never filled what was and remains missing. I must still search but I am tired of looking—looking for what, I do not know. So you see, my love for Camille is not the same thing and you should look for both."

"Easy to say. You looked and didn't find it. Why would I? I don't know if I could recognize it even if I found it. I don't know what I am looking for."

"Would you like me to help you?" Didier put his cool hand on Samuel's and looked at him intently.

"What do you mean?"

"Would you like me to help you, in your way, to fill the hole, as you put it?"

"Yes, why not?"

"Will you let me help you?" Didier said more seriously.

"Yes. Certainly."

"Good!" Didier said and he squeezed Samuel's hand.

"Then first, you move out of your hotel and into my house, here! You can see, there is much room for you. Tomorrow! You must move here tomorrow! I insist! Camille and Jeanne-Marie, she is twelve years old, will help you. You can learn *La Louche* and to drink absinthe too—perhaps see Degas' *L'Absinthe* here in Paris—and then we talk more, much more, about how we will make lots of money together, you in New York and I here. I think we can do well together, make a good team! *N'est-ce pas?*"

Samuel didn't know whether to move in after so short a time but he felt a connection and a kinship and was drawn to Didier. He enjoyed Didier in a refreshing and new way unlike anything he had ever known, and didn't want it to end so he accepted and moved into Didier's mansion at Park Monceau and stayed there for two weeks. They became very close to each other as partners and friends for a very long time.

CHAPTER SIX

Teo and Adrianna had walked out of the lecture room and started toward the University hospital.

"This is the first time we're talking outside of class," she said, inwardly proud and outwardly boastful, having forgotten the way Teo had just mesmerized her about her "internal compass."

Teo put his hoodie up over his head even though it was a sunny day.

"Will it bother you if someone you know sees us walking together?"

That hurt. He was perceptive, his aim was sharp, and he showed her a part of herself she couldn't deny yet didn't like.

"You're changing the subject. The subject is you. Tell!"

Teo took her through the main campus, past the government research building which was not a particularly welcoming place, and then toward the hospital. She had relaxed by the time they got off campus.

"Have you ever run away from home?" he asked.

"Teo—I mean René—are you reneging? You're supposed to tell me about you. You're changing the subject."

"No, really, I'm not. It's part of my story. I ran away from home when I was ten. I was a bright kid, good looking if you can believe that, and misunderstood. I didn't know who I was and I don't think my mother did either. She couldn't figure me out. But more than just misunderstood, I was ignored, nonexistent. I mean my mother didn't see me as anyone special to her, like her son. I was like a boarder in a rooming house. She felt nothing for me and in retrospect, I don't think she was capable of loving me, or anyone, not even my father. You're lucky to have two parents and a sister who can love, and love you and each other. Not everyone can love or be loved."

"I guess," she said, "but sometimes I have my doubts, not that I would ever run away. I know they love me. It's only my father doesn't see me the same way he does my sister. Maybe because she was the first born and isn't so pretty, so she became his favorite. Or, it could be related to a car accident he blames himself for when I was a little girl, not that we got hurt. I don't know but I wish he treated me the same."

She didn't bring up the apparition of the dead woman who had been thrown from her car and who just made another appearance.

"Maybe he's afraid of you."

"Why should he be afraid of me? Why do you say that?"

"I don't know. Maybe he's spooked by something he senses. Maybe it's not guilt but something else."

"I can't believe that. Anyway, you're avoiding 'you' again. It's your turn to tell. Come on. And what about your father, you keep talking about your mother?"

Teo hadn't planned on talking about his father or his mother and would have preferred to gloss over it.

"I guess I can't start and then not tell you about my parents. Well, my father died when I was eight. They said it was suicide but I'm not sure my mother didn't have a hand in making it happen, and sometimes I think she actually did it."

Adrianna was taken aback. He just told her something deeply personal and intimate, much more than she would have shared, and was surprised.

"That's awful. I'm sorry for you. You get more serious when you talk about personal things, you act differently and

I'm glad you feel comfortable with me to do that. Is this new for you, talking about yourself like this?"

"Well, maybe. Anyway, I liked my father. He told me the week before he died that my mother tried to have an abortion when she was pregnant with me but stopped. He said he wasn't sure he really fathered me cause he knew she slept around then. She had a fondness for Jewish businessmen who could show her a good time. It didn't matter to me since he was the father I knew and I loved him. I know he loved me even though she didn't."

"So you're not sure who your real father was? Did you ever try to find out? And it didn't make any difference to you? You loved the man you called your father the same not knowing for sure?"

"Sure, he was the one who raised me and loved me. It didn't matter to me one way or the other so why bother. He actually told me I should get away from her as soon as I was old enough and could, that he didn't know until after they were married she was a sick woman, sick in the head. He wanted to leave but didn't on account of me—he couldn't. He didn't have enough money to live somewhere else and still support all of us and he'd probably have to support her too since she didn't have any job that lasted. She wasn't really good at anything and everyone she worked for saw through her but she spoke like she was some knowledgeable expert or aristocrat so she could talk her way into getting a job. Trouble was, she didn't have anything to back it up other than her good looks, and acting sexy and seductive, which is how she manipulated my poor father into marrying her. She was four years older than he was and he couldn't see there was nothing behind her seduction and the sex. She used to sleep with me in my bed from time to time right up to when I ran away, and she didn't wear anything! She said it was very European and Americans are too obsessed with nudity. She went into rages and once held a knife to my father and said she'd kill him if he tried to stop her goings on but the next day acted like they had the most intimate, special relationship. I saw all that. I'm not making it up. And did she ever flirt and act theatrically! It was comical once you knew her but to someone meeting her for the first time, they were impressed. Like I once said, all is not what it seems. It was back then I began to keep myself to myself. I was—and still am—embarrassed to tell anyone about all this and after I ran away, I certainly didn't want to tell anyone about my past that could trace me back to her."

Teo stopped talking. He was on a roll and now regretted he told her what he did. He changed the pace and skipped over any more of that part of his life and went back to a matter of fact style to tell Adrianna about his running away.

"Okay, enough of all that. I told you too much anyway."

"No. I'm glad you told me," she said with obvious sincerity. "You know, telling me about yourself that way is more flattering to me than the stupid flirting nonsense I get."

"So what do kids like that do at ten? They run away. Except I really ran away. I never went back. I haven't seen nor spoken to my mother since then. That's almost ten years now."

"You're kidding! Ten, and you ran away for good? Never spoke to her since? That can't be true! I could never do that."

"Well, I might have gone back except it wasn't so hard the first week. I had the money my father had secretly given me before he died, and I took a long bus ride a few hundred miles away. Won't go into details about how I did that, but I did. I was surprised how many people—strangers—helped me. After the first week, I had only a little money left and I was hungry and dirty. I thought of returning but each day was another day I survived, and so for a month I went day to day.

I stole food and clothes, and got a small job when they didn't care how old I was. I ended up in New York City. I thought it would be easier in a big city and maybe find a job in a restaurant kitchen. I was so naive, I was amazed I actually survived a month but I was pushed along by a force within me."

"What about your mother, didn't you care about what you did to her? After all, she was still your mother. I couldn't do that to my parents no matter what else I felt about them."

"I was so consumed with how to get through each day, I thought less and less of her, and frankly, I didn't think she could feel a personal loss, maybe only a social embarrassment cause she didn't know what to tell people. I was feeling pretty miserable when I met this man. He was sitting in Central Park facing the back of the Shakespeare statue at the end of The Mall. I sat on his bench. I remember it because behind him on the backrest was a small brass memorial plaque like those on a lot of benches there, given in loving memory of someone, and this one had an unusual name, Didier Hermus, which I could barely see behind him. He looked like an old man to me—which he was—about eighty three. Eighty three, that's ancient! He had a small liver spot on his right temple like old men have. He looked at me. He studied me. After a while he motioned for me to sit nearer. His name was Samuel and he thought I had run away from home, that I must be looking for something. He didn't threaten me or tell me what to do or anything like that. He was kind and I liked him. He was reading from a notebook of green pastel colored paper and asked me if I could read French. A pity I couldn't, he said, because I might have liked those stories, fantasies written by a young girl he once knew named Mimi. After an hour, he said he felt a connection with me, and maybe because he felt that way, he made me feel comfortable with him. He said he could help me and asked 'Would you like me to help you?' and

I said yes. He put his old hand on mine and said, 'Will you let me help you?' I said yes again and he squeezed my hand and held it a little longer than was comfortable. I thought he was going to give me some money. Instead, he took me to his apartment and I moved in. Right then and there! At first I thought he would take advantage of me, if you know what I mean, but no. He really wanted to take care of me, and as it turned out, to be sure I grew up well. He gave me my own room and food, and after a while, clothes and spending money, and then he started me on my education. He took care of me, he was very generous. I don't know what I would have done if I hadn't met him. I certainly wouldn't be here right now. You wouldn't be here either if you looked left instead of right some time in your past. I owe him a lot."

They reached the cemetery where he took a paved pedestrian path until it came to an end. He led her on uneven ground through the trees, stepping over and between the graves and gravestones with the names of those who once lived and the dates of their arrival and departure neatly etched in the smooth granite stone. He stopped deep in the middle of the cemetery at a very quiet place where they came to an intersection of overgrown paths.

"I should remember the way," he said, "but now I'm not sure of which path to take. I think talking to you confused me. I'm not sure exactly where we are."

He sat on top of a footstone and motioned for her to sit down too. She didn't but kept her distance.

"I'm scared. I didn't want to be here," she said, "can't we go on? I knew I shouldn't have come. This isn't right. I don't belong here."

"But which way? You don't know either, do you? Besides, don't you want to be a little daring?"

"Daring? That's not a part of me."

"Why not make it a part of you? You can choose to be daring or not, it's not written in stone like these tombstones, you can choose what you want to be." He tapped a tombstone.

She turned scared and confused. The trust she thought she had in him in class was now pushed aside by doubts out here alone with him in the middle of nowhere. She wasn't sure if she should continue on with him, but she didn't want him to leave her there alone either. He had stopped and sat down in the middle of all those graves; she hadn't seen anyone since they entered the grounds of the cemetery. She stayed on edge watching to see if he made any advances toward her. She took out her cell phone but there was no service in the middle of the large cemetery.

"There's no service here, it's a dead zone," he said, amusing himself with his remark.

"But I saw you on your phone a couple of minutes ago."

"Oh, yeah, I was checking my GPS."

Adrianna's sense of fear and impending danger heightened. He knew she wouldn't be able to make a call from where he stopped. She didn't know what to do and her anxiety mounted.

After a long pause, and with no reaction to his pun, he said to her, "I think either of these paths on the left will take us out of here and should lead us to the backside of the hospital. We'll take the first one here on the right."

"I thought you said we should take the ones on the left. Are you sure you know where you're taking me? We're going to the hospital, right?"

His getting lost here didn't add up to her. He knew where to find the government research building that no one else knew much about and how to navigate around it.

"Oh, yeah, right. This first one on the left. Ready to go?"

"Yes."

She was relieved to be walking again on a path, any path, and hoped it would take her out of there. They started out and she stayed on edge until she saw the path lead to where the cemetery ended. She checked her phone and saw she now had service.

They finally reached the backside of the hospital complex and walked through utility areas hidden behind the connected buildings. Industrial pipes and aluminum ducts ran up stained brick walls and disappeared through glass windows covered in grime. Large motors and compressors rumbled and whined in underground vaults. Huge clouds of steam billowed up through metal grates and disappeared in the early grey winter sky.

"Here we are. This is the back where visitors are not allowed so no signs to tell you where you are or where to go. We're going to the eighth floor," Teo announced when they got to the rear service entrance.

As they started up the ramp, the door opened and an orderly was trying single-handedly to maneuver a gurney out. It had a white sheet covering the outlines of a small body.

"Afternoon Teo, how you doing?"

"Hello Liu. Have you eaten today? Let me give you a hand," Teo said.

"Sure. This one light. Not more eighty pounds. Here alone today."

They got the gurney outside and down the ramp to flat ground and headed over to a parked ambulance.

"Liu, isn't this Ken's ambulance? Liu, you're moonlighting on Ken and I bet he doesn't know you've got his ambulance!" Liu gave Teo a worried look of being caught in the act. Teo grinned and shook his head from side to side. "It's okay, don't worry. I won't say anything."

"Thanks Teo, one job not enough. Who your gal? You lucky!"

"Liu, if you don't watch out, your gal might just slip away from you!"

Whatever was under the sheet had shifted to the edge of the gurney. Liu laughed and pushed it to the middle while rolling the gurney. Teo helped Liu put the gurney into the back of the ambulance and Liu drove off.

Adrianna waited at the door experiencing Teo's curious world, and chided herself for doubting him back at the cemetery. She wondered: did she overreact, or was she right to be scared of him and prudent in her caution?

When Teo got to the door, she asked him, "Two questions. Why did you ask him if he 'ate', and was that a dead woman?"

"Chinese greeting, like 'How are you?' And yes, it was probably a dead woman. Must have been her time. From the size and weight, she was probably an old woman."

"Doesn't that scare you, to carry a dead body around? I don't even like being in a cemetery."

"Nope," Teo said. "And yeah, I saw how nervous you were in the cemetery but for me, Death, dead people—they don't upset me. We all die, we all get born, you know, some sooner than others. It's not spooky. Haven't you ever seen a body in an open casket at a funeral or a wake?"

"As a matter of fact, just once. I don't like looking at dead people. It upsets me. There's something, I don't know, unknown about it, frightening, dangerous. I don't handle it well it and I don't like it. But it seems to be around me more than other people."

Without thinking about it, she now wanted to tell him the reason for her fears, so she added, "When I was a little girl, I had to go to a funeral and they made me look at the woman in the coffin. I thought I saw her raise her arms to hug or grab me and I screamed out but of course it was only my imagination, though it seemed so real. And then later, when I was four years old, I saw a dead woman on the street and I've been haunted by her ever since. That really affected me, seeing her lying in the street—dead—so close to me, and it still scares me and gives me nightmares. She was so close. She didn't have any shoes on and she looked straight at me and I was looking back at her too. She had an odd expression on her face. I see her a lot and it really upsets me . . . a lot. Please don't tell anyone. That's why I said Death is around me more than others, she—Death—follows me."

"Of course. We all have our demons. You're lucky you can see yours. I can't see mine but I hear them when they take over, otherwise I don't even know they're there. Famadihana."

"What?"

"Famadihana. Good thing you didn't grow up in Madagascar where they dig up the dead of their ancestors, dress them in fresh cloth, and then celebrate and dance around the tomb to music. Death travels back and forth in time. Today it's here, yesterday it was in some other place and maybe in some other time. Death is always lurking nearby at different times, and in Madagascar at least, they accept it without regret. There are people who believe that not only do the living pay the price for the sins of their ancestors but your ancestors may have paid a price back then for your sins today. Hard to get your arms around that one, huh?" He then paused to make his next point.

"But, we can put up a fight or fool it and sometimes cheat Death out of an early victory. Right? Let's go. The kids are waiting."

They entered the hospital and began their walk through its subterranean corridors—long fluorescent lit corridors which connected one part of the enormous hospital to another and echoed their footsteps over the vinyl tiled floors so ubiquitous to hospitals.

While she followed Teo through the underground labyrinth, she thought, "What is he talking about?" She mused over an internal compass and a power to see he said she has, her anxiety in the cemetery alone with him and yet dependent upon him, tribal peoples dancing around an upturned grave, a dead woman without shoes, a white sheet over a corpse on a gurney, Teo's perception, his knowledge of things, his parents, and of course, his face. His self awareness and confidence in spite of his face highlighted for her her lack of it. Why didn't she have it? Was it buried in her somewhere? She was fine within her own milieu but she hardly ever ventured out of her comfort zone. He was on his own at the age of ten, if you can believe him. She gave him credit and wondered if she had the mettle to be like that, to get close to a dead woman on a gurney, to be unafraid. He was more complicated than she first unthinkingly assumed.

They finally reached a service elevator and took it to the eighth floor where Teo took her down a hallway past a small room made into a chapel, to a pair of doors surrounded by children's drawings on the hallway walls. They walked inside and no sooner had they cleared the doors when the children ran over to Teo and shrieked out his name "Teo! Teo!" They ranged in ages from five to twelve, and about seven of the younger ones grabbed and pulled him to the center of the room. "Teo!" they called out. They pulled his sleeve and made him sit down on a fold-up chair in the middle of the room and as soon as he did, all of the fifteen or so boys and girls sat down on the floor around him. He pulled out one of the storybooks from his knapsack.

"Do you know the story about the baby kangaroo who liked her pouch so much, she didn't want to leave her mommy's pouch?"

"No, no. Read that one! Read that one!" they shouted.

"Okay then, get comfortable and listen to what happened when the baby kangaroo suddenly fell out of her mommy's pouch. Once upon a time..." and he started to read the story he had written and illustrated for them.

Adrianna, left alone and feeling deserted, stood by the doors not knowing what to do or where to go. A heavy set black woman whose fleshy arms and body spilled out of her crisp white nurse's uniform came from across the room and headed straight for her. Adrianna nervously thought she would be asked to leave, that she didn't belong there.

"Is Teo a friend of yours?" the intimidating nurse asked.

"No, no," Adrianna protested, "just a classmate. We take one class together. That's all, that's all."

"Uh huh. I see. Classmates, that's all. Right. Know him long?"

"No, just a few weeks or so," although now it seemed like she knew him, or at least was thinking about him, longer than that. "Maybe only a couple of weeks," she corrected herself.

"Well, if you plan to spend any more time around Teo, you better stop wearing eye makeup."

"What?"

"Oh nothing, you'll see."

There was an unmistakable presence about this big black nurse who was formidable but likeable. She liked Teo a lot, a whole lot.

Adrianna asked her about the children.

"Didn't Teo tell you? These kids are terminal. Each one has a time stamp. Mostly cancer. Teo comes, cheers them up.

He can do that. He can do magic. We use only half the pain killers on these kids for the day or two after Teo comes. Don't know how he does what he does, but he does it. My name is Brenda. What about you?"

"Adrianna."

"Well Adrianna, if Teo led you here, he must have his reasons. You sure are pretty but that wouldn't be it for him." She made no effort to hide her skeptical and reluctant acceptance of Teo bringing Adrianna into her domain.

Adrianna hadn't considered that Teo had a life of his own outside of class, a private life, friends, and these children, and who knows what else.

"Does Teo live on campus?" Brenda asked. "He doesn't talk about himself. Sometimes he comes here toting one of those airplane carry-on bags so I don't know where he came from and he won't say. Funny thing about Teo, he doesn't talk much about himself, but get him started on something else and he's fine though he keeps a distance in spite of his friendly ways, except with the kids. Then I think he's more relaxed and himself, nothing to hide. Of course around them, he's in control and no threats there either."

"No, I don't really know where he lives. He hasn't said anything about that to me either."

"Yeah, he's real nice and real private, almost paranoid, or he's hiding something, not supposed to tell. I thought maybe he did something with that government research at the University. No matter to me."

Adrianna looked around and watched Teo read the story. He was at ease and animated, and hardly looked down at the book. The children were lost in the story and forgot about their pain and that they were in the children's cancer ward. They ooed and aahed and laughed and everyone leaned forward for a better look when he held up one of the storybook pictures for them to see. They looked at him oblivious to his face. They were stuck on a train platform waiting for an unscheduled train to come. No one knew when; time stopped for them. When he finished the story, a girl of about ten who wore a knitted cap which covered the top of her head, jumped up and sat on his lap. He put his arms around her and they both hugged.

"Who's that?" Adrianna asked Brenda.

"That's Amanda, his favorite. The doctors say she only has a month to live. They've been saying that every month for five months now. But Teo is fighting for her. More than the others. He's determined to win this one."

"Win?"

"He thinks he's fighting Death. He fights and cheats. He says Death has its arms around Amanda but he has his arms around her too, even closer and tighter. So far, it's a stalemate. She doesn't get better, and she doesn't get worse either. I have this crazy notion that while he's fighting Death here, it's somewhere else, near someone he knows or loved sometime, and when Teo wins, Death does something to get even. Anyway, Amanda has a lot of spunk, hurts a lot but doesn't show it, and smart too. We all have choices and that little girl decided to be brave and upbeat. She loves Teo and Teo loves her. Everyone knows she's his favorite, nothing wrong if Teo has a favorite."

"I suppose so," Adrianna said, and something quivered within her. "What's he doing now?"

"He plays a game with Amanda, and the others too. He keeps changing the game but in each one, he touches them that way. He knows about pressure points, or applying pressure. He never says what it is he does but he examines them and presses. Whatever it is, it works. They feel better afterward, and like I say, we use less pain killers as a result. Like magic. Oh, he also gives them his teas. He does that too. His teas. He gives their parents teas for them. Better than some of the drugs we use here."

Teo massaged Amanda's shoulders and then her neck and lower back while she sat on his lap. Not quite a massage but a manipulation of her small body and pressing inward at certain spots. Amanda was used to this and liked it; she knew it wasn't a game but played along anyway. When he was through, Amanda gave Teo another big hug and ran off to her parents who were sitting in the corner. Amanda's parents who had been watching Amanda listen and laugh at the story, have to take time off from work to be there when they can, and especially when Teo is there so they can see their little girl laugh again.

Teo got up and went over to Adrianna and Brenda. Brenda hugged Teo. She was too big for her white uniform.

"Seems like you and Adrianna already met. Brenda, you know I love you, but that uniform on you just isn't right. Can't you get another one? I thought you had the lowdown on everyone here."

"Sure do. But find me a few hundred dollars and someone to make a uniform that'll fit this woman's body, not for someone like pretty Miss Adrianna over here. Nothing personal honey." She looked at Adrianna with that last remark.

"I see what you mean," Teo said in the same good natured spirit. He took out his wallet. It was a European style which had inner sections to hold paper currency of different kinds, and opened it to show he didn't have more than about thirty dollars himself, as if he would have given her the money if he had had it. His hand covered and hid a separate, less visible section of the wallet which contained euros, pesos, British pounds, and two passports, one U. S. and one from another country in the E. U. They chuckled at the little joke as he put his wallet away.

Amanda's parents came over and excused their interruption but wanted to say hello to Teo before they had to get back to work. They said they were almost out of the last batch of the teas he gave them and he said he needs to bring different ones next time. They thanked him and told him he's in their prayers every night. "God bless you Teo, God bless you!" they said and left.

"Who is that Asian boy playing with Amanda?" he asked Brenda. "I haven't seen him before."

"That's Patrick, he's Japanese. He came in a few days ago. Very quiet. The doctors are still giving him the usual tests. We won't know exactly what he's got for a week or two."

"Patrick," she called out, "come over and say hello to Mr. Teo who read you the story. Did you like the story?"

Patrick was a small Japanese boy, about six years old. He didn't show much emotion and he was shy but couldn't hide the pain which coursed through his little frame. Teo said hello and asked Patrick if he hurt. Patrick nodded.

"Would you like me to help you feel better?" Teo asked.

"Yes," the boy quietly answered.

"Will you let me help you?"

"Yes," the boy said again shyly in a meek voice.

"Okay then, let's see if I can find the baby kangaroo in you that wanted to stay in her mommy's pouch and make her come out. Okay?"

The shy boy said okay and Teo put his hands on the boy. As he moved his hands over the boy's neck, back, arms, and legs, he leaned in close around the boy's head. In a few moments, he was done.

"Well, Patrick, I think she saw me coming and hid from me."

"Thank you anyway Mr. Teo," he said quietly.

Adrianna bent down and asked Patrick who was this stuffed bear he was holding. He didn't answer but held it closely.

"May I please see your bear?" Adrianna asked him.

He nodded his head yes and cautiously held it out for her and she took it.

"What's your name?" she asked looking at the bear. Patrick shrugged. "Well, I think we should give him a name, don't you? Let's see, he's got a tummy. Patrick, what's your whole name?"

"Hata," he said, "Patrick Hata," in his soft voice.

"Excellent, how about we call the bear Tummy Hata? Is that okay?"

"Yes, that's okay. Thank you." He took back the teddy bear and walked off to the window where he stood alone and looked outside at the grey sky.

Teo turned to Brenda. "Call his parents and tell them to come and put them up in a room. Tell them to come today."

"Oh no, not so soon," she said. Brenda took out a tissue to wipe away a tear. She knew what he meant. How can that be? The boy just got here. The tests aren't finished yet. "How long?" she asked. Teo said he thought maybe a few days before they put him in hospice and by then a couple of days more. Teo could feel and smell the effects of the cancerous poison which had spread throughout the sweet little boy's body. There was nothing could be done. His parents should say goodbye to their little boy while he could still talk to them. Death wins this one without a fight.

Brenda said okay and left to make the phone call and arrangements. Brenda had seniority in the hospital but even without it, no one wanted to mess with Brenda if they didn't have to. She knew where all the skeletons were hidden and somehow knew your dirtiest secrets, the ones you thought no one could possibly know. She was an intimidating, tough senior nurse with an imposing and overbearing demeanor. No one got in her way, neither nurses, orderlies, administrators, not even many of the doctors. If she wanted something, she got it. She allowed Teo to touch the kids when she was in the room and she could cut through red tape. Without Brenda, Teo couldn't do what he did there. She had no problem breaking rules; she enjoyed it if she thought it would do some good. In the short time she knew him, she saw his unlicensed and unorthodox ways worked so she made sure no one interfered with his games with the kids. And no one dared to say anything about it. Even the parents gave her a large and clear berth when she allowed Teo to touch their children, especially when they saw that Teo and his teas helped them.

He got his knapsack and started for the door. Adrianna followed. In the hallway, she stopped and sat down on a plastic bench. He sat next to her.

"How do you know what the doctors don't? How can you be so sure? Where did you learn all that? What's going on here? Who are you?" She was confused and angry.

She looked him squarely in the face. She wanted to know, not look away, to know who he was, the first time she acted naturally with him, face or no face, and he saw it.

"You should be careful around me," Teo said.

"And that little boy, Patrick? He's going to die in a few days?"

"Yes, I think so."

"He's so little. He doesn't look that sick." Adrianna shed a tear and her eye makeup started to run.

Teo said, "Let's go now. I have to stop off at the sports stadium on the way back." He pulled his hoodie up over his head and they left.

She was glad she didn't have to walk through too much of the campus with him.

CHAPTER SEVEN

Adrianna had a room in a suite on the fifth floor of Anstace, one of many campus dormitories. The University spread out over four hundred acres with countless concrete walking paths criss-crossed over and connecting dormitories, lecture halls, a sports stadium, gymnasium, meandering spring and small foot bridges. It was well endowed particularly with the grants it received for work being done at the research center at the edge of campus which no one knew anything about but speculated it was an international military project involving experimental drugs.

She needed to clear her mind so she put on her sweats and went out for a run. Phi Beta Kappa saw her, ran from the two fraternity guys playing with him, and joined her when she rounded the fraternity quad; she had dog biscuits ready. The frat guys yelled for her to bring Phi Beta Kappa back so they could flirt with her but she didn't want their attention this time. She put on her earphones to block them out and tuned into one of her music playlists.

For no particular reason, she ran along Stadium Road which has a long curve to the left along the full length of the football field before it ends at the sports stadium. Through the chain link fence, she saw the lonely bleachers waiting across the quiet field and the markings of the ten yard lines and white goal posts at either end. The morning rain had almost dried up but in the falling afternoon temperatures, a few wet spots began to freeze.

She was jogging on the right side of the road toward the sports stadium when she felt an odd cramp in her foot. She never gets a cramp from an easy jog and thought she might have pulled a muscle. She slowed down to a near stop, and as she walked slowly on the edge of the road, she saw a sneaker off to the right in the grass.

Out of curiosity, she stepped off the black macadam of the road, went a few feet onto the grass and sat down next to it while she took off her shoes to massage her bare feet and curl her toes a few times. She stretched out on the cold, damp ground and looked up at the late afternoon wintry sky which made everything bleak in that angled light of the early setting sun. Phi Beta Kappa played with her shoes as she tried to read the identity tag dangling from his pet collar chain, a worn and dulled stainless steel identity tag no longer readable. She looked at both sides of the metal tag but whatever had been written was now worn away.

She got up to take back her shoes and continue her run when she saw that the sneaker she first noticed, was not a sneaker at all but a stuffed teddy bear instead, like Tummy Hata, the one she named for Patrick in the hospital, something strangely out of place on a college campus. How could it have gotten there? She stepped over, picked up the teddy bear and held it for Phi Beta Kappa who dropped her shoes to give it a sniff. She sat down on the ground again while he played with it and she changed the music she was listening to.

At the same time, a car heading away from the sports stadium hit a patch of ice and slid silently across both lanes making its inexorable way to Adrianna. It undoubtedly would have hit her if she had still been jogging on the road; but she was now sitting on the ground with the teddy bear to relieve the cramp in her foot. The car couldn't see her playing with the dog and continued to make its way silently toward her. When it was thirty yards away, Adrianna stood up and the car went into its own lane. She had been playing with Phi Beta Kappa with her back to the road, and when she turned around to see what was happening, the car was already moving in its own lane again. She didn't see what the driver thought he saw, that is, a shoeless woman in a green dress standing in the road near Adrianna. Adrianna never knew that her unusual cramp and the sneaker-turned-teddy-bear strangely appearing on the campus grounds—and the appearance of that woman to the driver—led her out of harm's way. She gave the teddy bear to Phi Beta Kappa who held it in his mouth while she jogged back to the Anstace dorm now that the cramp in her foot was gone.

When she got back to her room, she showered, put on jeans and a sweatshirt, left her shoes off, and tried to do homework but couldn't concentrate. She put down her book of French poems and looked out the window. Students walked to and from Anstace on paths that crisscrossed the campus. Where does he live—Teo, René? She never thought to ask. There was a lot she didn't know; maybe she didn't care to know, maybe she was afraid to know, perhaps he didn't want her to know. He, on the other hand, was insatiably curious, remembered everything about her, and always left her unsettled. She tried to dismiss him from her mind but his face, that awful face, showed up unannounced and uninvited. She decided that after dinner, she would talk to her suitemates about him and maybe call Charlotte for her thoughts as well. In the meantime, she absent-mindedly began to copy into her notebook one of the French poems as she rubbed her freckle and waited for her suitemates, Samantha, Wanda and Erika, to go down for dinner.

CHAPTER EIGHT

They agreed they should meet regularly to go over suite issues like clean up schedules and use of the refrigerator so they decided to meet monthly and make the monthly meetings into a night off to coincide with their same time of month for Adrianna, Samantha and Wanda when they just wanted to lounge around and not do any schoolwork.

Samantha was Adrianna's closest friend and roomed with her every year since they were freshmen: a light spirited, down to earth and sensible girl, plain looking at her best, who never dated much until she recently met and started going out with Kendall, who, she proudly boasts, is on the wrestling team . . . well, sort of. She giggles a lot, which seemingly puts an unimportant gloss over what she says, as if she took nothing seriously but in fact belies her common sense intelligence and good sense of direction.

Whereas Kendall was Samantha's first boyfriend, Wanda, on the other hand, another suitemate, had too many first boyfriends. She never went out with anyone more than twice and was content with her frequent one night stands and the excitement of forbidden sex. Her promiscuity was common knowledge and spoken about openly.

On the way down to dinner, Adrianna asked Wanda, "Wanda, what's it like for you? You have so many first times with guys. You couldn't have felt a lot for each one. Did you feel anything at all for any of them?"

"No, not really. In fact, it's always been just okay, but I keep thinking it'll be different next time."

Wanda's cavalier attitude made Adrianna think. Wasn't that what it had been like with her Julian? Just okay? Shouldn't it be something memorable? Could it be memorable with Julian?

"Love can be ugly, very ugly," Erika interrupted.

Erika, the last suitemate, was an exchange student from São Paulo, Brazil: a taut, militant Sonia Braga look-alike, with an olive complexion, big dark eyes and thick black eyebrows. Quick to criticize and not interested in dating, she was often rude but went out of her way to cultivate a connection with Wanda even though they were opposites in many ways.

"Ugly?" Wanda asked.

"Yes, ugly. Why do you think love always has to be mutual, or even-sided and pure? It can be a one way street mixed with hate, and hurt and pain. You don't get it. None of you do. You don't see how mean people can be . . . mean to themselves and to each other. How they can let you fall in love with them and selfishly relish it, without caring a whit for you. Love may mean one thing to you and something else to them. You all live in a fantasy world. And I just can't get out of a rut, falling for someone who doesn't or can't fall for me."

"No, it's not ugly," Samantha said. "You should want to help each other do what the other doesn't do so well, help them be better."

"As I said, I don't want to depend on anyone anymore, male or female! Not me! Take what you can get. Be selfish!" Erika barked.

When they got to the dining room, Adrianna told them she wanted to talk about someone she had met, but later, upstairs, not over dinner. The tables were communal, first come, first served, and reserving a table of six for only four of them, was frowned upon so privacy was not guaranteed. Though

Anstace was a co-ed dorm, eating was usually by sex, the boys ate with boys, and the girls with girls. This caused a small social problem for Leslie, the one and only transgender student in Anstace. Leslie sat down with them. They didn't have a choice.

"Hi," Leslie said and was greeted with a civil but lukewarm "Hi" from them.

"I'm limiting myself to salads this week. I read if you do that, you kind of cleanse your system and it can do almost what a colonic does. I won't be able to test that since I never had a colonic. How about you?"

"Leslie, this isn't quite dinner conversation," Erika berated him. "Besides, we happened to have been in the middle of a conversation if you had been any bit at all observant when you sat down. Which part of you didn't see that?" she hissed.

"Well Miss—or should I say 'Mister' to you, or haven't you told anyone else about that yet?—you don't have to spray me with your pheromones to make a point! Tell me, does being so ugly come naturally to you, or is it something you managed to get past the customs officials when you flew in from the Amazon?" At that, Leslie got up, his head held purposefully high, and walked away to another table.

As he left, Erika held her right hand up high for all to see, extended her middle finger, and gave him the finger, thrusting it upward and toward him.

"Are all gays like that?" Adrianna asked.

"He's not gay, he's transgender, but he does have a bit of that affect," Erika answered. "I need something to read. Anyone have anything, anything at all you can recommend?"

"Most books I read now are in French," Adrianna said. "It helps me to speak it more fluently. I actually like the poems I've been reading, *Les Fleurs du Mal*. I don't think you want any of those!"

"Is that why you copy them into your notebook? I've seen you do that lately using a green pen," Samantha asked.

"I'm not sure why. I guess it helps but I do it absent-mindedly. I started doing it, that's all," Adrianna said.

"I finished one you might like," Wanda said.

"What's it about?" Erika asked, giving Wanda her focused attention.

"Well, it's an equal mix of romance and suspense. It's got sympathetic and interesting characters, subtle clues, the supernatural, social commentary, whimsy and sex all thrown into the pot. It held my interest and I can see it as a movie. It's a good beach read and in fact there are some delicious parts I want to re-read!"

"Great, just what I wanted. Can I borrow it when we get upstairs?" Erika asked.

"Sure, but leave it on the cocktail table when you aren't reading it so I can get to it when I want to, and I'll do the same. Okay?"

"Sure, no problem. Cocktail table it is," Erika answered thinking that was a bit overly complicated but typical of Wanda.

"Wanda, where are you going for Christmas?" Adrianna asked.

"I think I'm going skiing but I'm not sure. Want to come?"

"No," Adrianna said. "I don't ski. I'm not a skier and I'd be afraid to try. I don't want everyone to see me when I keep falling down! That's not me. Thanks for the invite though. And I think it's your turn to clean."

"Yes, it's Wanda's turn," Samantha said.

"Is it? I don't remember but if you say so. It's not my favorite job but I'll do it," Wanda said.

"No, it's not, it's Adrianna's turn," Erika said.

The others disagreed. Adrianna had cleaned last time.

"No, I'm sure of it. It's not Wanda's turn to clean. Absolutely. She shouldn't have to do it." Erika was set on sparing Wanda the job she didn't like.

It wasn't worth an argument so Adrianna volunteered to do this week's clean up out of turn. She didn't mind and thought it would end the confrontation.

"That's selfless and so admirable of you. Something new?" Erika said.

Adrianna replied right back, "As you said, there are people who don't care a whit for anyone else but themselves although you do make an exception for Wanda. Her fucking around so much must really get to you. Doesn't it?"

Erika gave Adrianna the finger.

CHAPTER NINE

After dinner, Wanda and Erika went directly to their rooms which gave Samantha time to talk to Adrianna.

"You know Kendall and I never said we love each other and if I say it first, he'd say it back because he'd think he should. I mean telling someone you love them doesn't necessarily mean you do, and not saying it doesn't mean you don't. Right? I've never been in love so how can I be sure? If I have a doubt, how can I tell him I love him? What if I don't really love him?"

"We all have doubts. I have doubts. If you're waiting for a soul mate, how would you ever know? How long would you wait, a year, a lifetime, before settling for second best?"

"And I think I might have to take care of him more than he would take care of me. I'm not ashamed to say I want someone I can depend on, someone I can lean on, someone more confident than me so I don't have to take a risk . . . and bear the consequences myself all the time!" she added with a giggle.

"I think," Adrianna said, "if he wanted to take care of me, that's got to be important. And I want that someone to be someone that I want to take care of too."

She then realized she didn't feel that way about Julian and doubted whether he could feel that way about her. She never even thought about depending on him.

"What do you think about what Erika said to Leslie at dinner?" Samantha asked.

"I thought she didn't have to be so rude though I don't like being around him either. He makes me uncomfortable. There's nothing like that in Bellevue."

"Adrianna, you really need to get with it. He won't rub off on you or contaminate you with something. Right? Anyway, so what do you really think about Kendall?"

"He's nice."

"No, come on. You've dated a lot, more than me. I'm not a great looker and neither is he but that doesn't matter to us. He adores me, yet he's immature and clumsy, and even more inexperienced than I am!" she giggled. "I'm his first real girlfriend so naturally he wants to spend all his time with me. Something nags at me and stops me from jumping in totally. Know what I mean?" she giggled again.

"Well, from what you say, what you see is what you get with him and there's really nothing so negative, and when I get my turn to talk about someone, I'll give you negatives! Questioning yourself is healthy. I bet he's got doubts too. You say you feel something pulling him to you and I would go with that. Trust what you feel more than what you think. Don't overthink it. That's my advice for what it's worth."

Adrianna then wondered if that was her own thought or one she got from Teo.

Meanwhile, Erika had gone into Wanda's room where Wanda was sitting up in bed applying lipstick to her thick lips and examining her work in a hand held mirror—and spending too much time on it, thought Erika. Erika sat down next to her on the bed. All around them on the bed and on the floor, were Wanda's clothes, and books, and shoes, and just plain stuff lying about and covering everything. By contrast, Erika kept her room like a military barracks—stark, neat, precise. While Wanda fussed with the lipstick, Erika scanned the room and fingered all the papers and the heaped up clothes which engulfed them on the bed, and kept her hand on Wanda's thigh.

"So, let me see the book you mentioned," Erika said patting Wanda's thigh.

"These earrings," Wanda said, as if she hadn't heard Erika, "I don't know if I can keep them. They looked good when I bought them but they might irritate my skin. I should return them. What do you think?"

"The book, Wanda, I came to borrow the book," Erika said and slapped Wanda's thigh as a gentle punishment for not paying attention but kept her hand there, moving it back and forth and feeling the fabric of Wanda's pants.

With mirror in hand, Wanda got up from the bed and rummaged through a bookcase which was the repository for books and anything else that could be jammed in. She extricated a book from the mess and handed it to Erika as several things fell to the floor. She then continued to put on lipstick while uttering self-indulged staccato phrases without actually closing her lips, trying not to smear her lipstick when she spoke. She didn't look at Erika for any answer, just at herself and her handiwork in the mirror.

Erika took the book and went into the livingroom but not before eyeing the excessive lipstick Wanda had put on, still looking at herself in the mirror.

Adrianna was about to join the others in the livingroom when she heard someone at her door. She turned around to see no one and knew it must have been the barefoot, green-dressed woman, this time unseen.

All of them were sitting on the couch or on the floor around the Parsons cocktail table which they had bought for the suite in a thrift shop, when Adrianna told them she needed feedback about someone she met.

She told them everything she could think of: how Teo spoke up in class for her, his initial arrogance toward her and the professor, how he puts her off balance, his sketching, the sandwiches and teas, how he frightened her in the cemetery, the hospital, Amanda, Brenda, Patrick, the gurney, and of course, his face. When they wanted more lurid details about his face and twitching lip, she had a strange urge to defend him against a foreign sick interest.

"Why does he keep popping up in my head? When I'm not with him, I feel like my normal self but he's on my mind. When I am with him, it feels right too, but a different kind of right, like a different part of me comes out. It's strange. I feel secure and insecure, and somehow afraid of something too. Should I stop talking to him which is pretty much only in class? I don't want to hurt him even though we're not really friends. I want to be with him and at the same time, I don't want to be with him. Am I being selfish?"

Erika, the Paulista, said "Drop him without another word, everyone knows guys are a different kind of animal but they're animals and under that face of his, he's still an animal. Besides, he's a control freak, so run girl, run!" She sounded like a drill sergeant.

Wanda, the indecisive, looked at Erika, barely nodded agreement and asked them if they thought the lipstick gloss she put on looked good. She wasn't sure if she should take it off, or maybe it was the wrong color for her.

"Hullo. Earth to Wanda, Earth to Wanda. Come in please," Adrianna chided. "You're flying solo again in your spaceship. Come down out of orbit and join us, okay?"

"Leave her alone," Erika said. "That's who she is and she can't help herself. We all know that. It's what makes Wanda, Wanda."

"Sorry," Wanda answered, somewhat, but not altogether apologetically. "I was listening and well, I think his face would give anyone nightmares and you should tell him you didn't want to see him anymore because, 'being brutally honest', you couldn't take it." Erika and Wanda gave each other a high five.

On the other hand, Samantha the sensible and true to her nature, was empathetic. "Talk to him about how you feel or what's going on. Aside from his face, he seems kind and gentle, maybe a little spooky—and okay, he's controlling—but quite extraordinary. I'd like to meet him," and she added one of her giggles.

"Really, you want to meet him? I'm ashamed to say I don't want to be seen with him, and yet you want to meet him? I can't even imagine what my mother would say if I brought him home! Maybe you won't feel that way after you see him. He's really repulsive to look at. His face is so unnatural, and no one you would ever consider going out with. He has a face only a mother could love and then I'm not so sure! It's pitiable."

"I don't know. So he looks like that. Really, so what?" Samantha asked. "You say he stood up for you in class, well, sort of. He helps those kids in his free time, and that Chinese guy Liu and the big nurse like him. He remembers everything you tell him. I wish Kendall was like that. Is Julian? Adrianna, I didn't grow up looking at life through pretty prisms like you do. Let's face it. You always had good looking boys who want to go out with you and everyone tells you how pretty you are. You are pretty. That's who you are, and your life since, well, since ever!" and she added one of her giggles to highlight the point. "Listen, there's nothing wrong with that. Sometimes I wish I were pretty," with another giggle, "but, at least for me, I don't measure up things that way. Look, all I'm saying is like it or not, the problem could be you might actually like this guy with a face and it doesn't fit for you. He's a challenge and shouldn't have made it past your front door, but he did. Your pretty prisms aren't filtering him out as well as they used to and aren't as strong as they used to be and that's what's going on in you."

Adrianna was silent.

CHAPTER TEN

She didn't talk to him at the next class but at the one after that, before she could say anything when she passed his row, he asked her if she would come with him to visit the children again. He needed her to read a story so he could be free to sit with them on the floor. She was thinking about it when he handed her a storybook.

She hesitated. She hadn't made up her mind yet about what to do with him. It would mean another walk with him on campus and alone through the cemetery. She fought both sides of a tug of war. Go with him, or don't; be seen with him, or not. She could go just to be nice, to fulfill a social obligation, nothing personal. Or, she could act from her gut without overthinking it, as he would say, and go because she wanted and chose to go. She can't say no to him even though she was torn and can't bear to look at him. She wasn't sure why she ultimately decided to say yes, she just had to. And anyway, she wanted to see the kids and help them too.

They started to walk to the hospital, Adrianna had a headband to show off her face, and Teo a hoodie to cover his. On the way, she wanted him to tell her more about himself, and he did, at least a little. He told her briefly some of Samuel's story leaving out parts about himself. He thought she might find Samuel's story interesting and be satisfied with just that. So he told her how Samuel and Didier met at a café in Paris back in 1952.

Life was good then for Didier, Camille, Jeanne-Marie and Samuel. Even though Camille worked for Didier and had a husband, and Jeanne-Marie later got married and had her own family, the four of them became very close to each other, and went on picnics, to Jeanne-Marie's wedding and the christening of Mimi, her baby girl. Didier and Samuel went with them—and everywhere else—together, and Samuel lived in Didier's mansion with Didier whenever he came to Paris which was more and more as the years passed. When Camille's husband died, Didier insisted she move into the mansion and take care of the house and live with him.

When he died later at seventy seven, Camille was sixty four and long a widow, and while she could have moved in with Jeanne-Marie's family, she stayed at the mansion until she died, which was Didier's wish.

Teo told Adrianna some other stories about Samuel, but there was much more he could have said. She was disappointed he stopped, particularly since he wasn't comfortable talking about his background, but they had reached the children's ward and he couldn't—or simply didn't want to—continue.

Brenda stood by the doors and asked Adrianna what was she doing there... again? Adrianna faced Brenda squarely and told her she came with Teo.

"Are you friends yet?" Brenda rejoined. "Maybe so, maybe not, you're still wearing eye make up."

Teo got the same exuberant greeting from the time-stamped kids. He told them he had a special treat. He brought a real princess, Princess Aimée, who, if they asked her, would read one of the stories but Princess Aimée might be a little nervous so they should make a special effort to welcome her. Amanda took Adrianna by the hand and led her to a chair in the middle of the room and asked her in a loud, grown up voice to please read them a story, and there was no need to be nervous, everyone would help her. Actually, she was nervous.

She took off her shoes and sat on the floor instead of the chair and curled her toes. She put her bag on the chair, opened the book and began to read the story about the itch who was looking for a foot to belong to. She read it competently with a stage presence and an unknown thespian flair. Like the kids, time stopped for her too, and then she was content, with herself and these little people who sat on the floor all around her—children waiting on a platform without a clock, waiting for the last train to come for many of them. While she read, Teo sat on the floor and play acted the story. He invited one at a time to sit in front of him, take off their shoes and socks, and as he pretended to look for the itch, he massaged, and pressed, and stroked their feet and calves. Each time he said he couldn't find the itch and it was okay for them to put their shoes and socks back on.

At the end of the story, he asked them if he should look at Princess Aimée's feet to find the itch. Of course they all laughed and squealed for him to do it. He knelt in front of her (told her the touching of an elder's feet in India was a sign of respect), and massaged each foot up to her mid-calf but carefully not any higher. He said out loud he found the itch and put it in his pocket and if anyone misbehaved or didn't take their medicines, he would take the itch out of his pocket and put it on their nose! More shrieks of laughter and Adrianna thought it felt good and wondered if he wasn't showing off for her.

Amanda's parents came by to say hello and Teo gave them a new batch of tea with instructions for its preparation and dosage. They said their goodbyes and God Blesses.

Standing nearby almost out of sight, a Japanese couple waited patiently. They approached Teo with formal respect and bowed their heads. The man, in understandable but broken

English, said they were Patrick Hata's parents and they came to thank Teo. Because of Teo, they were able to say goodbye to their little boy when he was still conscious. They valued those few days Teo gave them before Patrick could no longer be the boy they knew and loved. They had taken photos of Patrick smiling and he took one of the photos in both hands and with a slight bow and both hands extended, presented it to Teo.

Patrick's mother, who stood behind her husband, kept her head in a bowed position, and spoke very quietly in Japanese. Her husband began to translate. "My wife says she would like to . . . ." Teo interrupted and began to speak softly in Japanese. He was privileged to help them see Patrick off and he will keep the photo to remind him of the beautiful boy he and they could only have had for a short time. He said other words of comfort and the mother began to cry and apologized for her crying in front of Teo. He asked if they were Buddhists and they said yes, they followed Shinto and Buddhism. He would like to perform a Buddhist ceremony for Patrick if they would permit, that he had some training by Buddhist monks. They were speechless, bowed up and down, and said they would be honored.

He took them to the small room made into a chapel down the hall where he carried his backpack behind a screen and came out wearing a thin orange robe over his street clothes, barefoot, carrying a small bowl and a stick of incense. He lit the incense and in Japanese said a few words and they responded with a few words as the smoke of the incense wafted up around them. Patrick's name could be heard. Amanda, Brenda and Adrianna followed them and watched the ceremony from one of the few rows at the back of the small makeshift chapel. It lasted only five minutes when Teo took off his orange robe, folded it carefully and placed the bowl on top and handed them to the father. The father bowed and took it from Teo with both hands; the mother cried and apologized again for her unseemly behavior. They thanked Teo, and after he, Brenda and Adrianna left, Mr. and Mrs. Hata sat down in the first row of the little chapel and cried, holding each other, rocking back and forth.

Amanda, who had stayed behind, went over to the Hatas. She sat down next to them and told them Patrick was a nice boy and she liked him. She said she knows that many of the kids there are going to die. And when that happens, she doesn't get a chance to say goodbye, not even at a funeral because the funerals are outside the hospital. This was the first time she could say a goodbye and thanked them for letting her sit with them. Mrs. Hata put her arm around Amanda's shoulders and gently drew her close. Amanda put her little girl's arm around Mrs. Hata's petite waist and leaned her head against Mrs. Hata.

"Can you come back and visit me?" Amanda asked in her girlish voice, and Mrs. Hata nodded her head yes.

In the hall, Brenda saw Adrianna's eye makeup had smeared. Adrianna caught sight of Brenda's knowing look that said, "I told you so." Adrianna asked Teo where did he learn that, and Brenda chimed in with where the 'hell' did he learn that?

"Some other time," which had the intended effect of ending the inquiry without answering it.

Outside of the hospital, Teo said he needed to stop off somewhere so Adrianna should finish walking to the dorm by herself. She stopped and faced Teo looking at him in the face from under his hoodie. It was such a hideous face but she had something she had to say.

"I am going to be brutally honest. That's what you want. Okay, here goes, brutal honesty. You're bothering me! I think about you when I don't want to. It pains me when I see your face and I can't look at you for too long. You and I will never be together. Do you understand? It's not going to happen. Never. Understand? I don't mind walking with you on campus because I know everyone knows I'm just being nice. If we can have that understanding, then we can keep this up. Otherwise, I think you'll be crushed in spite of what you say and I don't want to be responsible for that. So there it is!" She said it sternly, defiantly, triumphantly.

He waited until she finished. He was unmoved. He got into a somber mood and spoke in the faint, hollow voice that wasn't his own.

"Aimée, listen up . . . . Be careful . . . . Listen to what I say . . . . If you fall in love with me, it will be very, very hard on you. It will come over you like a tidal wave, the undertow will drag you under. You'll feel like you're drowning and you won't know up from down, who you are or what you are. You won't sleep. It will be hard and if you fall in love with me, your life will never be the same and nothing like you could have ever imagined. You should know that now."

She was dumbfounded. As soon as she knows what she's going to do and regains her footing, he knocks her off balance, uniquely, abruptly, with brute force. She had neither the tools nor the words to deal with this. She said nothing.

Teo didn't make the stop he had planned to make. Instead, they walked back together. Neither said anything until after they had gone through the cemetery and past the research center, and got back to the campus grounds. She said she thought he had to stop off somewhere and he didn't have to walk her the whole way. When they got to Anstace, he walked in too.

"It's okay, you didn't have to come into the dorm," she said.

"Of course, but I live on the third floor, and I think you said you live on the fifth."

CHAPTER ELEVEN

None of his suitemates nor anyone else had seen Teo's room. Keeping his privacy meant no fraternization. He was up early before anyone else, and frequently slipped away for a few days, and no one even knew if he was in or not. He stayed up until 1:00 a.m., and woke up at 6:30 a.m. He was almost as invisible to them as he was to everyone else, except now for Adrianna.

He had moved in and set up his room in the summer before the semester started so no one saw the expensive high-tech equipment he brought in: computers, audio, video and other equipment, a hot plate and a high priced table, chair, wall unit, and lamp. Walls that weren't covered with the wall unit, were covered with sound-minimizing fabrics and *objets d'art*. In spite of its smallness and crowding, the room was nonetheless harmonious and calm, helped by his use of traditional *feng shui* elements.

He barely spoke to anyone on campus except Adrianna. When he wasn't doing that, or planning for it, or going to the hospital, he was reading, writing, sketching, sewing, playing on his portable piano keyboard, taking care of his emails, working out in a gym at unusual hours, or meditating on the tatami mat in his room. Or, he was mysteriously coming and going. He was never bored or lonely but knew having been aloof for so long exacted a price which, perhaps, he should stop paying. Adrianna was a beacon pulling him in. He could neither make it out nor understand it but he was mysteriously drawn to it. She was certainly good looking, but that wasn't it. She didn't seem to have anything else that helped him explain his attraction to her.

* * * * *

Adrianna called Charlotte. She described Teo to her and went on and on so much Charlotte finally said she wasn't herself and wondered if she was okay. Adrianna slowed down and asked her for advice. Charlotte didn't have any; she didn't know Teo and besides she had one of her migraines so now wasn't the best time to talk on the phone, maybe this could wait until she came home for Christmas? Adrianna was eager to go home and talk to her big sister. Good thing Christmas break was only a couple of days away.

CHAPTER TWELVE

Teo packed only a few things for his carry-on bag. He drove to the airport about thirty miles from campus and pulled into the long term parking lot. A car with a couple in the front seat stopped in the middle of the parking lot aisle behind him. He took no special notice of them while he parked his car. The lot was busy and almost full with Christmas in two days and there were so many people traveling on one of the busiest travel days of the year.

His first stop was the Upper West Side in New York, to Samuel's apartment in one of those buildings built in the 1920s and 1930s when the name of its architect meant something. It was a large classic seven room apartment which had ceilings over nine feet high and walls made of real plaster instead of hollow sounding sheetrock. The housekeeper comes every week and had stocked the refrigerator with freshly squeezed orange juice, eggs, yogurt, and cream cheese with scallions, and left a fresh loaf of multi-grain bread (unsliced) from Zabar's on the counter. He sorted through the accumulated mail which had not yet been forwarded, checked his emails and answered several of them. A quick shower and a change of clothes from his wardrobe in the master bedroom, and then a walk down Broadway and across Central Park South to an office building on Park and East 54th Street. He went up to the modern offices of a law firm which occupied the entire 34th and 35th floors. Its grand client reception area had clubby chairs and couches that offset a well decorated modern decor. He was taken into a glass walled conference room for his meeting where the glass walls became frosted and opaque for privacy at the flip of a switch.

When the meeting was over, one of the younger lawyers, an attractive brunette whose tight fitting white blouse and dark blue jacket and slacks hinted of a body well maintained, invited him out for a drink and then dinner. She was too young a lawyer to be a rainmaker to entertain clients; she actually hoped he would join her. Teo thanked her but said he had things to do and not much time before he flew to Paris.

His next stop was a small nondescript mid-block building in the Plaza District not far from the Grand Army Plaza on Central Park South. There were video cameras on the outside which pointed to the street, the sidewalk and the entrance door; on the inside, other cameras were set up in the hallways along with plain-clothed security guards standing in front of some of the doors. Access through those doors required both digital and biometric retinal identification.

Teo had a series of short meetings, and in the last one, Portman, a tall well-built fellow, gave him an envelope and said he'd have more later that day. They arranged to meet for dinner at the Red Rooster, a restaurant on Lenox Avenue in Harlem.

By the time those meetings were over, it was late afternoon but already dark and nippy outside. The streets were bustling with tourists and office workers who wore scarves and gloves against the cold air. The police did a good job keeping the bumper-to-bumper traffic on Fifth Avenue moving and the intersections clear of the hoards of people who otherwise would have blocked the cross streets causing an enormous gridlock. Store windows were aglitter and decorated for Christmas and the excitement in the air was palpable. Bergdorf's, as usual, had the most imaginative and stunning window displays, the best in the City, where tourists and locals alike stopped and crowded the sidewalks. Everyone tried to get close enough for a good look at their windows which were jam-packed with ingenious delights, and be awed and marvel at all their creative intricacy.

He had time before his meeting at the Red Rooster, so with his scarf wrapped around his face, he walked down the west side of Fifth Avenue and stopped at Henri Bendel to see what they did for their decorations this year. They had a splendid make-believe, bare limbed tree painted in shiny gold, hug upside down from the high ceiling. From luminescent gold branches hung imitation red and green semi-precious stones and diamonds which sparkled against iridescent branches like a giant mobile of glittering gems. For the young at heart, red candy apples hung down from golden lolly pop sticks. Shoppers didn't know what to look at first when they came in from Fifth Avenue: the magical gold tree hanging over their heads or all the beautifully gift wrapped Christmas items festively displayed. Teo picked up one of them, a snow globe, and shook it. He saw Santa and his reindeer fly over the skyline of Manhattan and he saw himself in it, and the snow falling all around them.

He went down Fifth to Rockefeller Center. Sightseers mobbed the huge Christmas tree towering seventy eight feet above their heads. They took photos on their tablets and phones of the beautiful Norway spruce and its countless sparkling tree lights. Looking down to the ice rink below, sightseers tried to see it all, bunching up four deep against the railings. Skaters moved to the sound of piped in organ music, and festive triangular flags that seemed to be made of silk, undulated smoothly in the gentle evening breeze, silently billowing their red, blue and white folds of color. It was as exciting as it always was. Of all the far off places he had been to, he thought no place could compare to New York City at Christmas time.

Across from the tree, he stopped to see the spectacular sound and light show projected onto the facade of Saks Fifth Avenue, and then went up the east side of Fifth to take in the windows at Cartier and then Tiffany's, where he looked at the jewelry dazzlingly and cleverly displayed, all in Tiffany blue. Inside Tiffany's, he picked up an antique oval hand mirror which had a patterned silver handle, chrome tourmalines and a fleur-de-lys of semi-precious stones on the back. He looked at it and then held it up; he lowered his scarf and examined his face carefully in the mirror, from his forehead to his neck, and ear to ear, watched his lip twitch, and he shrugged his head.

He finished his tour with a walk up Madison Avenue to see the brightly lit holiday windows of its high-end stores. Ralph Pucci seductive mannequins showed off elegant designs in expensive fabrics and furs. Precisely aimed halogen spotlights made the jewelry sparkle brilliantly. Most people wondered: who could possibly afford all that?

The last stop on Madison was the mansion Ralph Lauren converted into a store which reminded him of the mansion in Paris by Park Monceau which he would leave for tomorrow.

From Ralph Lauren's, he walked down to 68th and over to Lexington and got on the local 6 train to 125th Street. He sat quietly as he vanished into the populace of the subway car where everyone stood or sat next to each other on the seats that stretched along both sides of the subway car minding their own business or discreetly looking at the others sitting across from them. A little girl and boy were side by side, on their knees pressed against the backrest looking out. They held hands and pressed their noses against the window, fogging it and laughed at the swooshing sound the subway car made as it sped past the flashing green signal lights in the dark underground. When the little girl saw Teo reflected in the window, she and the boy turned around to look at him through the crowded train, and they smiled. It was a peculiar adult-like, knowing smile. They nodded their heads to him in unison, turned back to the window on their knees and pulled their pants up to show Teo their red Christmas socks and the sewn-on green elves playing tug of war. With their cheeks pressed to the window and noses touching, they looked at each other and laughed. Teo got off at the next stop, 125th Street, and walked west to Lenox Avenue and the restaurant.

He enjoyed the anonymity of the City where no one in particular stood out no matter what you looked like. It was a melange of peoples of different colors, sizes, dress and speech. In other cities, you can isolate yourself and feel invulnerable in the confines of your car. But once you step outside and mix with the melting pot, you feel less secure, at risk, perhaps a target. But in New York, in this city, you're not in a car that much. You walk or take subways or buses to get around. There is no privacy nor escape from "the others", the many different kinds of people who surround you constantly, the people who belong there as much as you do. You don't feel vulnerable as you meld into the amorphous background. Teo liked the anonymity the City gave everyone.

He met Portman at the restaurant where they had the medley of Southern and comfort food the Red Rooster is known for, and went over the matters they wanted to discuss. Portman gave Teo another envelope. After dinner, they walked back to the subway station at 125th Street. On the way, three young men stopped them and started a banter which was clearly a prelude to a mugging. Teo and Portman separated from each other and went into a defensive stance, getting ready for trouble. Teo said to Portman this could be resolved "without that", when Portman was about to take out his holstered Smith & Wesson 380. The three would-be muggers got closer and demanded their watches and money as they brandished their knives. Teo said very calmly to wait a second and he took a step back. He crossed his arms over his chest in a meditative way, took a deep breath and then said no one wants any trouble so they should all just leave. The muggers laughed as they rushed and lunged at them.

Teo and Portman struck back. They delivered swift kicks to knees and groins, and rapid jabs to throats and kidneys, professionally and instantaneously executed. Quickly, Teo used his arms and hands to fend off one of them, and with his right leg, kicked and broke the kneecap of another about to pounce on Portman. Portman grabbed hold of one and swung him into another, knocking them both down. The muggers were incapacitated in seconds and left groaning on the sidewalk. Before they walked away, Teo took the knives from the muggers and threw them down a sewer drain.

"You okay?" Portman asked.

"Yeah. You?"

"I hate that right after I eat," Portman answered and they continued on to the subway.

* * * * * *

Grand-Mère Jeanne-Marie greeted Teo at the mansion with kisses and hugs and tears of welcome. She took his carry-on and put it near the door leading out of the sitting room, and then squeezed his arm and pulled him to the sofa. He simply had to tell her everything about school! What was it like in a class with so many others? What was he doing? His designs, was he keeping up with everything else? His time in New York? She wanted to hear about everything, like a school girl wanting to know about her best friend's first date and kiss. He said of course, but first he wanted to wash up and then had to say hello to Samuel. She cautioned him, Samuel had aged more since his last visit. He slept all the time, was forgetful and his memory was slipping. He leaned over and kissed the forehead of his grey haired *Grand-Mère* and left to find Samuel.

He was resting in the library amidst the oak paneled walls and sconces of a distant, more elegant time in history, his diminished body swallowed up by the large leather arm chair. They embraced and Teo gave him four cheek kisses the way Mimi used to. He told them in general terms of his life at the University, that he was bored with the curricula and the professors. He went to New York to see Samuel's lawyers and now he absolutely had to have Jeanne-Marie's goose dinner before he went back. It was Didier's favorite, and now Teo's too. If they wanted, he would help take Samuel to visit Mimi's grave, the anniversary of her death was only a few weeks away and he knew Samuel and Jeanne-Marie would want to go and to visit Didier's and Camille's graves too.

Samuel asked him if he made any progress to find his missing part. Teo gave a vague answer not wanting to expose his doubts about Samuel's unshakeable belief that Teo should be looking for his other half just as Samuel was, and wasn't surprised to learn Logan and Ralph were coming to visit and stay for a week. Samuel had met them in the States several years ago and thought he had identified in them a missing element in their lives like he did with Teo. They reinforced it wholeheartedly and agreed that indeed, they had to find what was missing, a hole as Samuel put it, in their lives.

Logan was married and took care of her husband and family in New York; Ralph was from New Jersey; and they knew each other very, very well before they met Samuel in Central Park. It didn't take long for them to make Samuel realize they too were looking for something. He invited them to come to the mansion and paid for their annual visits where they shared this common longing to find the missing part of their lives, all the while enjoying Samuel's (and Jeanne-Marie's) extreme generosity! Teo had met them before and knew he would have to see them if he was still in Paris.

The next day Teo took Samuel who needed help walking, to see his lawyers and then, with Jeanne-Marie, to the Père Lachaise cemetery in the Twentieth Arrondissement to visit the grave of her daughter Mimi. Teo bent down to place flowers on the graves of Didier, Jeanne-Marie's mother Camille, and Mimi, and then they all stood silently. The earth around Mimi's footstone had pushed over it and half buried the footstone so only her last name "Durand" showed and the year of her death, 1995. Jeanne-Marie would take care of her daughter's footstone later; she made sure the grave sites were kept in repair and the grass cut. She mumbled aloud to remind herself to take care of that, a bad habit of hers; Samuel never knew if she meant to talk to him, or was she talking to herself like a crazy person.

That night, over a roast goose dinner, Teo told them about Adrianna although there wasn't much to tell. He met her in one of his classes, very pretty, who reminded him of Mimi, at least from the photos he had seen of her. She was bright, and yet despite her lack of any particularly remarkable characteristics, he felt a connection even though she hadn't expressed any feelings for him. Their relationship was not romantic and limited to short meetings after class, and only in class, except for the visit to the hospital, hardly a relationship at all. No, he told Samuel, he didn't think she was his "other half" because without knowing at all what that meant, he couldn't tell. After dinner, in a totally non-French custom, and to Jeanne-Marie's constant disapproval, Samuel ate his *pain au chocolat*, and got buttery pastry and chocolate all over his fingers and the fresh white damask napkin she had set for him.

The next day, Teo and Jeanne-Marie reviewed their sketches, ones he had brought and ones she had been working on. They compared them to old sketches Mimi had drawn years earlier on paper now brittle with age, some of which Teo kept in the flap of his sketchbook. Aside from their separate designs, they worked together on one dress at a time, helping and criticizing each other, and when they were both satisfied with it, they started a new one. She insisted Teo know how to sew if he was going to design, and taught him on her mother's old heavy duty sewing machine, the one Samuel had brought from New York and given to Camille as a Christmas present many years ago. Jeanne-Marie was an expert seamstress, taught by Camille to have that skill to help support herself, and probably could have worked for any haute couture designer if she had wanted; nonetheless, she was content to just take care of Mimi, Samuel and the mansion.

The day before Teo left, Ralph and Logan arrived and spent Teo's last night in Paris with him and Samuel, talking about the part that was missing in their lives, as they had done for the last six years. They enjoyed Jeanne-Marie's excellent cuisine, the wines, the brandy, and staying in a Paris mansion by Park Monceau. Too many times had Teo heard their own particular descriptions of what was missing from their lives which they repeated once again in wistful camaraderie. They sat around and lamented their fates that they, unlike Samuel, never filled the top half of their glass, and they never would, given that each was married and had a family in the States. Teo wondered how they managed to go to Paris on an annual, fully paid trip, and stay in a mansion by the park, when each one had a family back home.

Samuel mentioned Teo had met someone who might be his missing part, which started a round of questions. How did Teo know? What does it feel like? Does she know or feel the same? Teo quashed their enthusiasm when he informed them she wasn't his other half. He left out he still didn't know what the hell they were referring to, whether it was all bunk, and whether they were the real thing or sycophants who took advantage of an old man and his largesse.

CHAPTER THIRTEEN

While Teo went to New York and Paris, Adrianna went home to Bellevue for the Christmas break. Charlotte filled her in about their cousin's wedding in June and what was going on with her job as a bookkeeper for the accounting firm. While she yearned for a more independent and exciting life, she did nothing to help herself. Living at home didn't cost her much and Mr. Bittfield said she could stay for as long as she wanted so she ended up doing nothing else but that.

Adrianna, on the other hand, told Charlotte she would live on her own as soon as she could, maybe in a big city. Not that she didn't love her family but she knew there was more to life than Bellevue's non-existent offerings, and hoped there was someone or something out there for her. She'd be better off looking if she wasn't under the family roof.

Charlotte asked her where she might go, after all, graduation wasn't far away and Adrianna hadn't applied to any graduate schools.

"I don't know," she said. "I might stay here for a little while until I figure it out."

"That's dangerous," Charlotte admonished. "I thought the same when I finished college. I had no specific goals and figured the future would take care of itself, that there was plenty of time. I knew I had to move out, but I was living here during college and it was easy until I had to make up my mind. I got the temporary job at the office, and, well, you know, I'm still there—and living here!—five years later. I know I have to go but it's hard for me and frankly, I don't see a way out now. I was naive but so many others did the same thing and didn't make plans either. Be careful if you move back. Besides, you have student loans to pay off so better do something sooner rather than later. It's time for you to make the break and have definite plans. There's more to this world than Bellevue. One of us has to break out."

"I know, I know, but I still have a little time," Adrianna said. "And I know how much you want to be on your own. Look, maybe you did get derailed but don't that let stop you. Even if you can't see the light at the end of the tunnel, you feel something pointing you in a direction out of here. Follow where it's pointing. It's in you, go for it, follow it. Even if it is hard or seems impossible, don't let that stop you."

Adrianna didn't know if she came up with that herself, or was it something else she got from Teo, when he told her about her "internal compass". Things coming from somewhere else; she had trouble knowing what was hers and what was his, but if it's hers now, did it matter?

"Tell me more about Teo. He fascinates you, doesn't he?"

"Fascinates? No . . . no, it isn't fascination, at least I don't think so. He's on my mind a lot more than I want. Maybe it's his face or spastic lip. But I wouldn't call it a fascination. I like him and feel something for him, but certainly nothing physical, and that's the problem. Physical attraction was always first and foremost. You know how Mom feels about that. He is not like anyone I ever met. He does things that . . . I don't know how he does them . . . good things. He knows things. He's smart and sensitive but he's hiding something and he scares me sometimes, especially when he speaks in a weird voice and says weird things. Most of the time he's really interesting to be with and strangely, I feel both comfortable and tense with him, all at the same time. But there is no way I could date him, or bring him home and meet Mom. I think I should stop talking to him after class. And then there's Julian. I know Mom would love him, and maybe she's right."

"And have you told Julian or Teo your nose isn't your nose, that you had a nose job?"

"No, I haven't and it's not any of their business."

"Here's what I think," Charlotte said. "Now that I'm out of school and working, I have to accept I've grown into the woman I'm going to be. Growing up here—maybe more for you than me—has been living inside a bubble. Remember those bubbles we used to make with soap and water and blew through a loop? We used to watch them float in the air until they touched another bubble or the sidewalk, and then they burst in a splash. Well, you've been living inside one. It filtered stuff coming in but also held you back. Everything has been cozy but distorted. You see only what gets in, or what you let in, or let yourself touch—and maybe that's been limited to safe and familiar things, like a Julian, fashion magazines and headbands. This guy Teo comes along. Normally he wouldn't be able to reach you, and you wouldn't see him or touch him, but somehow he's pushing in on your bubble."

"Bubble or no bubble, trust me, he's hard to look at."

Mrs. Bittfield came in and overhead a little of the conversation.

"Boy trouble?" she asked. "And Adrianna, please put on socks or slippers, why must you always be barefoot in the house? Just because your father goes around barefoot is no reason you have to. You may have gotten my good looks not his—thank goodness—but you sure do have his bad habits! He won't listen to me so I can't stop him walking around like that, but in my house, I can have you put on socks at least. I've told you a thousand times, the bottoms of your feet will get rough and coarse, and no boy wants that! You have to look nice if you're going to get someone who looks nice. Well, at least you got your father's good business sense though Lord knows how that happened! And are you rubbing your freckle? It seems larger and redder than I remember. Stop doing that!"

"Yes and no," Charlotte answered.

"What was the question? I forgot the question," Mrs. Bittfield said helplessly. "Maybe I can help."

Charlotte answered her mother dismissively. "Mom, you and Dad were high school sweethearts. You said you never dated anyone else and got married early, too early. I don't think you ever had boyfriend problems."

"Well, I suppose maybe you're right. I didn't have much experience except for your father though everyone said I was a real knockout. I'd say to both of you, just be careful whatever you do, if you know what I mean, and I don't have to draw you any pictures! You know exactly what I mean. I think you take after your father in this regard," she said to Charlotte, "and you Adrianna take after me when it comes to boys. Be careful, you know what boys want, especially the pretty ones. Don't let them pressure you. Okay, let's all finish decorating the tree. Your father is down there and I don't want him standing on the ladder alone, and Adrianna, put something on your feet!"

On the way downstairs, Adrianna spoke to Charlotte.

"It's amazing how totally clueless Mom is."

"Not so," Charlotte said. "Mom isn't so clueless and don't be fooled or taken in by her. Living here for so long has taught me a thing or two about Mom."

"Charlotte, do you think Dad is afraid of me?"

"That's a strange question. Where did that come from?"

"Teo asked me when I said I thought Dad treated me differently from you."

"I never thought of it that way. He respects you more than me. I do his bookkeeping but you really help him in the family business and he knows that you have a better business sense than he does. You do, you should think about a career in business. Afraid? I have to think about that one. There is something there between you and Dad, but I can't put my finger on it."

"Yeah?" asked Adrianna.

"Look, let's go down and help old Dad, okay?" she said abruptly to put an end to Adrianna's questioning.

Unlike his wife and especially Adrianna, Mr. Bittfield was not attractive. He was overweight and had an enormously round and protruding gut that buried any belt he cinched below it. His chubby face was clean shaven and pinkish, accentuated by the slick black hair he combed straight back. He had gone to school, married and raised his family in Bellevue and ran a small plumbing supply business there. Not exciting for most but for this taciturn and unassuming local, it was enough to go to work, come home and watch baseball on TV, and of course, oblige his wife to go out from time to time when she wanted, and to take the girls out too.

The next day on Christmas morning, they sat in the living room admiring this year's tree which glittered with lights and decorations and was laden with nostalgic ornaments—a typical Norman Rockwell family scene. Dad sat in his big leather chair which groaned as his large girth filled it and his bare feet atop a plaid ottoman. Mom sat on the couch while Adrianna and Charlotte spread out on the floor handing out the presents. Mrs. Bittfield gave Mr. Bittfield a pair of tan carpincho gloves from Argentina and he gave her her favorite perfume and they threw kisses to each other. Other presents were torn open as red and silver Christmas wrappings littered the carpet.

"This one is from Dad for Charlotte," Adrianna said, handing it to Charlotte. It was a cashmere and wool scarf.

"Oh, I love it! Thank you Dad. You always get me a present I can use!" She got up and kissed him on the cheek and they hugged.

"And this one is, let's see, it's also from Dad, and let me see if I can guess, it's for me," Adrianna announced. It was a gift certificate from Amazon. He always gave her a gift certificate. "Thanks Dad, I saw some headbands there I'd love to have. Great! Thank you." She got up and kissed him, but no hugs, he was fumbling to take off the new carpincho gloves.

"You know I never know what to get you so I let you decide," he said sheepishly. For birthdays, Mrs. Bittfield bought Adrianna presents from them both, but for Christmas, on his own, he gave her a gift certificate even though he managed to buy a personal gift for Charlotte each year. Adrianna accepted the gift certificates with mixed emotions, one of his blind spots she regretted.

Mrs. Bittfield asked Adrianna about the boy she was seeing, Julian, right? A good looking fraternity boy? Is it serious? Whereas some mothers are interested in the economic prospects of a suitor, or his character, or family background, her mother's first interest was always his looks. Adrianna unenthusiastically covered her dating Julian when Charlotte brought up Teo.

"Who's Teo?" her mother asked, obviously eager to get every detail of a new beau.

Adrianna threw a darting glance Charlotte's way who responded by mouthing "I'm sorry," and realized she may have opened a Pandora's box. She told her mother he's someone she met in her psychology class whom she only talks to in class, and she joined him once or twice as a volunteer at the hospital to read stories to children. That's all, nothing else, they're not dating.

"Is he good looking?" she wanted to know.

"No, in fact, he's quite ugly, to say the least."

"Well, you shouldn't spend too much time around this ugly Teo. Julian might not like that."

With that comment, her mother unwittingly electrified Adrianna. She found a nerve that ran deep in Adrianna, tore off its protective sheath and clawed the raw nerve with her nails. An excruciating violation rushed through Adrianna and she reacted with a primal urge to defend herself—and Teo.

She exploded.

"Mom, you always want to know if a boy is good looking! Is that the most important thing? Nothing else matters? That's all I ever hear from you. Is he good looking? Is he good looking? And what if he isn't? Then what? Am I only to go out with good looking boys? You know in fact I like Teo but I never would dream of dating him or having anyone think that, let alone bring him home. Why? Because he is ugly, and disfigured, and you've brainwashed me to think I shouldn't even consider the possibility I might date him, not that I necessarily want to. But you've made it so I don't even have that choice. You've made me into someone I don't like. Samantha told me I see through pretty prisms, and she's right. Charlotte said the same thing, I've been living inside a bubble. My God! Twenty years of telling me I should only think about someone's looks, that that's all that matters. You made me believe being pretty was the most important thing. Shame on you mother! Shame on all of you! Shame on me for letting you do it! Why did you do that to me, and not Charlotte? What happened to you to do that to me?"

Adrianna buried her face in her hands and cried.

"I should bring Teo home to spite you so you can see how ugly a boy I can go out with but I'm not that cruel. Cruel to him, not you. I won't show him off like you show me off. He doesn't deserve that and besides, we don't have that kind of relationship. Why not? Because I can't get over the way he looks but I'm sure there are others who would at least try to, but not me. If he isn't good looking, he's no one. Well, it's not too late for me. My eyes are beginning to open. I can see, see there are parts of me I don't like and don't want. I will choose, not you, and I also see I don't have to accept who I thought I was, who you told me I was, whether you like it or not! I'll pick and choose what's good for me and what's not. Not you or anyone else. I'll make whatever I want, my own, me. You know Mom, until now I didn't question it. Sometimes the one in the pretty wrapper isn't the best choice."

She thought of the two sandwiches Teo made and she cried for herself.

"You're making me—no, you've made me—crazy over this! Just because I have good looks, doesn't mean I have to go out or marry someone good looking. You certainly didn't!"

Silence thundered through the room. The Norman Rockwell scene started to peel off its paint and reveal another family scene underneath it. Charlotte looked at her mother and then her father. Mrs. Bittfield was frozen and Mr. Bittfield squirmed in his chair. Everyone was stunned by Adrianna's outburst and the elephant she brought into the room.

"Dad, I'm sorry, so sorry. I didn't mean that about you. I'm sorry Dad. That was awful of me. Mom got me riled up and I guess I finally lost control. I shouldn't have said that about you. I'm so sorry Dad." She continued to cry.

Finally, Mrs. Bittfield spoke.

"Your father and I love each other very much and I only hope you find someone as loving and understanding as your father. I only want the best for you, for you both. And besides Ms. Snotty, your father is good looking, or well, he was before he got so big after you were born. Charlotte, don't you remember him before then, he and I made such a nice couple."

She was oblivious to, or simply chose to ignore, everything else Adrianna had said about her awakening and feelings.

"Let's have breakfast," Adrianna said. She controlled her sobbing as the anger toward her mother which had suddenly welled up in her took root—as well as the disappointment in herself—all of which she would now have to deal with.

"Yes, I remember Mom," Charlotte said. "Look, let's clean up this mess and then have breakfast and talk about the wedding in June. Do we really have to go? I hate formal weddings and the loud music and lousy food."

Charlotte gave everyone the excuse they needed to put the episode behind them and they all went to breakfast pretending nothing happened except for Adrianna who just jarred loose her internal compass.

CHAPTER FOURTEEN

Back at the University, things were quiet after most everyone left for the Christmas break. Erika stayed on campus; she didn't want to go home to São Paulo and the inevitable bickering with her parents about her lifestyle and past, and decided to save the travel money they sent her.

Wanda couldn't make up her mind where to go: maybe skiing, but that meant a trip with the college ski club and she didn't like half the people there. Maybe somewhere warm with a pool, but going by herself would be lonely and her neck was bothering her despite buying and returning a special pillow five times in one week that was supposed to help her, and she wasn't sure if she'd be able to sleep on a hotel pillow. (Erika thought that was crappy and eagerly volunteered to complain to the online store who sold her the pillow.) She ended up going nowhere and stayed with Erika. They had the suite to themselves and spent Christmas and New Year's Eve watching movies and drinking cachaça which Erika had brought from Brazil.

Samantha and Kendall had wanted to spend the holidays together but couldn't, their parents wanted them to spend it with them respectively. For Kendall, wrestling practice started before classes resumed and although he could have skipped it easily, they hoped if Samantha could come back early too, they'd have a chance to at least spend some time together. She made up an excuse for her parents and came back early. She said Wanda asked her to come back so Wanda wouldn't have to be alone the entire Christmas break.

Teo came back from Paris early too. Earlier in the first semester he had joined the University wrestling team, and with a championship competition in February, the coach wanted the team back early from the Christmas break to prepare for it. Teo and Kendall had met at the wrestling practices and paired up to practice together which gave Kendall a chance to talk to Teo. He was shy and socially awkward but if you weren't high up on the social ladder and you showed any interest in him, he had no problem opening up; Teo qualified in both respects. He looked up to Teo notwithstanding his face.

Teo asked how his Christmas was and how things were going with his girlfriend Samantha ... wasn't that her name? Now that he had someone he could talk to, Kendall eagerly shared his excitement and bragged he had his first real girlfriend, and they both came back early. And confidentially, just between Teo and Kendall, they went to get her an IUD, leaving the obvious reason unspoken.

Kendall had a good heart, a decent lad who came from an agricultural valley town, and who probably never suffered any personal tragedies that might have put a reality check to his rosy view of life. He was happy Samantha liked him and had no reason to think they wouldn't just keep going merrily along. In fact, he didn't think much more than that, anything deeper was beyond his ken. Fortunately for him, Samantha took the lead. Teo listened patiently to Kendall and wondered what, if anything, might befall him to shake his provincial pollyanna nature.

CHAPTER FIFTEEN

When classes began, Adrianna stopped by to ask Teo about his Christmas. He avoided a direct answer and said he had to be on campus for wrestling practice. As a new addition to the team, the coach wanted him to train for the February competition coming up. He didn't tell her about New York or Paris. She said Kendall, Samantha's boyfriend, was also on the wrestling team but probably wasn't good enough for a team meet and asked if he knew him. Yes, he knew Kendall, he was a decent sort, a bit shy and naive and, no, he didn't remember if Kendall mentioned Samantha.

Over the next couple of weeks, they saw each other frequently but always in class, ate lunches he brought, talked freely about Adrianna's family and friends, including Julian where Teo detected Adriana's growing ambivalence, but scarcely little about Teo. He never revealed anything about his day to day life. She didn't ask, and he didn't say.

He showed her his latest dress designs which intrigued her, how he took a blank sheet of paper and then created something in one of her fashion magazines. She wanted to try it herself, so he gave her her own sketch pad and helped her develop a confidence as they worked together on a design. He volunteered to make a dress from one of her own designs but she said no. She was hesitant to increase her physical involvement with him; she thought he might misinterpret it and take it as a sign she might be interested in him that way. She decided she shouldn't do anything to encourage him beyond what they were doing, but she didn't want to give that up either.

In one of their after class conversations, Teo took an old sketch from the flap of his sketch pad to compare it to a new one they were working on. When she leaned over to look at it, she got dizzy and a déjà vu experience came over her as if she had already held the old sketched paper and looked at it before. And then the dead woman showed up. Adrianna didn't like her more frequent appearances. She told Teo she attributed the dizziness to bending over and looking down like the last time she got dizzy when she looked at one of the old sketches. He thought she seemed frightened but said nothing.

The only time they spent together outside of class was to visit the children's ward. Neither one initiated anything else. Although she enjoyed his company, physically he was still a leper, an untouchable, and she couldn't bear to be too close nor look at him for too long without feeling a physical disgust—something visceral she would have liked to get over but just couldn't. She was glad the distasteful physical repulsion she felt didn't seem to bother him.

Unanswered questions kept popping up. What did he do after Samuel took him in? Where had he gone to school? Where did he live before? What does he do after class? Who was he? Each time she asked, he put her off.

Finally, Teo relented and cracked open the door an inch to tell her what it was like growing up with Samuel and Jeanne-Marie Durand, more than he ever told anyone else.

Soon after he moved into Samuel's apartment in New York, Samuel said he'd like to give him a very special education, partly because registering Teo in a regular public or even private school, would raise questions about his parentage both wanted to avoid, and because Samuel missed having a better education when he took over his father's fur business. Instead of schools, classrooms and classmates, Teo had private tutors, lots of them, for all the academic subjects, and for a host of human endeavors that could be taught, from Art to Magic and Martial Arts, and Mentalism to Zen. If tutors couldn't come to Teo, he went to them, wherever they might be, in or out of Paris or New York, his home bases.

He went to every continent to learn and further his unique education with private lessons, never stepping foot in a customary classroom. He learned two monumental things early on that shaped the rest of his special education and his life: first, how to meditate and put himself into a deep sleep and wake up after only five and half hours, refreshed and ready to go, and second, how to speed read, enabling him to read and remember a huge quantity of books. For the last eight years, he told her, and even now, he slept five and half hours a night leaving him more than eighteen hours a day to read, learn and practice, every day, seven days a week, without any breaks or vacations. It's incredible, he said, how much you can learn and do in eighteen hours a day, every day, day after day, for so many years. He couldn't even begin to imagine the number of books he read over all that time, and the number of private lessons he took.

"Is that how you learned to speak Japanese and do acu-manipulation? And you trained under Buddhist monks too? Wasn't that tiring, so much work, every single day? And you didn't need more sleep than that? And what about friends, didn't you have any?" she asked, beginning to understand how he can know as much as he does, and also how isolated he must have been growing up.

"None of the above. I got used to that and it became my way of life. Remember, I started this when I was much younger. I liked and still do, learning and knowing about so many things, particularly when most everyone doesn't know what I'm talking about. I think I'm driven to do it. It's been non-stop, working on it all the time. Besides, Samuel was, and still is, very generous to me and I knew he wanted me to succeed and do well. I owed him something in return, and for me, it was to work as hard as I could and learn everything he set out for me. I wanted to please him. Don't you do things to please your parents?"

"More than you know, and more than I should have," she said.

"I'm not sure if I can handle everything he's giving me. I may be over my head but there isn't anyone to talk to. I've been a loner for as long as I can remember so staying a loner was easy and comfortable. I buried myself in this crazy lifestyle he paid for. The more I learned, the easier it was to keep myself from other people since no one knew what I was talking about and I could hide behind that. But here at the University, something in me wants to change and reach out. As generous as he is, Samuel is not a particularly loving man and brought me up that way. I never quite realized the price I paid."

"So Samuel was the only father you had since you ran away? No other family or friends?" She didn't address the other intimate details he revealed.

"Yes and no. Samuel is an old man, spends most of his time in Paris and is more like a grandfather than a father. *Grand-Mère* Jeanne-Marie, on the other hand, in addition to caring for Samuel, took care of me. She loves me and spoils me and helps me design, and my French too. She's the one who taught me how to sew. I love her like the mother I never had."

Teo wanted to tell her more but was afraid to, he didn't think it would be safe—any more could lead to unwanted questions. He also decided to keep under wraps Samuel's lifelong quest for his other half, what a Frenchman named Didier, told Samuel to search for and Samuel's *idée fixe* that Teo had to look for and find his missing part, his other half.

CHAPTER SIXTEEN

Samuel was convinced that the young Teo he met in Central Park suffered from what he and Didier suffered from, an incompleteness, a compulsion to search for something, something they did not know or understand. He likened it to a glass half full: no matter how much you poured in, it never rose more than half way. You couldn't fill the glass no matter how much you tried, the top half was always empty which left you to crave more, search more. Teo never understood what he meant and doubted it could be true.

But Samuel told Teo that after many years, he actually did find what he was supposed to look for and it was Jeanne-Marie's daughter, Mimi.

* * * * * *

Paris, circa 1974 - 1995

In the year Jeanne-Marie turned thirty four, her mother and then her husband both died. Samuel had promised Didier he would always look after Jeanne-Marie and so he asked her to move into the mansion with Mimi and to continue as housekeeper. The mansion (which Samuel had inherited along with Didier's share of their businesses) was too big for just Samuel, and Jeanne-Marie, now a widow, was happy to move in with Mimi and live in the home her mother had lived in with Didier before they died.

Over the next twelve years, Samuel spent less time in New York and more in Paris. It was about then Samuel said it happened, when he was sixty five years old. He had seen Mimi working in the house, coming and going, and it came to him—Mimi was the missing part he had been looking for! What a surprise, to feel that way for a young girl forty years his junior, not a paramour or an equal which is what he long suspected would be the case. For reasons he never understood, he was convinced that Mimi was the one he was destined to find and take care of, his other half. It was something he had never experienced.

He tried to understand why but never found an answer. Didier had said it wasn't love, which Samuel doubted back then, but it now seemed Didier must have been right because he didn't love Mimi. Samuel never trusted emotions and believed he owed his business success to that. He thought his rejection of emotions was blinding him to the reason he was drawn to Mimi, that it must be an emotional reason which he couldn't recognize. But his feeling for her was not an emotion, it was something else. He was confounded that after finding her he was bewildered by why she was the one.

Jeanne-Marie believed it involved something Didier must have said or passed onto Samuel and she told Mimi to simply accept it without question and enjoy her good fortune!

Mimi was tall and had a large purplish birthmark which covered a part of her right cheek and neck but it didn't take away from her pleasant appearance and warm smile. She kept to herself when possible, read a lot, and always thought about what she would say before speaking. Aside from drawing, she spent hours writing short poems about lost love or other romantic fantasies on the pale green note paper Samuel had given her. She was prim and proper, and dressed conservatively.

As Camille had taught Jeanne-Marie, Jeanne-Marie taught Mimi how to sew and help design the dresses Jeanne-

Marie sold to her few clients. With a trim figure and a pleasing manner, Mimi enjoyed modeling them. Not that they needed the extra money the work gave them; Samuel provided whatever they needed and they were content to remain as housekeeper and daughter, well taken care of by Samuel. Mimi had her own room, she came and went as she liked, and passed many pleasant hours in the sewing room which held all their fabrics, designs, mannequins, and everything else they might possibly need.

Samuel increased Jeanne-Marie's household allowance with specific instructions to spend more on Mimi who reciprocated by adopting him as her grandfather, called him *Grand-Père*, and always gave him a special four cheek kiss. Jeanne-Marie was pleased Mimi had an adopted grandfather who doted on her, no matter if he wasn't related by blood and the reasons were murky. It was fate, she said, which brought Didier to Samuel, and Samuel to Jeanne-Marie and lifted Mimi up from one life to the path of another, better life.

One day, Mimi went to visit a girlfriend in the country whose grandfather took them on a hay ride with his old horse drawn cart. They took off their shoes to lie down on the hay and look up at the large plane trees they passed under. They came to a small stone bridge over a spring where there was some commotion. A car had gone over the edge of the road and fell into the shallow water. No one was hurt but the driver needed help to get out through the broken door of her car and up the steep bank of the spring. Several people joined hands, one to another, stretching and reaching down the slope to help her climb out.

A young man on a bicycle had stopped on the roadside just past the bridge to look and to help if he could. When the horse passed him by, the horse got spooked, reared up and the cart broke loose from its harness. Mimi's friend fell from the cart and hurt her ankle. The young man ran over to help.

"Excuse me. I'm sorry if I made the horse rear up like that. Are you okay?" he asked the girlfriend.

"I'm not sure. I think so but I'm not sure if I can stand on it," she said.

"Well, I don't think that's a good idea. You should get an x-ray first. I'm a nurse at the local hospital just ahead and was on my way to work when I stopped to see if I could help the woman in the car over there. I'm sorry if I was the cause of your falling down. It seems like I did something to the horse."

"No, it wasn't your fault," Mimi interjected. "No one can say why the horse got spooked. It must have been something around you or near you that she sensed, nothing any of us could have seen."

"Well, would you like me to look at your ankle?" he asked the girlfriend.

"If you're a nurse, then yes, please, if you don't mind," the girlfriend said.

"So, you'll let me help you?" he asked as if he wasn't sure she had said yes.

"Yes, please," she said and she moved her leg to let him get to her ankle.

He was shy and blamed himself for the horse rearing up though he hadn't done anything. He touched her ankle gently, examining it. He didn't think anything was broken but she should have an x-ray to be sure. They lifted her into the cart to take her to the hospital for the x-ray.

The horse was still agitated from something it sensed, something that spooked it. The young man went over and gently stroked the horse's shiny, dark brown mane and spoke to her softly, and calmed it enough so they could continue.

He didn't talk much as he walked with his bicycle by the side of the cart over that country road to the hospital. He kept to himself while Mimi and her friend sitting in the back of the cart, agreed how nice he was, and so shy.

While Mimi sat in the waiting room for her friend to be finished with the x-ray, she took off her shoes and crossed her legs beneath her. She sat like that working on a sketch when Philippe, the nurse who helped them, came by to say her friend would be finished in about twenty minutes. He watched her as she sketched, what she was wearing, how she curled her toes absent-mindedly.

"What are you drawing?" he asked.

"A design for a dress. It's a hobby except my mother and I make the dresses we design and sell them to a few clients. I'm the model," she said and showed him her design.

"Could you design a uniform for me? As a male nurse, there isn't much in the way of uniforms for me to choose from."

"Do you like being a nurse?"

"I would have preferred to be a veterinarian but here in the middle of nowhere, without money, it wasn't possible. Those dreams will have to wait. But in my spare time I study alternative medicine. There's a place in a hospital for both traditional and alternative medicine but country doctors are so conservative, they absolutely won't allow it and frown on my doing anything like that, like helping my patients with a hands-on approach, so I have to do that surreptitiously. What do you do, if you don't mind my asking?"

"I help my mother take care of my grandfather and his house in Paris though he's not really my grandfather. He promised someone a long time ago to watch over my mother, and indirectly me too. He pays us to take care of him and the house, and he treats me like a granddaughter. He says he was waiting his whole life, looking for me for a long time. Now that he found me, he is very protective and generous. It doesn't sound so strange to me even though we don't understand what he means."

"What else do you do, aside from that? Do you have a boyfriend?"

She smiled at his leading question.

"No. Maybe I'm waiting to find someone too."

"You shouldn't have to wait too long. What do you do while you're waiting?" he bantered.

"I write poems and make believe love stories."

"I'd like to read one if we meet again."

"I think that would be nice," she said.

They continued to touch and play like this, and savored their blossoming courtship. He fought his shyness to ask her out and within a few months, they were engaged.

He took her on bicycle rides in the country by small country villages and meandering rivers. He loved the serenity and bucolic feeling of the countryside and shared it with her, and introduced her to one of his favorite musical pieces by Debussy, *Prelude - Afternoon of a Faun*. This one time, they stopped at a small cemetery to rest and listen to the music and afterward went to the neighboring village. Although Mimi had never been there before, it seemed familiar and she was comfortable there so they lingered. They talked about the future and Philippe again brought up his regret he couldn't become a veterinarian and make more money for them but he didn't see how it was possible.

"Well, why don't you?" she asked.

"That would be so hard now. I mean, school is expensive and we couldn't afford it and I'd have to quit my job at the hospital."

"I think it would be a good investment. We can figure it out. Maybe my grandfather Samuel would help us. He's always been very generous and I think he'd like to see me, and us, succeed. What do you think about my asking him?"

"I don't know. I don't know him well and I don't want to be beholden to anyone. If he agreed, and if I did this, then what would happen if I failed? I would have a hard time facing you and him if I failed."

"You won't fail. And if you do—which you won't—at least you will know you tried. Please darling, don't be afraid. I'm not. Being a nurse is admirable but you've said and I believe it, there is more to you. Please, let me speak to Samuel."

It was late when they got back and Jeanne-Marie worried they might have been in an accident biking on dark country roads. Mimi told her they lost track of time. They had stopped for a few hours at a quaint village with a small cemetery by a river that seemed strangely familiar to her though she never had been there before, at least not that she could remember. She was sorry it upset her but something good might come of it. She told her about their plan for Philippe to quit his job as a nurse and go to school to become a veterinarian if Samuel would help them. It would be the best wedding present she could think of.

Jeanne-Marie and Samuel were happy Mimi found someone with ambition who clearly cared for her. Samuel insisted on paying for the wedding which he and Jeanne-Marie helped organize and he agreed to pay for Philippe's schooling as a wedding present. They began work on the wedding plans and Jeanne-Marie and Mimi began making the wedding dress and her trousseau. They also took Philippe under their wings; he came from a humble background and didn't have much of a family.

Mimi bought him a puppy to keep him company at the beginning of their engagement so he wouldn't be lonely at night. It would have been out of the question for her to spend any night alone with him until they were married—even in those times. Their faiths and love for each other and for the full life which awaited them, helped them fight their urges and so they waited for their wedding day.

Their abstinence was for naught.

It came to a violent and tragic end, when in 1995, on a grey winter's day, they were struck down by a car as they crossed a street in Paris. The traffic light was askew, and instead of pointing its green light directly facing one street, and its red light facing the other, the green light was angled and flashing so both intersecting streets seemed to have the same light. The driver thought the light was green in his direction and sped through the intersection at the same time Mimi and Philippe were crossing. They saw the same green light and neither one thought to look the other way. They died instantly spread out on the cold street facing each other holding hands.

Samuel and Jeanne-Marie were utterly devastated. Mimi and Philippe had been a beautiful and loving couple cut down without warning. It should not have been ordained this way and it shook the foundations of any faith they had. Who could have caused this punishment of such an early death? Why? Jeanne-Marie lost her only child, and Samuel a granddaughter and his other half. She was gone and their remaining years would be lifeless.

They buried Mimi at the foot of Didier's and Camille's graves and so began their mourning of her which never ended. Jeanne-Marie never finished the wedding gown but kept herself busy with the trousseau and threw herself into designing and making other dresses and clothes she imagined Mimi would have designed or worn herself. Except for a necessary business trip to New York three times a year, Samuel became a recluse in the Park Monceau mansion.

They spent the next ten interminable years in mourning, ten years of an arid, lifeless existence, a depression of soul waiting for their own time to die. But something happened, unexpectedly, one afternoon in Central Park. A very old, sad, spent Samuel met a very young runaway Teo. In that brief encounter, Samuel felt something about Teo, something that reminded him of his quest for his other half and Mimi. It was enough for an old man to spend more time to see what that feeling was and so he invited Teo to his apartment. The feeling grew stronger to the point Samuel believed it was Teo who had a missing part like he did—a revitalizing sensation for Samuel.

With no one other than Jeanne-Marie in his life, Samuel had the time and money to take on the self appointed role of guardian for Teo, to watch him, guide him, make him flourish so one day, he could find his own missing half. It became a *raison d'être* for Samuel, and Jeanne-Marie didn't hesitate to end her mourning as well and become Teo's foster mother. After ten years of mourning for Mimi and nothing to look forward to except death, they were both ready to live again.

They called him René.

* * * * * *

Samuel was convinced that Teo should also spend his life looking for his other half. Teo couldn't quite bring himself to buy into this as Samuel did so readily with Didier on that day in a chance yet fateful encounter by the Canal Saint-Martin, but it was a small price to pay for all Samuel bestowed on him. Yet, was Samuel right, he wondered?

This was on his mind when last year he decided to give himself space away from Samuel, Jeanne-Marie and all his private lessons and tutors, space and time to think about it. It was time for him to go mainstream, start living like others his own age and at the same time, get a college degree which they knew he didn't need. Samuel already had dealings with the University and through his contacts made arrangements for Teo to enter as a senior having passed all entrance exams they could devise for his special case. He moved in during the summer and set up his room the way he liked including special, high-tech security door locks so no one could casually—or otherwise—get in.

He explored the campus, scouted the neighborhoods, and found out where to eat and workout. He visited the children's ward at the University hospital and started volunteer work there before classes started. He was bored in class and didn't expect to learn anything. He was actually taking his first long vacation away from his special private education. He still read voraciously, practiced his piano, martial arts, traveled to and fro, maintained the things that needed practice, and kept up his eighteen hour a day schedule.

CHAPTER SEVENTEEN

Teo did not tell Adrianna any of that.

"Your birthday is this weekend, January 30 I think, and I made a dress for you, not quite what we worked on but similar," he said.

"How did you know that?" Adrianna wondered how he knew her birthday. She knew she never mentioned it.

"I don't remember, I must have overheard it. You can wear it over the weekend. I assume Julian is taking you out somewhere?"

He handed her a package wrapped in pale tissue paper. She looked at it for a moment.

"Shall I open it now?"

"Yes, please. You must come from Korea where you're not supposed to open a gift when it's handed to you."

"No, just Bellevue."

"It isn't like the other sketches you saw but I thought this would look good on you . . . and be more useful too. Those others were more formal. But I'm not sure it will look good with a headband. Can you go out without a headband?" Teo had never seen Adrianna without a headband and he probably could remember each one and what she wore with it.

She took a pale green dress out of the package and held it up. "It looks like a good fit. How did you know my size?"

"By looking at you, of course."

"It feels nice. I like it. And the color and these stitches look so well done and . . . they must be hard to do. What are these stitches?" she asked marveling at his workmanship.

"The one at the bottom is a reverse tulip, some of these others are pick stitches and slip stitches, in addition to your garden variety cross and chain stitches, and there are others too. You need the right machine for many of them," he answered modestly but pleased to show off.

"Well, I love the design and everything about it. It's fabulous!" she said a little humbled. "I'll try it on as soon as I get back to my room. And if it fits—I mean I know it will—I'll wear it for my birthday. Thank you, this is really a nice present, and let me add, appropriate and personal, but not too personal. And you designed and sewed it too!"

"Yes, ma'am!" he said in a mock military reply.

"René . . ." she started to say but didn't finish.

"Yes?"

"Nothing. Only that I . . . I don't know what to say. Thank you so much. This is special, truly, better than any birthday present I ever got." Her eyes moistened and she wanted to do something like hug him, but didn't know what to do, and couldn't anyway.

"You are most welcome, Princess Aimée. Is Julian taking you out for your birthday?" His upper lip twitched.

Julian hadn't said anything about that. She didn't pay attention to his lip, she was thinking about Julian and why didn't he remember her birthday like Teo.

"I guess we'll go out. Well, I'll just have to run back to my room and try this on, won't I? Thank you again and I'll see you Tuesday."

"I have to go too. Wrestling practice awaits."

CHAPTER EIGHTEEN

Adrianna never missed a class except the one a couple of weeks later in early February, and when she came back, she wore the same headband she wore the first time she spoke to him, the one which made her freckle almost disappear but today the freckle was much more noticeable.

"Didn't see you the other day. Everything okay?" he asked.

"Sure," she said and then thought about what to say next. "Wanda and I had a pajama party, just the two of us the night before and we stayed up late, too late, and I wasn't feeling so well. I'm okay now."

When they next met, he asked her if she had ever been to a wrestling match. He was going to be in the intercollegiate wrestling championship and had four tickets for her if she and Julian and her friends wanted to go. Kendall wouldn't be competing so he could go with Samantha, and Adrianna could go with Julian.

While she wasn't the least bit interested in going to a wrestling match, she did want to see him in a way which didn't involve a one-on-one meeting. So later that day, while in her room reading one of the *Fleurs du Mal* poems, she heard Samantha and went out to invite her. She knew Samantha was there, yet she wasn't, no one was, only the dead woman standing in the hallway.

When Samantha came in later, she asked her if she and Kendall wanted to go and they could make it a double date and go to Julian's fraternity party afterward. Kendall was eager to go but hesitant about a double date with a fraternity guy.

Samantha explained it was a package deal, he had no reason to feel awkward and needed to improve his social skills. In the end, he wanted to see the championship competition with Samantha, more than he didn't want a double date with Julian, and so they all went.

Almost every seat in the stadium was filled, not just by students, but others too, including a couple in their thirties or forties who didn't stand out except they kept looking through the crowds, looking for someone in the stadium.

The meet started off with the Star Spangled Banner and then the first match, followed by several others. Adrianna wasn't impressed nor interested especially since Teo hadn't wrestled yet. She asked Kendall if Teo was going to wrestle. Kendall laughed.

"You don't know about Teo?"

"What do you mean?"

"I didn't know it but like he has an underground reputation as a terrific amateur wrestler. This is his first public event and it's been word of mouth; pretty much only the cognoscenti know. He works out off campus in addition to the team practices, and so they must have seen him there. Like this stadium never gets full on other championships. It's Teo. They want to see him. I can't wait to see what he does."

They announced the next and last match which Kendall explained was an elimination match and will determine who wins the championship. Each team enters seven members. They start with one member of one team against one member of the other team. The winner stays in, the loser is out, and the losing team sends in another to take on the winner. This continues until one team no longer has any of its seven members left.

The match started and after a few elimination rounds, one powerful wrestler of the visiting team was the current winner and his team still had four members left to put in if needs be while the home team had only two. It was Teo's turn to try to catch up. He had on his ear and chin protector which covered most of his face. Before he got to the fighting circle, he dropped his head to his chest, crossed his arms, closed his eyes and meditated. He put himself into a state of serenity where there was no one around him except his one adversary. Then he bowed a slow bow in martial arts fashion, and entered the circle. They took their respective positions and when the whistle blew, the fury began. They grabbed, feinted, pushed and pulled. They used their arms, legs, knees and weight to get an advantage. They dropped on one knee, swirled, and lifted the other's leg or torso to throw them off balance. It was fast and furious. They grabbed and squeezed hard at a neck, leg, foot, wrist, stomach—any part of the other guy's body they could keep hold of. They were intertwined, you didn't know whose leg or arm was whose. In spite of greater size, his larger, strong opponent never got the advantage. Teo used arm and leg movements to constantly keep him off balance and finally maneuvered to hold and press against the guy's neck and groin where he exerted pinpointed pressure in two specific spots, a move no one noticed, not even his opponent. It slowed him down briefly but enough for Teo to pin him and win that round. The crowd cheered and Teo remained by the circle to wait calmly for the next contestant. This continued for each of the visiting team's remaining but dwindling number of members as Teo used various unbalancing techniques and hand and body holds—and applied pressure—to overcome and keep winning until the visiting team had no more members to put in and Teo won the match for the University.

The crowd stood up and cheered, including the couple who were now no longer looking for someone. Teo's team ran over to him to high five him and slap him on the back which he tolerated quietly. They all meandered into the locker room, and the stadium began to disgorge the crowd.

"That was pretty cool," Kendall said. "Did you like it?" addressing that to both Samantha and Adrianna.

Samantha said it was interesting but very sweaty and macho and asked Kendall why he would ever want to take part in that. Adrianna said it was certainly different from other sports events she had been to and was impressed by Teo, and of course, her home team won. She didn't mention she had a more personal interest in watching him. Julian thought Teo did a great job and he liked the match too, but now he was thinking about spending time with Adrianna at the fraternity party and then upstairs in his room with her.

They went to Julian's fraternity party from the stadium. The snow which began in the morning and lasted all day, was tapering off and the skies were clearing. His fraternity house was one of eleven houses which surrounded a large grassy quad now covered in snow, five on a side and one at the end. Each house had three or four large white pillars in front and the Greek initials of the fraternity written near the top of the gabled facade facing the quad. Trees dotted the spaces between the houses and in nice weather, they played frisbee or ball on the grassy quad.

Inside the Alpha Sig fraternity house, the party room was crowded. Julian took Adrianna's hand to dance a slow dance and held her tightly, the way he always held her, a little too tightly for Adrianna which he never sensed but not enough for her to ask him to ease up. They moved to the slow music, not really dancing but holding each other, wrapped in each other's arms as they had done many times before; he had his hand on her breast like many times before. Nonchalantly, she took his hand off her breast. She didn't feel like going up to his room afterward like they usually did.

She wasn't paying attention to the music nor Julian, her mind was elsewhere. She was going over what she saw at the wrestling match. The wrestlers' interlocked bodies brought up her dream of being pushed off a path and the human chain of bodies pulling her out of the darkness below.

Out of nowhere, she asked, "Julian, what size am I? For clothes I mean."

He stepped back, looked at her from head to foot, and in a playful way said, "Oh, let me see, I think you must be a size ... uh, small. I'd say you were a small. Am I right? I never had to guess that before. Was it a good guess?"

Adrianna spoke slowly, "Do you think this dress is a 'small', and, by the way, do you recognize this dress?" She was wearing the green dress Teo made for her.

"I don't really know. Why do you ask?"

"The dress, have you seen it before?" she continued.

"I think that's a loaded question or I'm being trapped into something here. What am I missing?"

"Do you know my sister's name?"

"Why the questions?"

"Do you know when my birthday is?" she quietly asked.

"Uh oh, is that was this is about, I forgot your birthday? When is your birthday? Around now, right? If it is, I'm sorry. Happy Birthday! So let me ask you the same questions. What is my size? And when is my birthday? And have I worn these pants before? I bet you can't answer those either! Right? Come on, let's dance and I'm really sorry about your birthday if I missed it. I see it upset you and I'm sorry. I'll try to make it up to you."

No, she told him, she didn't know the answers to his questions, while she mumbled to herself, "I don't really care". At that, she said she was sorry, she was leaving and didn't want to stay. She left abruptly and told Samantha she was going back. Julian stood on the dance floor surrounded by couples swaying to the slow music wondering what just happened.

She was thinking about Teo, poor Teo. He wasn't invited to the party and wouldn't feel comfortable there anyway, seeing couples dancing, and holding each other, and kissing (if not more). What a sad sack who happened to win the championship. Why didn't he mention how good he was? He must have wanted me to see him but why did he invite me and Julian? He knew every answer Julian did not, and he wanted to know every answer. He listens. He cares. He understands. He knows me much, much better than Julian! Why did he have to be so ugly and strange! Why couldn't Julian be like Teo?

She left the fraternity house and started to walk to the dorm but took a sudden detour toward the stadium. Phi Beta Kappa recognized her and started walking next to her, eager for a dog biscuit. She started to walk faster and then into a careful jog on the snowy paths to get to the stadium with Phi Beta Kappa as an escort. She asked someone who was cleaning up where the locker room was, and was anyone still in there. No, the last guy finished showering and left a short time ago. She started to jog and then began to run toward the dorm. She spotted his silhouette standing perfectly still on the white snow covered path.

He was looking at the grounds, the trees and the sky. He was a solitary figure, the only one visible anywhere. He had all the trees and snow to himself. Everything was covered in a hushed white and the stars were points of twinkling light against the ultra clear, black sky. Phi Beta Kappa saw Teo and sprinted through the snow toward him.

"Wait up," she called out. Teo stopped looking at the trees and grounds, and turned around. They stood alone on the path. Phi Beta Kappa had run up to Teo, found his legs welcoming and nuzzled against them. He petted and rubbed him behind the ears in a familiar way and quieted him down. He held up his index finger to his mouth for Adrianna to be quiet and then pointed it all around.

"Shh," she heard him utter in that far off hollow whisper she'd heard before.

There was nothing else in sight, only the untouched snow which glistened and blanketed the grounds and morphed everything into soft, undulating, shapeless shapes, muffling all sound to nothingness. The snow stuck to the limbs of the trees in pleasing stark contrast to their near blackness. The boughs of the majestic evergreens lowered their arms to offer respect to the heavy soft snow. The only existence was this hushed, soft quiet white of purity to be savored in stillness. He inhaled the air and the moment, and let it out slowly. His breath made a little cloud of mist that drifted out from under his partially hooded face.

He pointed to the sloping roof of the Asian Study Center nearby and then waited amidst all that stillness, looking at the snow covered roof. It resembled a Forbidden City Hall in Beijing, and he kept his finger extended, pointing to it. He stood that way, and after standing still and pointing, and waiting, what he was waiting for, happened, as if he had willed it to happen and he only needed to concentrate for it to begin. The deep snow which had accumulated on the sloped roof silently began to slide down in one piece, like a thick, soft, continuous blanket of pure white snow which then fell off as if it were one solid, velvet curtain that for an instant stopped in mid air and became a drape on the wall of the Forbidden City Hall. It finally fell upon the ground with a barely audible soft whoosh. A cloud of snow-dust billowed up creating a surreal diffuse white screen that rounded up on itself to hide the side of the Asian Study Center in its eery fog so only its pointed roof could be seen peaking out of the whiteness like a mountain top holding its head high above its cloud covered mountain. Had he not stopped and waited for the blanket of snow to slide off the roof, had not looked and willed it to happen, it would have been forever unseen and his sentient connection to it, and the evocations of ancient memories and wonder would have been lost forever. It was as if he knew it would have been a lost-forever, never known, never seen, moment in time if he hadn't stopped and waited.

He finally broke his oneness with that unique moment and returned from wherever it had taken him. He faced Adrianna, himself again.

"I thought you went to the Alpha Sig party."

Adrianna didn't share the moment equally. She just walked out on Julian and ran over and was catching her breath.

"Did you make that happen? Did you actually make the snow fall off the roof?"

"I'm not sure, it puzzles me. Things like that have spooked me."

"Really?"

"So why are you here?" Teo asked.

"Well, I didn't feel like being with Julian tonight."

She took a moment to catch her breath so she could speak calmly. "I don't know. I wasn't too nice to him. I left him alone on the dance floor. But I didn't want to be with him right then and there. Samantha and Kendall are probably still there." She fidgeted. "That's not like me and I never did that to him before. I don't feel so good about that. Maybe it's because he didn't remember my birthday. I don't know, maybe I had to leave because he wasn't who I thought he was. I mean, he's okay but I think maybe he likes me mostly cause I'm pretty and isn't interested in much more than that, at least not for now anyway. Maybe in a couple of years it'd be different but tonight I didn't want to start waiting for that to happen."

She paused again. "By the way, thank you for the tickets. The seats were great, and so were you. Can we walk back together, please?" She asked for his permission, she didn't take it for granted.

"Sure. It's dark out, no one will see that you joined me." He pulled the hoodie further down to cover his face.

"That's not fair and I didn't deserve that!" she said indignantly and hurt.

Phi Betta Kappa got startled and Teo patted his rump and made him go back toward the fraternity quad, making a parallel set of fresh, four footed dog tracks in the snow.

"You're right. I apologize. For a moment I mistook you for an uncertain girl in a pink headband I met a couple of months ago. Are you wearing a headband? I can't see it under your hat."

"Yes and it's green. I thought it would actually look good with your dress ... which I am wearing, thank you."

"Yes, you wore a green headband when you read the story about the itch. You've changed. You're coming out of your chrysalis."

"What?"

"You're eclosing."

"What's that?"

"You'll have to look it up," he said, his old controlling arrogance peeking through.

They got to the dorm and Teo stopped in the lobby to let her go on ahead. "Aren't you going to your room?" she asked.

He hesitated before answering, "Yes, yes I guess I am."

"I think I still have the book you lent me. I'll give it back to you now if you're not tired. Can you come up to the fifth floor?"

"Sure, if you like. I can go up if you want."

They got in the elevator together and rode up to the fifth floor. He left his hood over his head making it hard to see his face. He waited in the hall outside of her suite until she brought out the book.

"René, I've been wanting to ask you a personal question, a very personal one but didn't have the courage before. Now I do. I know you say I ... I mean we ... have to be brutally honest with ourselves and each other but even so, there are things that are hard to talk about, at least hard for me if not for you. So ... you told me once when you ran away from home, you were a good looking kid. What happened to you, and why don't you try to have plastic surgery on your face?"

He casually took the book that was still in her hand, perhaps to buy some time for an answer.

"First, that took courage to ask me that. Good for you. It's a legitimate question. This face you see, or which you and others choose not to look at, came on me suddenly. No more details than that. As for plastic surgery, I don't want to go that route. Too drastic and although you won't understand this, I like the privacy my face gives me. I can't give you any more details. It may not be as complete an answer as you'd like but that's all there is. Anyway, I'm glad you came to the match, and I'm glad you came back to walk with me. I think that's a first."

They stood there and each felt the shared intimacy. He waited for her to speak, it was apparent she wanted to say something.

"René, you know I like you ... and I know you like me ...." She stopped there and paused.

"No, please don't," he interrupted her. "Don't say any more. Stop right there. I don't want anything out of pity, or charity or kindness. Thank you, but I don't want your pity or your charity. Don't get me wrong, if and when the time ever comes—and I say if it ever comes—then it has to be for real, it has to be what you're sure you want, no pretending. Don't ever pretend for me. Thanks, but let's say goodnight now. See you."

He turned and went down the stairs as Adrianna stood in the doorway and watched him leave.

CHAPTER NINETEEN

A month later on an early Sunday in March, Adrianna was in Anstace coming down in the elevator when in a chance encounter Teo got in at the third floor. They chatted about her latest design and the Baudelaire poem *Le Voyage* she just read, and he teased her about her orange headband. He said he was going over to Lorinda's, a dive on the wrong side of town for some Southern cooking. He had a craving for it and since the dining room in the dorm was closed for Sunday dinners, he thought he'd go there. Why didn't she come too? It was the best Southern cooking within driving distance and maybe even further.

"What is Southern food?" she asked. "I never had it. Between Bellevue and here on campus, I haven't tried that many different restaurants. Is it safe to go to? I'd like to try Southern food if it isn't expensive."

He assured her it would be cheap and safe but she probably shouldn't try it on her own.

"How would we get there?"

"I'll show you, come on."

They left Anstace and walked to one of the many parking areas on campus. As he was looking around the parking lot, a car was slowly tailing him at a discreet distance. Two people were in it, the same couple who had been to the wrestling match, that same couple who seemed to be looking for someone there. Teo kept walking, vaguely aware of them behind him when he came to a parked car where he opened the door for Adrianna.

"Whose car is this?" she asked.

"Mine. Like it?"

"You never said you had a car on campus."

"Never said, never been asked. I'm not walking there so let's get in, huh?"

"Okay by me!" and she slid in and buckled up.

The car was dirty, a little beat up and showed signs of age and neglect. He drove, like he said, to the wrong side of town, and parked on a one way street in front of Lorinda's. They got out and he locked the doors and told her this is it. As soon as she got inside, she was Alice in Wonderland tumbling down a well into a strange and foreign world, a place she never would have allowed herself to go into.

It was a seedy bar and restaurant with old stain splattered tables and chairs, and a small platform with an upright piano. On the near end of a worn, wooden bar was a creaky narrow staircase to an upper floor which had just a single rickety handrail. Beyond the far end of the bar, a kitchen could be seen through the cracked dirty round windows in each of the two swinging doors. The lighting was whatever they could put together so it was dark in spots, and light in others. They hadn't heard about the no smoking rules and the room was redolent with a mixture of old and new smoke.

From behind the bar Lorinda came out to greet them as if she were welcoming them to an upscale restaurant. She wore a white flowing silk blouse that hung perfectly over her black wide-legged suede pants, and she had short leather boots to finish the look. She was a black, trim and elegant woman, and so well dressed, coifed and poised, she could have been the hostess at any international three star restaurant. She certainly was out of place in the seedy restaurant-bar that bore her name on the wrong side of town.

"Well, my oh my! See what the cat just dragged into Lorinda's!" Lorinda said.

"Hello Lorinda, you make me feel so welcome here!" Teo countered.

"Oh, come on, behind that ugly face of yours, is a thick skin," she said as she stepped forward to give him a hug. "Well, aren't you going to introduce me to your friend? I haven't got all day you know."

"Is that right? I see half the tables are still empty," Teo said with a playful smile.

"They all have reservations and it's early. Do you have a reservation sir?" she kidded him. "Listen, I can't wait for you to behave nicely," she said and faced Adrianna. "I'm Lorinda, welcome to Lorinda's," and gave Adrianna one of her smiles that made you love her instantly.

"Okay, okay. Lorinda, this is Adrianna. She knows I'm ugly but she's punishing herself for being so pretty so she talks to me and looks at me sometimes. Say hello to her and be nice. Adrianna, this is Lorinda, our sassy lady owner of this dive."

"Weren't you listening. I just said hello, and you're the one in college! Don't they teach you to pay attention there?" Lorinda teased him. She looked at Adrianna and asked her, "Tell me Miss Adrianna, did you really come here with him? Now, I know I just saw it, but I can't believe it. Aren't you afraid he might rub off on you?"

Adrianna fidgeted. She was out of her milieu. She didn't know the social cues and this repartee was new to her. She hesitated and suddenly realized she was glad Teo was there to lean on.

"Lorinda," Teo bantered back which took the onus off Adrianna to answer Lorinda, "be careful or I'll make sure I rub off on you and your expensive haute couture looking outfit!

It's very nice, but it's a knock off—but a good one! By the way, when are you going to fix up this place? And aren't you a little overdressed? You're no longer the hostess at the Red Rooster back in New York."

"Well," she said more seriously, "as a matter of fact, you can congratulate me! My financial backers just left. I showed them my plans and I finally got them to agree to invest in me here. They said they were just the agents for the real investor so I'd only deal with them. No matter. I needed to look the part of the 'professional restauranteur,'" she said flamboyantly with a dramatic wave of her hand, "launching a new chic hot spot. It paid off. They think I can do it so I now have the money to make it happen!"

"Congratulations! If anyone can do it, you can. What are the plans?" Teo asked.

"Frankly, if I didn't get that money, I'd have to walk away from this. I've been renting and couldn't fix it up. With the money they're investing, I'm going to exercise my right to buy the building. There'll be a new kitchen, tables, chairs, lighting—you name it, all of it has to be replaced with high end materials and design. Except the bar, I have a soft spot for an old wooden bar like this."

"Sounds fancy," Teo said. "But when you draw in that clientele to this part of town, don't you price out the locals? Your humble crowd won't be comfortable here, let alone afford those prices."

"That's a challenge, to straddle both worlds and make this a go-to place for the high end and also for the locals. I've lived in both those worlds. I went to private schools and had opportunities but I was also close to my grandparents and spent a lot of time in their world. That's a different world. They worked hard and struggled, and taught me a lot. I feel obligated to them in a way, that I'd betray them if I moved on and up and forgot them. Growing up and living as a black, you face bias everyday of your life. You can't even imagine how pervasive and subtle it can be, every day, day after day. I want this place to be for everyone. I'm hoping that when you boil it down, pardon the pun, everyone who wants good Southern cooking in a friendly place can feel welcome here. I can adjust the menus so everyone can find something they can afford, and allow me to make a profit too. Wish me luck!"

"Good luck! I'm rooting for you. I don't suppose we can sample some of that Southern cooking now?" Teo grinned and asked.

"You two park yourselves over here and I'll see what I can get. Teo, did you just come to eat, or can I get Black Jack to come over?"

"Well, it's early, and I'm in the mood so why not get Black Jack and anyone else who can help liven up this fallen down shack of forgot-to-pay electric bills, and I'll do my best with that miserable excuse for a piano."

"Oh that's great! We're going to have a good time tonight! Thanks Teo." She called over to a teenager standing behind the bar, "Mary, tell Black Jack Teo is here and we need him and Hammie, and then get more chairs from behind the stairs and put more beer on ice. You got that young lady?"

"Yes Ma'am," Mary said. She was a thin, sullen, listless black teenager who looked like she spent most of her life in that bar.

"Teo," Lorinda said, "this will take a little time so how about you go upstairs and pay a nice visit to Mama Lou, she'd like that."

"Glad to. Aimée, you'd better come with me. Lorinda, what's Mama Lou's story? Did you bring her here from New York with you?"

"Lord no! She came with the house. Whether I rented it or bought it, she gets to keep her room upstairs. They say a long time ago she was a Candomblé priestess, a *Mãe-de-santo*, of her own house in a favela outside of Ondina. That's in Salvador, in Bahia. Something happened and she left—or had to leave—and went to the Creole bayou in Louisiana. She somehow ended up here, in the Midwest of all places! No one will ever know. Anyway, everyone loves her and treats her like their favorite grandma. I've managed to buy some caipirinha from Brazil for her. She likes to drink that, it reminds her of her old times."

Teo and Adrianna climbed up the creaking staircase which led them to a narrow hallway. Pieces of old grey paint peeled off and curled down from the walls; a couple of bare hanging light bulbs lit only some of the hallway, leaving other parts in shadows. A voice came out of the first room on the left.

"Is dat you Teo? I know it is, come here and help me," said the voice.

They went into the room. They saw odd artifacts lying around including a bowl of cowrie shells on the floor and pictures of a harp, a trident and the Star of David lying next to it.

"What are all those things?" Adrianna whispered to Teo.

"They're part of Candomblé. It looks like she took it from her house when she was a priestess and made this room into something of a holy place for herself," he whispered back.

Mama Lou, dressed all in white, sat with her stockinged feet atop a worn hassock. She had brown, wrinkled skin and wore a white headdress wrapped around her hair like a wasp nest, a long necklace of three strands of multi-colored beads draped down and lay on a fluffy, crinoline stuffed, white hoop skirt. She must have been eighty though she looked older. She had a cackle to her voice and coughed a lot.

"Come here and let me look at you," she said.

Teo came close and Mama Lou examined his face with her hands since she was nearly blind.

"Why you still keepin ya self so ugly? Shame on you boy! Now let me see the girl standin next to you."

Teo moved Adrianna closer so she could be examined too.

"Don't be afraid'a me girl, nothin I can do can hurt you. But please let me get a good look, okay?" Mama Lou started examining Adrianna's face. "You are some pretty thing, aren't ya? Let me see what else you got."

Mama Lou moved her hands down to Adrianna's neck and arms, and then held her hands for a moment. She moved her hands onto Adrianna's breasts, stomach, thighs and behind. It was done so quickly and softly, Adrianna didn't have time to react.

"Teo, what you want with such a pretty little thing. You need a full sized woman by now. Maybe your face'll clear up if you get yourself a real woman," Mama Lou cackled. "But I'll tell you this, she's good and ready! You better be careful or like it or not, you'll be a pappy!" She cackled again. "Now, is you or ain't you gonna do your magic on me?"

"Sure Mama Lou. Would you like me to make you feel better?"

"That's what I said, go ahead, quit your yakkin."

"Will you let me help you?"

"Yeah, yeah. Why do you always make me answer those same dumb questions?"

Teo told Adrianna to look in the bathroom at the end of the hall for a basin, soap and a towel. She should find them there and to fill the basin half way with warm water and bring it all here. He took off Mama Lou's stockings to reveal varicose veins which covered her swollen, brown-skinned legs. He told her to close her eyes and relax while he went behind her and massaged her neck and shoulders applying gentle pressure. She started to hum a tune while she enjoyed a dreamy memory of a mirage shimmering way off in the distance. Teo kept this up for a few minutes until Adrianna came in with the basin of soap and water. She put it on the floor by Mama Lou and then Teo gently washed and massaged Mama Lou's hard cracked feet with his bare hands, stroking up as far as her knees. For ten minutes, he applied pressure to her feet, swollen ankles and calves as Adrianna sat and watched Teo care so lovingly for Mama Lou, undaunted and not in the least repulsed to touch her unsightly legs and feet. Mama Lou hummed the tune, lost in an ancient memory. Finally, Teo dried her with a towel and put her stockings back on.

"Aah, Teo. You got the magic. Who taught you all that? It's so good. My mother got her magic from her mother and she taught me. You got blessed with your magic too. Help me up, I want to see about walkin. You know, I used to be a great dancer in my house, a long time ago."

She put her feet on the ground, and with Teo and Adrianna helping her, she stood up and tried to dance a step or two with her arms circling in and out and her overflowing white hoop skirt spread out and swaying just like her old days.

"Wonder how long this'll last? Thank you kindly Teo, Miss Adrianna, bless you, bless you both. Come here children, come closer."

She took their hands and put them together in hers, and with her eyes closed, began to chant in a mixed African and Portugese dialect. She stopped abruptly midway and opened her eyes wide. She was startled by something and stared at Teo and Adrianna. She then nodded, closed her eyes, smiled to herself and resumed her chanting.

"Okay, tell Mary to come up and help her Mama Lou. Poor Mary, poor girl, afraid she's a lost soul. I see connections everywhere. Teo, you got the magic, the power, but Miss Adrianna, she got the gift, she can see. I see why you two are always goin to find a life together ahead, but Mary, she ain't got no life, no one else to help her."

Mary came up from the bar and helped Mama Lou walk a few more steps around the room before easing her back into her chair. Teo left Adrianna with Mama Lou and followed Mary into the bathroom down the hall who had taken the basin of water to be thrown out.

"Mary, Mama Lou worries about you."

"Yeah, don't do no good though."

"What would do some good?"

"Look, you and your girlfriend are nice, white college kids, you don't know, you haven't got a clue what my life is like, so don't come down here with your do-gooder attitudes and think you can wave a magic wand and change things. You can't. It's a bad joke if you think you can make a difference and I'm not laughing. Leave me alone if you know what's good for you. No one asked you, so fuck off! You want to see what it's like here? Here, I'll show you."

She rolled up the sleeve of her shirt to show the scars across her wrist and the needle marks up her arm.

"I turn tricks so I can take some stuff and escape. That's my life. How's that compared to yours? Pretty picture? I bet that girlfriend of yours is still intact. Me, already had two abortions. You gonna come here and tell me how to live? Fuck off. I can't even remember when I had dreams, when I could see some way out of this place I'm in. So, fuck off!"

CHAPTER TWENTY

Teo was no crusader. He got the message and left her in the bathroom cleaning out the basin. He picked up Adrianna, said goodbye to Mama Lou, and they went downstairs where the room was full of folks talking, eating and drinking beer. Lorinda told them to sit at the bar and then brought them two dishes heaped with food. It was Southern cooking like none other. Teo and Adrianna dove into it and scarfed it down and then used the bread to wipe the gravy off the plate. Adrianna got the diet cola she asked for, and Teo a beer.

By now Black Jack and Hammie were sitting on the platform waiting for Teo. Black Jack was a black albino: a lanky, easy going, slow talking, banjo strumming, ex-card dealer who kept a worn deck of cards in one pocket or another. He laid his banjo on top of the piano bench while he stood and played a game of solitaire on top of the upright piano. He was wearing his signature outfit, a grey corduroy vest over a white shirt and black slacks which hung from his trim, malnourished waist. A cigarette dangled from his mouth. Its curled ash, as long as the unsmoked white part, refused to fall off.

Hammie sat next to him. He wore a cap to cover his grey and white short hair, and had a constant three day old stubble in want of a shave. He was warming up by playing riffs on his harmonica.

"Before I start playing, would you like to meet them?" Teo asked Adrianna, indicating Black Jack and Hammie.

Lorinda interrupted to ask Teo something so Adrianna had a moment to answer. She was rudderless. It wasn't her way to do something like that, and of course she had never been in this situation. She looked around the room, studied the people who sat at the tables and the bar, and Teo talking to Lorinda. She did it slowly, she let it all seep into her and saw them now for what it simply was, not distorted by her pretty prisms nor kept at bay by the bubble Charlotte said she lived in.

"Yes," she told Teo, "I really would like to meet Hammie and Black Jack. Yes, I would, please. Yes."

He took her around and through the tables and chairs in order to get to the platform.

"Adrianna, this is Black Jack. Black Jack, this is Adrianna," he said.

"Pleased to meet you Adrianna. Is this ugly no-talent really a friend of yours?" He extended his albino white hand. She looked down at his hand and hesitated to touch him. It would have been awkward if she had waited any longer, but she finally took his hand, and then shook it firmly and sincerely.

"Thank you, pleased to meet you too Black Jack, very pleased, and yes, we're classmates," she replied.

"Black Jack was one of the best card dealers at the casinos, weren't you?" Teo said. "But you also play a real mean banjo. Which came first, playing the banjo or card dealing?"

"Well, you know all great card dealers played the banjo and I started to play even before I stopped sucking at my mother's tit," Black Jack said.

"Is that so?" Adrianna kidded, and added, "Must have been hard to find a banjo that small!"

"You think you were a great card dealer? Ain't so. And watch your language!" interrupted Hammie.

"Yep, true as I'm my mother's son!"

"Adrianna, this is Hammie. He was and is one of the best harmonica players ever lived," Teo said.

"That's right, just like you say Teo." Hammie tipped his cap to Adrianna.

"You think you can play the harmonica like a Hammie?" Black Jack said, getting even now.

"Sure thing! Like Teo says, one of the best ever lived!" Hammie proudly replied.

"Right, that's about as true as what I said!" Black Jack said, throwing a taunt back at Hammie.

"That's exactly why I can't believe anything you say, like for instance, 'you're your mother's son!'" Hammie retorted.

Before they could layer on more insults, Lorinda came over to shut them up and ordered them to start playing.

"You come with me," she told Adrianna. "I have some pecan pie to put meat on those bones of yours." She put her arm around Adrianna and walked with her over to the bar. Adrianna said she wasn't sure and didn't know what it would cost.

"Don't you fret about that," Lorinda said. "No one ever turns down a free piece of my pecan pie! And you're not going to be the first!"

Adrianna put her arm around Lorinda's waist and they walked back to the bar together, holding each other like that.

Teo waited for Black Jack to collect his cards and banjo from the piano before he sat down on the bench. The folks quieted down and the three of them started playing without introduction. They improvised and did a hodge podge of soul, blues, ragtime and jazz. It was good old fashioned music not played or available commercially. They played songs and tunes that dated way back, hollered out or sang and talked to each other as part of a tune. Folks kept time with their feet, some danced in the small spaces around their tables. A man in a wheelchair danced with his woman as he rocked one wheel forward and the other back, making fast turns and twirling himself and her. They moved and grooved better than most white folks thought Adrianna, and had a great time doing it.

A slick haired, tall thin guy in a white suit, talked side by side with sullen Mary at the end of the bar near the stairs. After a while he sidled up to Adrianna who sat at the other end of the bar near the kitchen where Lorinda was going to and fro to get the food out to her customers.

Teo quieted down the music and shouted out to the guy, "Hey, dude, you come one foot closer to that honky and you'll be playing tunes with this lousy piano from the inside every time you take a shit." The folks laughed and clapped and Lorinda came out of the kitchen and told the dude to peddle his wares somewhere else, and then told Adrianna just sit where she is and don't worry cause Teo and Lorinda have her in their sights.

After an hour and a half, Teo got up to leave. They all said he couldn't, they hadn't heard enough and it wasn't even seven o'clock. But Teo had to go and thanked them, wished them all well and thanked Lorinda for the food. She gave him a big hug and hugged Adrianna too.

"You and Miss Adrianna are always welcome here, you know that! And be sure to come when it's all fixed up—and order something expensive!" she said as they left the bar.

Adrianna got in the car first and when Teo was about to get in, the tall thin guy from the bar approached Teo with an open switchblade in his right hand.

"Hey, you're pretty cocky in there but maybe not so much out here, huh? I see you here before, none of my business but when you start messin with my rice bowl, then that is my business. So, if you're plannin to talk to Mary again, then your business and my business going to have a problem."

He brandished his knife in front of Teo who stepped back and took a stance in case he needed to fend off the knife.

At that moment, a guy started to get out of a car parked across the street, and shouted out, "Hey, dude, I got something for you, maybe you got something for me?" The tall thin guy closed his knife, pointed his finger at Teo in a menacing gesture and sauntered over to the car across the street. It all happened so quickly that between the time Adrianna got into her seat, closed the door and fumbled with her seat belt, Teo started to drive away and she didn't see the encounter. He said nothing to her about his few words with the tall thin guy.

Adrianna had never been to a place like Lorinda's. The first time to sit at a bar—a black bar with all black people—a tired and dimly lit bar, tired because of no money, not because of an interior designer's idea of shabby chic. Her initial nervousness wore off when she saw them simply as folks who ate, drank, had a good time and enjoyed each other and the music even if they talked and looked different from what she was used to. Not a revelation but a thinning of her insulating bubble, that they were not so different from anyone else who goes out to have a beer and listen to some music.

She wanted to know what Mama Lou was chanting. It was a Candomblé blessing, he told her. She still didn't know what that was and didn't ask but kept jabbering away about the people she saw, how they dressed and talked, about Lorinda, Mama Lou and that sad looking girl Mary and that dude in the suit. And where did he learn to play the piano and know all those tunes? And how did he know what Mama Lou was chanting, and what made her stop and look at them so surprised and tell her she has "a gift to see"? Teo drove to campus and kept nodding his head in agreement while she excitedly went on and on. He parked the car in the same parking area as before; the other car with the couple in it had gone.

Back at the dorm, Teo got out of the elevator on the third floor and Adrianna thanked him for a great time.

"Was that a date?" he asked.

"Whatever," she answered cutely and the elevator door closed.

CHAPTER TWENTY ONE

Samantha skipped breakfast and stayed in bed waiting for her cramps to die down. It was Sunday, no classes. This was her worst period and she thought it was because she was so late. She finally got dressed and made coffee but could barely drink it. Her flow was heavier than any time before and the cramps kept getting worse, not better. She was glad she was alone to get through this. All the others were out for the day so she laid down on the living room couch instead of her bed. That's where they found her when they came in, curled up with a blanket she had thrown over herself.

Erika and Wanda came in first at about 7:30 p.m. Samantha was rocking back and forth and sweating, moaning, holding the blanket over her stomach, and managed to say she was having a really bad period. They got her water but she couldn't drink it and tried to engage her in conversation to take her mind off the pain but she wasn't paying attention. Ten minutes later, Adrianna came in, eager to tell them about her time at Lorinda's but was brought up short by Samantha lying on the couch. The three of them never saw a period like this. After a few minutes, Samantha began to cry out in pain and became less responsive. It was clear she was in trouble and needed help. They asked each other what they ought to do. Wanda and Erika hadn't a clue and kept discussing it when Adrianna said she was getting Teo and ran out and down the stairs to his suite. He answered the door and was surprised to see her so soon.

"There's something really wrong with Samantha. We're not

sure what to do, maybe you do. Do you think you can do something? Can you come up right now, please, can you? Hurry."

He hesitated a moment and saw Adrianna was worried. "Of course," he said. He ran into his room and came out with a small box.

He and Adrianna ran up the two flights and into the living room. Erika and Wanda momentarily moved their attention from Samantha to Teo's face. For that moment, his face took center stage, not Samantha writhing on the couch.

"Teo, this is Wanda and Erika," Adrianna said looking at them, and then "this is Samantha," pointing to Samantha.

"Hi Teo," Wanda and Erika said and Wanda continued, "she was like this when we came in half an hour ago. Maybe we should call a doctor to come over. Do they make house calls here... on Sundays?"

Teo knelt down by Samantha's side. He looked at her quickly and took her hand in his.

"You're not feeling well and you hurt. Would you like me to help you?" Samantha could hardly hear what he was saying, she was almost delirious.

"Do you want me to help you?" he asked again.

Adrianna got close to Samantha and screamed at her, "Say yes, Samantha, say yes!"

"Yes," she murmured.

"Will you let me help you, will you?" Teo asked.

Samantha was incapable of understanding what was happening, her pain and distress overcame her.

"Yes! Samantha say yes! Samantha say yes! For God's sake, Samantha say yes!" Adrianna screamed at her. A feeble yes came out.

Teo put his hand on the blanket and moved it gently over her distended belly. When he pressed, Samantha cried out in pain. The blanket was wet.

"Aimée, does Samantha use tampons?"

"No, she doesn't," Adrianna answered without pausing to think what kind of question was that.

"Go to the bathroom and pull down, yank it off if you have to, a plastic shower curtain! Bring it here now and bring me rubbing alcohol and towels!"

And to Wanda and Erika, "We have to move her to the floor."

Teo took the blanket off of Samantha. Her dress was soaked in blood and the couch was drenched in it. Small puddles of blood had formed on the cushions.

"Take off her dress!" he ordered Wanda and Erika.

Samantha now had on only her bra and panties.

"Help me get this off," pointing to her panties and they slid her panties off. He again moved his hand over her belly gently pressing and feeling.

Adrianna came in with the plastic shower curtain and was shocked to see Samantha nearly naked, Teo by her side and the couch now turned a reddish black from the blood. He pushed away the cocktail table and laid the shower curtain on the floor next to the couch. He took command and no one dared question him.

"Take her feet! We're moving her to the floor."

They put her on top of the shower curtain. When they moved her, more blood poured out from between her legs and made puddles on the shower curtain. He put his clean hand on Samantha's brow and told her she'll feel better soon and be fine. It seemed she understood even though she was no longer cognizant of what was happening. He told Adrianna to boil some water and then fetch some of Samantha's things for an overnight in the hospital. He told Erika to take Wanda and go to every floor from the lobby to the top floor, get friends to help, and not allow anyone to use the elevator and to keep the elevator doors open and waiting in the lobby. Do whatever they had to do but block out the elevator from anyone using it until the ambulance arrived. They understood exactly what they had to do and left to do it. When Adrianna came back from the kitchen area, Teo was on his cell phone.

"Ken, Teo here. Look, I am calling in a Code Orange. I repeat, this is a Code Orange and not a joke. Come to the Anstace dorm at the University, fifth floor. We'll be waiting. You'll be taking a female, twenty years old, severe loss of blood and continuous hemorrhaging. Call the state troopers and give them your route. Tell them you are requesting Code Orange assistance. And tell them it was called in by Brenda. I need you here really fast and don't forget to activate your traffic signal priority preemption."

He hung up and called another number. He told Adrianna to get overnight things for herself and to make a special tea as he opened his box of teas: one part from the red bag, one from the blue and one from the grey.

"Brenda, it's me Teo. I just called in a Code Orange. No, not for me. Can you have an operating room and an OB-GYN and an anesthesiologist scrubbed and ready as soon as Ken gets us there, maybe in about thirty five minutes. And a crash cart too. I'll be coming in with Adrianna's friend Samantha. Twenty year old female with a loss of blood of about . . ." he looked down at the couch and shower curtain, "two maybe two and half or even three pints, it's hard to say, and still hemorrhaging out her vagina and probably going into hypovolemic shock. I'm not kidding and there is no time to talk about it. Get a clear path from the emergency entrance up the elevators to the operating room. Brenda, we can win this one if everyone acts fast. By the way, I called the Code Orange in your name."

He hung up and took the tea Adrianna prepared. To her surprise, he drank half of it.

"Samantha, you can do this. Drink a little."

He held up her head and tried to have her take a sip. She couldn't. She was only semi-conscious. He drank the rest of it.

Adrianna got a sheet from her bedroom and draped it over Samantha who was naked except for her bra. She got a black plastic garbage bag and threw in her overnight things along with Samantha's. And when she saw the box of teas, she threw that in too.

Teo moved his shirt sleeve up on his left arm and poured rubbing alcohol over it. He took a deep breath, closed his eyes and sat perfectly still, cross legged on the floor until he heard Ken wheeling a gurney into the room. Right behind Ken was an EMT who carried an impressive array of equipment and despite her small size was no nonsense.

"Open an IV on me and one on her and get a flow going from me to her. I'm type O negative."

"I never did that before. Does it work?" the EMT asked him.

"I hope so. I don't see any other donors around here."

"I don't know about that. It's not in any of the manuals I had to read and your blood hasn't been screened for pathogens and the rest."

"If you don't do it, Ken will and then this girl on the floor will continue to bleed to death and die. So do it. It's legal."

The EMT stopped quibbling and decided action was in order. She connected Samantha and Teo with one IV, put an oxygen mask on Samantha and started a mobile EKG on her.

They got Samantha onto the gurney with the IV connected to her at one end, and Teo at the other. They quick stepped to the elevator where three girls from next door kept it open. It later became the news that everyone had cooperated in keeping the elevator reserved for Samantha.

Adrianna wanted to sit in the back of the ambulance but the EMT told her to sit in front with Ken so there was more room in the back for the EMT, Samantha and Teo. Ken went as fast as he could, hitting sixty miles per hour on some roads and with his signal preemption activated, he had green lights most of the way. He called ahead to the hospital and gave them his ETA.

The EMT was busy doing what seemed routine to her. She took off Samantha's bra and cleaned the blood from her legs. She checked on the IV and saw it worked and the blood was moving well but adjusted the flow rate slightly. She made Teo lie down and kept on the phone with the emergency room crew who were expecting them. Teo told her what he thought was causing Samantha's condition and the EMT made her notes and passed it on to the waiting personnel at the hospital. She ended by saying, "Roger that." She took out a safety razor and began to shave an area about eight inches in all directions around Samantha's vagina and partly up her abdomen.

After a few minutes, Ken picked up an escort of a state trooper whose sirens and flashing red lights helped clear a lane in front of him. Because of the Code Orange, major cross roads had been blocked by other state troopers so Ken made good time getting to the emergency room entrance.

When he arrived, the trooper in front of him kept moving ahead so Ken could pull right up to the entrance. Doctors, nurses, orderlies, another gurney and others, were waiting. Ken had not even come to a full stop when the back door of the ambulance was opened and everyone went into a concerted frenzy of effort. Samantha was rushed out with Teo attached. Someone opened another IV line on Samantha's arm and held up an IV bag. Teo was still attached so he was pushed alongside the gurney and two male orderlies nearly held him up and carried him as Samantha was brought in. Doctors and nurses raced alongside the gurney feverishly working on Samantha, calling out orders and results. They had already been told what to expect.

The elevator door was held open for them. Everyone in the emergency room was either a participant or an active observer. They had trained for a Code Orange several times but this was the first time it was being done for real. Someone's life was hanging in the balance. In a brief span of forty five seconds, Samantha had been lifted out of the ambulance, had additional IV lines started, was intubated, cardiac monitoring was begun, and was in the elevator surrounded by a team working on her. Just at that time, one of the nurses detached Teo from Samantha and closed off his IV to stop his flow of blood, and attached Samantha's freed up IV line to a bag of clear fluids.

"You'll have to stay down here," the nurse told Teo. "Someone will come to help you in a minute." She stepped back into the elevator and the doors closed.

Teo began to feel the affects of his surge of adrenaline and loss of blood. Samantha was out of his hands and into the hands of others. He got her to the hospital where she had to be if she was going to survive and now his own body called for attention. He needed rest and fluids to make up for the blood he had given her. Adrianna had followed the gurney up to the elevators too and now walked by Teo's side to two empty seats in the emergency room. It was quiet there after the intense, high speed activity which just took place. Teo and Adrianna were lost in the hubbub and weren't noticed much except for a good looking girl now holding a black garbage bag, and a hideous looking guy with an IV stuck in his arm.

CHAPTER TWENTY TWO

Brenda marched into the emergency room ready for action but saw she was too late for that. She saw Adrianna and Teo.

"You got here fast," she said. "I was on my way home when you called and I turned right around. Is she alright?"

"She's in O.R." He took his time to catch his breath and said slowly, "Brenda, we shouldn't lose this one. I want to be up there. Can you do it?"

Brenda ushered them out of the emergency room as if she were going to treat them but took them instead to a service elevator. They went up to the O.R. and sat down on the floor outside in the hallway while Brenda went into the O.R. and said she would keep them posted. She came back in a minute. Samantha had lost a lot of blood and they weren't able to stop it. They looked for the IUD Teo told them about but there was no IUD. They said there was a lot of internal damage and it was messy inside and hard to find anything.

"It's there. Did they take an x-ray?" Teo asked.

Brenda went back in and came out with an x-ray. "They say they can't find it on the x-ray. It's old Dr. Letum in there. He's in charge. He's been here a long time . . . too long . . . and he's got the lowest success rate of them all, if you know what I mean."

Teo grabbed the x-ray from Brenda and looked at it intently. "Have them look here, it's probably way up and out of the way."

"Where?" she asked.

Teo pulled his IV out of his arm which dripped blood and used it as a pen. He drew a small circle in blood around an area on the x-ray. "Please, ask them to look here. They have to find it. I'm sure it must be there."

Brenda went back in. Teo should have been nursing himself but was getting another adrenaline rush and got antsy just waiting and not doing something, anything. He stood up and paced. Adrianna had never seen Teo behave like this, nor for that matter, like he did since he came up to help Samantha. She wanted to help him, take care of him, but nothing seemed like the right thing for her to do.

Brenda burst out of the room. "They found it! Close to where you marked. They removed it and are about to close her up and it seems like it stopped the hemorrhaging."

Teo showed no signs of relief. He kept pacing. Adrianna told him that was great news.

"Her heart," is all he said and he shook his head from side to side.

From inside the O.R. they heard loud voices and a different level of furious activity, and then a high pitched sound followed by "Clear!" and a thud, repeated again, high pitch, "Clear!" and thud, and repeated again. Brenda ran inside and stayed there. After a few agonizing minutes, all went silent and Brenda came out slowly, shaking her head in disbelief, and tearful.

"She's gone. I can't believe it, I just cannot believe it. Her heart stopped and when Dr. Letum tried to revive her, it was too late. They gave her CPR and everything else they know. They're speechless. He called it just now, this second. It's unbelievable. Just like that. Gone. I'm so sorry Teo."

"Oh God, no! No! No! No! No!" Adrianna cried out.

"Not good enough. She should be alive!" Teo yelled.

"They couldn't save her. Apparently her heart couldn't take it. She lost a lot of blood and it strained her heart. Teo, you did everything you could. You know you did and you know you don't always win even when you really want it."

"Get me in there! I'm not losing this one yet. Brenda, do this, PLEASE!"

"They won't let you into an O.R."

"Brenda, find a way, and find it right now," he pleaded. "And don't let them stop the CPR!"

"They absolutely won't allow it," Brenda said.

"Look. She's dead, right? It's not like they're allowing me in during an operation. Cleaning people go in there. Orderlies move dead people around. Tell them that. Tell them anything but get me in there!"

"Look, I can bend the rules and let you touch the kids especially when their parents don't object and with your teas and all. But getting you into an O.R. is not anything I can do. But I'll try to get Dr. Letum to come out here and you can talk to him. Then it's up to you. Okay?"

"Yeah, but hurry and keep up the CPR." Teo paced frantically as Brenda left.

She went into the O.R. and asked Dr. Letum to come out into the hall. She conveyed a sense of urgency and immediacy, and not knowing what was happening, he responded by quickly going out. He welcomed any reason to leave the room. Brenda followed him into the hall but on the way out told everyone to continue CPR until she came back.

"Okay, what is this about?" Dr. Letum asked.

"This young man wants to go into the O.R. to see if he can revive her," Brenda said not having a clue how else to present it.

"You're kidding! Right? You dragged me out here for that!"

"Just listen to him," she said. "Remember, he's the one who showed you where to look for the IUD."

"I know this is bizarre to you," Teo quickly said, not wanting to lose any time nor Dr. Letum's attention. "There isn't a lot of time so I'll make it real brief. You did what you know using Western medical procedures to save her. Okay, but it didn't work. I know about traditional Chinese medicine, things like acupuncture, acu-point manipulation and stuff. No, don't scoff at it. Please, she's dead right? Give me three minutes to see if I can do something. Just three minutes. It's a long shot. I'm not sure about it either. But it's worth three minutes, isn't it? I wouldn't do anything invasive nor inject anything into her. It's based on centuries old Chinese practices and studies that show there are pathways within the body that physically connect one part to another, including to the heart muscle. Please, there's no time to argue this. Please, for God's sake, give me three minutes. Your patient is already dead! I couldn't do worse than that."

"That's very noble of you son, but no way," Dr. Letum said who clearly wasn't going to allow any of that nonsense in his O.R.

"I'm her sister. She's my sister and I'm permitting it," Adrianna joined in.

The doctor was unmoved and didn't believe her anyway.

"Sis?" Teo looked at Adrianna, and then at Brenda, "Brenda?" begging her to do something.

"Doctor, it's your call, your patient and your O.R.," Brenda said. "But this young man knew enough to call in the Code Orange and nearly saved her life as a result. I was hoping not to do this but you have to let him in to try. Look, I know all about your dirty secrets and skeletons you keep locked away out of sight. And you know I know about them. I've never brought it up to you, and you know I could have, lots of times. I'm willing to keep the keys to all that nasty stuff in my pocket. I never used that information against you before because we both knew it would ruin you here, or at least make you a pariah.

That's not something I ever wanted and I never used it against you for my own personal benefit. But this is different."

Brenda took out a set of keys from her pocket to dramatically emphasize her point, and dangled them in front of her.

"Doctor, I'm sorry to have to do this, but either you give him those three minutes or I open the door to your shameful secrets. That's not something you want so close to the end of your career here. If you agree, I promise never to bring it up to you again."

"You bitch!" he screamed.

"Doctor, you've got very little to lose, just a failure to follow administrative protocol if you let him in. But look at what you stand to lose if you don't. What'll it be, come on. There's no time to think about it. He can't hurt her if you said she's already dead, right? Yes or no?"

Brenda knew she had a reputation in the hospital for being a tough son of a bitch, but in a good way, not like this. She knew she'd lose sleep over this one even if Dr. Letum was no one's choice for a doctor.

"Are you blackmailing me, you black c—."

Brenda interrupted him in mid-sentence. "Don't you dare say that to me like you do other women here! You pull that on me and three minutes or no three minutes, you'll wish you never did!"

"You c—!" He wanted to finish it but forced himself to hold back. "You . . . you . . . ! This is out and out blackmail! You'll be the one to regret this! You're blackmailing me!"

"Yes, I guess I am."

He tightened the muscles to his mouth, squeezed his eyes shut and shook his head from side to side. He had two abhorrent choices and he had to pick and live with one, awful as it would likely turn out.

"Well?" Brenda asked. "It's only three minutes of your life."

"Okay," he reluctantly let out, "but only three minutes, nothing invasive, no injections and you stop when I say so. And, you . . . ." He pointed his finger straight at Brenda as if he were about to send it darting through her. "You better keep your mouth shut and promise me never, I mean never, to bring this up again. Do you understand me?"

"Yes, Doctor."

"And you young man, do you understand too? Three minutes, stop when I say so?"

"I understand," Teo said, "and we both agree nothing invasive and no injections. That's what we said, right?"

"Yes."

Brenda opened the door to the O.R. and said to Teo when he was about to follow her in, "Make it quick, you only have three minutes. Here put on a bunny suit." She handed him surgical scrubs and a face mask and helped him get into it.

Teo rushed in with Dr. Letum right behind who nodded to everyone indicating his approval of this unorthodox breach of protocol. Samantha lay on the operating table under two bright lights shining down on her body and everyone else standing nearby. They had on surgical greens and face masks and stepped back out of Teo's way. No one wanted to be any part of this.

"Keep the CPR going! You, yes you, keep it up. Keep it all going. It won't kill her if she's dead, right?" And after getting a nod of approval from Dr. Letum, they continued the CPR, oxygen and everything else.

He went near Samantha's head, grabbed a nurse by the arm and brought her closer. He felt for a spot at the base of her neck. "Here, take your thumb and press here. Press hard and keep pressing until I say so. Don't ask questions. Just do it. You want to save her life don't you?"

He grabbed another nurse and had her press a spot on the inside of her wrist. He was so forceful and assured, and with Dr. Letum's acquiescence, they did what he asked.

By her feet, he felt for a spot on the sole of her right foot. He quickly looked around for a tool he could use and picked up a vaginal speculum which had a strong metal cylindrical end. He used the end as a hammer and jabbed the thick metal end into that spot on her foot.

"Is that heart monitor still attached and plugged in?" The anesthesiologist said yes.

"Keep feeling for a pulse and yell out if you see anything." He jammed her foot again. "Come on Samantha, you can do this." He hit her foot again with great force. And again. And again. And again.

"Look young man. I don't know who you are or who you think you are, but your three minutes are nearly up just like her time was up. It's time for you to leave. Brenda, I gave him his three minutes, now, please escort this young man out of my O.R. As we agreed, remember?" Dr. Letum said, making an obvious reference about her promise.

Teo ignored him and jammed Samantha's foot again.

"Brenda, you have to take him out now. I was afraid this would happen."

Teo repeated jabbing three more times. "Come on girl, your heart remembers how this works," he said to Samantha.

"Brenda, he has to go now," Dr. Letum said more angrily, not accustomed to disobedience in his O.R. He approached Teo about to grab him by the arm and force him out.

"I feel something," the anesthesiologist said.

Teo ignored Dr. Letum who had now grabbed Teo's arm. They saw the spot on Samantha's foot which was badly bruised. Teo took aim and hammered her foot again.

The anesthesiologist blurted out, "There's another beat! It's thready, very, very weak... it's not steady... wait, there it is again... still thready... very weak... still there... weak... thready... something is there, something is happening. Wait... wait... it's... I think I have a rhythm! There's a rhythm! You can see it now!"

Teo pressed the bruised spot and said out loud, stop the chest compressions but keep up the respiration. He told the nurse pressing near Samantha's neck to reduce the pressure slowly and the same thing for the one pressing on the inside of her wrist.

"Rhythm is becoming more steady but still quite weak."

"Okay Samantha, time for you to take over." He told the two nurses to stop pressing completely.

"Rhythm is becoming steadier, a little stronger now... a little bit stronger but still weak."

"She's breathing on her own now!" someone said and stopped the manual respiration.

Doctor Letum let go of Teo's arm and ordered someone to administer an injection of vasopressin and moved toward Samantha to take charge again.

"No! No. Please. Don't give her anything right now, it's too soon. She needs time for her heart to remember what to do. Don't! I got her this far, her heart is beating, let it beat. Wait. Please. We both said no injections, right?"

Teo looked at Dr. Letum and then Brenda, and then stared at Dr. Letum. Brenda took out the keys from her pocket and dangled them in front of her. Dr. Letum understood Brenda's pernicious reminder but told his assistant to give her the vasopressin anyway.

Teo massaged her chest. Everyone had stood silently by and frozen as they watched Teo do the strange things he had done, things they never saw or read about. They stood that way watching as Teo massaged and they listened to the heart monitor begin to beep more and more steadily. Everyone waited and listened, second by slow second, as the sound on the monitor grew from very weak to not too weak. No one made a sound or moved. After five, long breathless minutes, Teo said there wasn't anything more he could do so he would leave. He thanked them for letting him help and asked them not to inject anything else into her so long as her heart was beating even if it wasn't fast enough for them. He gave Brenda a look as he left, and before he went out, she spoke to him for a moment. He nodded.

As he left the O.R., he heard a string of "Holy Shit!", "Unbelievable!" and "That was incredible!" coming from behind those green masks standing around Samantha lying on the operating table.

Teo left, and Adrianna, who had been standing in the doorway to the O.R. watching it all, left with him. Brenda came out.

"God must have been watching Samantha cause I've seen you do some pretty impressive things, but this one. Wow! They're stunned in there. I'm stunned. They're speechless. No one has ever seen that or even heard about it. Doctor Letum is going to have to figure out how to write up how his patient, whom he pronounced dead and stopped treatment, came back to life! With help from a stranger, a college boy, not a doctor! I gotta see what he writes. Lots of witnesses in there. Teo, how did you do that?"

"It's a long story," he said automatically but wearily and with a look of immense satisfaction. "Thanks Brenda, you made it happen."

"Well, you just cheated Death big time! Be careful yourself, you know how I feel about all that."

"What do you mean?" Adrianna asked.

"Like I told you before, you do that to Death, Death finds a way to get even, now or at another time," Brenda answered.

"Maybe it's me getting even with Death!" Teo said.

They began to come out of the O.R. Each one looked at Teo and for the first time saw him without a face mask which only confused them more. They looked at him with incomprehension, respect and awe.

A Filipino doctor said, "You saved her life back there. You alone. Not Dr. Letum, not us. I still have a lot to learn. Good job."

After a few minutes, both doors opened and Samantha was wheeled out. "We'll take good care of her, don't worry. We'll let you know how she does. She goes to post-op intensive care now. Get some rest yourself. That was only amazing!"

Brenda took Teo and Adrianna to an empty private patient room and told them to get some sleep. Teo had started to shiver.

"I'll get blankets. The O.R. is always kept very cold. I'll bring you something to drink also. You need to hydrate."

Teo got into the bed and pulled the covers over him. He was shivering. Brenda came in carrying blankets and said she would be back with water or juice, hot water if she could find it.

Adrianna put an extra blanket on Teo and sat in the chair by the bed when Brenda came back with water and juice which Teo started to gulp down.

"Girl, what are you sitting there for? Your man is ice cold and shivering and you're keeping your warm body in that chair? Don't you young girls know anything? How to take care of your man? Or is he just your classmate? No eye makeup, I see. Get your cute hot bod into that bed or else!" Brenda left with a smile on her face.

Adrianna should have been totally amazed at what Teo did but somehow not as much as she once would have been.

He's not my man but he is cold she thought, and Brenda was probably right. She took the plastic bag and went into the bathroom near the bed, took off her clothes and changed into a nightee. Back in the room, she lifted the covers off Teo and moved close to him.

"What are you doing?" he asked.

"You heard Brenda. I'm going to warm you up. I don't want to get on her wrong side and have her bear down on me."

"So, you're getting on top of me and you're going to 'bear down' on me? All because of Brenda?"

"Be quiet or I'll change my mind!"

She went on top of him and pressed her head to his neck and shoulder. His cheek rested against her blond hair. His whole body was shivering underneath her. She felt his cold hands and tried to warm them in hers but then took them between her thighs to warm them better.

"Don't get any ideas," she said a little playfully. "When you warm up, out they come."

She wrapped her legs around him too which was awkward with his hands between her thighs.

"You know," Teo said in a shiver, "some girls get a reputation for sleeping with a guy on their first date but yours is to sleep with him before your first date, or was that a date at Lorinda's?"

"Shut up, just shut up for a change!" she said and smiled to herself as she snuggled herself into place. This felt right she thought and they fell asleep.

CHAPTER TWENTY THREE

Hospitals wake up early but not as early as Teo. Before dawn, he got up and took a shower. The sound of it woke Adrianna who needed a moment to recognize where she was and realize he was in the bathroom. She got out of bed and couldn't help but peek in. Through the partially opened door she saw him get out of the shower with his back to her. His back, buttocks, arms and legs were muscular, firm and well proportioned and she would have kept looking except he started to turn toward the door. She moved away and said when he was through, she'd like to get in there to wash up and get dressed herself.

They didn't say anything else and respected each other's limited privacy in the hospital room until both were dressed and ready to leave. They wanted to check on Samantha so they found the intensive care unit where they had put Samantha and not surprisingly, at that hour in the morning, no one stopped them when they entered the area.

It looked like she was sound asleep. Medical equipment surrounded her bed: IV bags hung down and dripped into clear, thin plastic tubes connected to catheters in her right and left forearms; a machine counted with a beep, each drop that came out; nasal cannula tubing delivered oxygen to her nose; wires hidden by her blanket reached up to cardiac monitors; green glowing sine waves and lines moved across the screens. It was quiet except for the repeated beeping of the life sustaining and monitoring ICU equipment.

A nurse came by to ask them if they were relatives but before they could answer, she said they must be Samantha's suitemate and her friend who brought Samantha in under the Code Orange. They nodded.

"Well, she hasn't woken up yet, and I know I'm not supposed to tell you this, but since you did save her life, the doctors aren't sure when she will wake up. That's all I can say for now. You should leave, there's really nothing to do and who knows when she'll wake up. By the way, what you did was awesome!"

They left and were standing outside the ICU when Samantha's parents walked quickly toward them. They recognized Adrianna and asked if Samantha was inside.

"Yes, but she's asleep," said Adrianna.

"I'd like to talk to you for a minute if I may before you go in," Teo said to them.

"Oh, excuse me," said Adrianna. "Mr. and Mrs. Jordan, this is Teo. He helped get Samantha here yesterday." She paused, looked at Teo and then back to the Jordans, and added, "He's a friend of mine."

"Thank you Teo. We appreciate that."

"Please, give me a minute, it's very important and Samantha is sleeping. Please, it's really important," he said.

Samantha's mother sensed Teo did not have good news. They went into the waiting room and sat down.

Teo began. He explained there are three versions of what happened. The first is what they and the others in the dorm saw, that Samantha had a very bad period and was hemorrhaging and an ambulance took her away. The second version is what Samantha knows, that she got an IUD and had a bad period as a result.

"She has an IUD? Adrianna did you know that?" Mrs. Jordan asked.

"Only a little while ago."

Teo took a breath which made Samantha's parents uneasy. They waited for him to continue with the third version.

"Samantha doesn't know what I am about to tell you. It wasn't a bad period," he continued. "The IUD had cut into her uterus and caused some of the bleeding. She lost a lot of blood before they found the IUD and took it out."

"I see," said the mother, and the father started to get up.

"Dear, I don't think he's finished yet, are you?"

"No."

Teo paused again, looked down at his hands, and then at Adrianna, and then the parents. He looked at Mrs. Jordan who returned his look with trepidation.

"It was a boy, a baby boy. She had a miscarriage from a ruptured ectopic pregnancy. I don't think they'll know if the IUD caused it or not. And it seems she was one of the few where the IUD didn't work. The doctors will tell you more but they won't be here for a while and in case she wakes up before then, I thought you should know. I'm not a doctor so you should ask them for the details."

A long silence. Mrs. Jordan began to cry. Adrianna began to cry. She didn't know about the miscarriage.

After a minute, Mr. Jordan started to get up. Mrs. Jordan put her hand on his arm.

"He's still not finished," Mrs. Jordan told her husband, "are you Teo?"

Teo paused. They all stared at him and held their breath, and he continued.

"She may or may not be able to have children. The odds are in her favor but she's been damaged. Maybe with proper care."

They were all hit hard by this last one. They became even more somber and continued to cry quietly at the enormity of the great loss they just heard that their Samantha, their baby girl, may not be able to have her own children. Mr. and Mrs. Jordan got up and held each other and she continued to cry. The father turned to Teo and said, "Please, please say there isn't any more."

Teo took a long time to answer and when it looked like he had something else to say, they froze. As they waited for him to speak, dread filled their whole beings so there was no room for any thought or emotion. They could hardly breathe. Finally, he continued.

"During the operation, her heart stopped. She lost a lot of blood and went into shock, hypovolemic shock. The heart is affected when you lose a lot of blood. They tried to revive her and eventually her heart was started again. But there was a period of time when there may not have been sufficiently oxygenated blood to reach her brain. She hasn't awakened since the operation and is probably comatose now. She may or may not wake up. If she does, she may or may not have neurological damage .... That's all .... I have no more to say. From what Adrianna tells me, Samantha is a good person. I think I would like her if I knew her. I truly hope she recovers fully. I mean it. If and when she wakes up out of her coma, and you see what her condition is at that time, you'll have to decide what to tell her, and when. Her friends at school only know the first version. No one outside the hospital knows about the miscarriage, not even Samantha. And remember, I'm not a doctor. I happened to have read about this stuff and spent time in, let's say, health care."

Mr. Jordan put his arm around his wife who had her face in her hands rocking herself. "Oh God! Oh God! Oh God! My little girl! Oh my little girl!" she kept repeating. Adrianna stared at Teo in shocked disbelief, tears wetting her face.

Teo got up to leave. Adrianna rose up and spoke.

"There is one more thing you have to know. The entire hospital knows by now. Teo saved Samantha's life. He alone, not the doctors, saved her life. He gave his blood to her. He alone knew she needed to be taken to the hospital ASAP. He ordered the Code Orange. He told them to look for the IUD and where to find it. And . . . and when her heart stopped, and they weren't able to get it going, they said she was dead. They pronounced her dead and I don't know if the doctors will tell you that. She died. They stopped working on her. It was over. They said she was dead, pronounced her dead and wrote down the time of death. He . . ." pointing to Teo, "he didn't accept that and he fought to get himself into the O.R. and they let him in only because they had declared her dead, and he, not the doctors, doing what he does, got her heart to start when they couldn't and had given up on her. He fought Death for her and saved her life, more than once yesterday. I thought you should know all that since he didn't tell you any of that and for sure the doctors won't tell you either."

They were all standing now. The mother looked at Adrianna and then Teo. "Thank you so, so much" and she hugged Teo. The father shook his hand, thanked him and hugged him too. "Thank you," the father said again, and he and Mrs. Jordan, sobbing and crushed, walked slowly through the doors to where Samantha lay comatose.

Adrianna looked at Teo in the face, that ugly face.

"It's a long story, right?"

"Yeah, I'm tired. Let's go," he replied.

CHAPTER TWENTY FOUR

For a week, they kept Samantha's condition a secret since they agreed it wasn't up to them to give anyone the true details. They lied and said they didn't know anything more. Adrianna wasn't comfortable having to lie and keep the secret but knew she had no choice. Other than Charlotte, Adrianna had no one else to talk to, to tell them how worried she was, to share her feelings, no one other than Teo. It was hard to concentrate on anything when all she could do was think about Samantha lying in a hospital bed in a coma.

She got a phone call from Mrs. Jordan. Samantha had opened her eyes and begun to move her arms and legs. She woke up with no apparent neurological damage and would be released later after they ran tests but only if they determined she had not lost any functioning. The Jordans would then be able to take her home to be followed up there with any needed out-patient therapy. It was too early to know about having children but under the circumstances, it was the best news they could have hoped for. They looked forward to a good prognosis and seeing Samantha come back to school.

More at ease now, Teo had time to knock off a few things from his to do list, and one involved Amanda. Since Valentine's Day, when she was upset she hadn't received any Valentine's Day cards from anyone in or out of the hospital—including none from Teo!—he wanted to give her a special present to cheer her up and make up for his forgetting it. She loved fairy tales and he thought for a change, instead of his usual manipulation of their afflicted bodies, he would enact a simple play of a fairy tale, and what could be more fun for a romantic little girl, with only hopes and dreams to get her through the night, than the story of Beauty and the Beast, Jeanne-Marie's favorite. He would play the Beast and Adrianna would play Belle except he changed her name to Princess Aimée, and his Beast did not ask for her hand in marriage.

Adrianna enthusiastically took on the assignment and studied her part, confronting and overcoming her fear of performing in front of a group. The all too obvious parallel to Teo and Adrianna was not lost on her and she thought this might actually be his first attempt to even suggest they could be more than just friends. She knew he wouldn't confront her directly with anything like that, she had to be the one to make that first overture. He wouldn't do it and she physically couldn't.

At the hospital, Teo found Brenda. Before he could ask her to help out in the play, she told him about Dr. Letum.

"You haven't heard, have you, about Dr. Letum?" she asked him.

"No. Is he in trouble for letting me into the O.R., or saying Samantha was dead when he could have done more?"

"No. He's dead. He just died."

"Oh?"

"Yeah. He had back issues which flared up from time to time. After the operation on Samantha, his back went out real badly. He took Cyclobenzaprine. It's a strong muscle relaxant which relieves pain but makes you very tired. He also insisted that the therapists here put him into traction to relieve the pressure on his back. He fell asleep and must have moved. The neck brace they put on him slid into a spot which pressed into him, the same spot you pressed at the base of Samantha's neck. He had cardiac arrest and no one knew it until they came back and found him there thirty minutes later. He was dead. There was nothing they could do."

"I see," Teo said. "I never realized what that spot can do to someone without a heart problem and a muscle relaxant. It saved Samantha and killed him. I can't say I feel sorry. I don't really feel anything for him. I guess he won't have to explain now why he let me into the O.R. or what happened to Samantha."

"Teo, you be careful. You played with Death and it might have given you a warning shot. It's a sign. I've been telling you, Death will get even with you. Watch out and don't be so cocky."

"Of course, but can I tell you why I came to see you?"

"Sure, but be careful. Now, what's up?"

He told her about Beauty and the Beast. He needed a narrator to read it while they acted, and wanted her to do it. She chuckled and said she didn't want to ruin his production but Amanda's mother would be perfect, and she was. Before long, news of the little play in the cancer ward circulated and by the time of the performance, there were more parents than usual as well as nurses and orderlies who just happened to come by. Even Mr. and Mrs. Hata, who began visiting Amanda, were there and spoke to Teo before the show thanking him again for his help with Patrick.

Teo and Adrianna got the children to help move furniture and set up crude props from whatever they could find lying around. They loved doing it and it made them even more excited about the play. Most of them had never seen a play before and the anticipation gave them something to look forward to instead of their frequent chemo or radiation treatments. For Adrianna's costume, Teo made a dress fit for a princess (which everyone in her suite marveled at!) and put together a leather cape over a dark shirt for his costume as the Beast. He made a mask for himself which he could hold up on a wooden rod to look more like a beast from a fairy tale. He gave Adrianna the magic mirror—the jewel encrusted one he bought in Tiffany's during the Christmas break—that allows Princess Aimée in the story to see the Beast in his forest castle even when she's not there. Amanda's mother sat to the side of their makeshift stage reading aloud the revised story while Teo and Adrianna acted it out.

Everything went according to plan: the telling, the costumes, the acting. Near the end, Princess Aimée, back in her family home, looks into the magic mirror and sees the Beast dying from a broken heart. She returns to the forest castle as Teo is lying on the floor acting the dying Beast and holding the mask to his face. As Amanda's mother tells the story, the Princess sheds a tear and bends down and kisses the Beast who thereupon becomes a handsome prince freed from a witch's curse. Adrianna bent down to play this out but Teo surprised her by removing the mask to reveal his own beastly face. This wasn't in the script and Adrianna froze, unable to put her lips on his face. He waited a few seconds but when he realized she couldn't do it—she couldn't even play act a little kiss directly on his face—he lifted his mask and covered his own face with it. She recovered and kissed the mask whereupon he flipped the mask to reveal on its other side, a handsome prince who rose up with the Princess, and Amanda's mother pronounced that they lived happily ever after.

Everyone applauded. Teo, Adrianna and Amanda's mother took their bows and came to the center of the room to shake hands and everyone told them how great they were. Amanda ran up and hugged Teo and Adrianna, and said that was the best story she ever heard and Princess Aimée looked just like a real princess.

"Princess Aimée," Teo said, "you told me you needed a lady-in-waiting to help you as a princess. Do you think Amanda could do that for you? She would have to keep and guard the magic mirror for you until you need it again? It's a big responsibility."

Adrianna, still wearing her princess costume, knelt down to Amanda's level.

"Well, I don't really know. Amanda, do you think you could be my lady-in-waiting and help me with my princess duties, and keep and guard the magic mirror for me, and help me when I need help. Do you want to do that?"

"Oh yes! Oh yes! I could do it! I can do it! Yes, and I'll help you whenever you need me and I'll keep the magic mirror always and take care of it and not break it, and, oh, I love you Princess Aimée!" and she hugged Adrianna with the biggest hug she could give. Adrianna gave Amanda the mirror which Amanda took as if it were the most precious thing she ever held in her hands.

Adrianna got up to leave with Teo but she didn't see him. Brenda thought she saw him go out the doors and assumed he'd be right back. She checked the men's room but he wasn't there either. By now, the room was back to normal with only the few children and hospital personnel around, but still no Teo. No one knew why Teo had left without saying goodbye, and eventually Adrianna, rather confused and upset about Teo's disappearance, left too.

CHAPTER TWENTY FIVE

She hadn't heard from him since he vanished after Beauty and the Beast last Tuesday. He wasn't in class Thursday or Friday and it was now Monday. She had become accustomed to seeing him in class and it wasn't like him to miss one. He certainly never went six days without some contact. True, although they were getting along well, they didn't exchange phone numbers or email which she purposely avoided to quash any obligation to be in touch. There was no understanding they should reach out to one another. Neither one should have expected the other to call to say they'd be out of touch—except Adrianna did. She never initiated anything outside of class except that time when she walked out on Julian and ran to catch up to Teo after the wrestling match. Other than that, she always went along when invited but never made the first move.

The day after their play, she began to obsess over why he left without saying goodbye and why didn't he contact her, which after six days had fomented into a maelstrom. She became distraught and her mind started to race.

Maybe he decided to call it quits when I couldn't bring myself to kiss his face in the play. Maybe he thought I decided it was time to stop. But that's not true. What is he thinking? Why doesn't he call me if he knew he wasn't going to be in class? But why should he call me? I should see him and explain, but what would I say? Where is he? He's probably holed up in his room. I'll call him on the intercom. No, I'll just go downstairs again to see if he's okay. What am I getting so worked up about? I wonder if he's okay? I bet he decided it would be better for me if we stopped. Stopped what? What would we be stopping?

On and on she had worked herself into a state of incoherent anguish, day and night. She couldn't eat much nor sleep well, didn't wash and looked awful and after six days, she was a total wreck. She was barefoot as usual and wore her jogging sweats, and by the looks of it, it's what she wore for the entire week. When she did finally fall asleep, she woke up in the middle of the night frightened by the visions of the barefoot woman lying on the cold street, who began making even more nocturnal and daytime visits. Someone was always in the next room or hallway or standing in her doorway, or so she thought, but no one was ever there. She saw Teo wrestling and the human chain of bodies from her dream. She saw Teo's sketches and the old ones in the flap of his sketchbook. She kept rubbing her freckle which got even redder and bigger. When she couldn't sleep at night, she took up her sketch pad to draw something. Though she started with a dress, it always ended with a sketch of Teo's eyes, the eyes she focused on so she wouldn't have to look at his face. She hadn't meant to draw his eyes but her hands did it of their own accord, she couldn't control it. She had dozens of sketches of his eyes strewn all over the floor and furniture in her room.

Wanda and Erika saw this building up over the past few days but were, as usual, somewhat useless in terms of helping. Samantha had been released from the hospital to go home the day before the Beauty and the Beast play, and her parents were finally bringing her back to the dorm later tonight. Erika and Wanda had been out all morning and when they came in, they saw Adrianna stretched out on the couch and told her she was getting worse and looked like shit, that she needed to take control of herself, eat, get cleaned up and put on fresh clothes.

"How did you come in?" Adrianna asked. "I could have sworn you were both in Erika's room all morning but obviously you weren't. You weren't here all morning? It didn't feel like I was alone. You know, I'm really losing it! I don't know. I . . . I don't know what's going on. I keep thinking about Teo. He's been AWOL. I haven't heard from him for almost a week. I don't know what to do. Should I be doing something? What? I don't know. What's wrong with me? Why do I feel so . . . so I don't know how I feel but I don't like it. Everything seems upside down and inside out. You're right, I do feel like I'm spinning out of control. Why? Because he hasn't spoken to me for a week? So what! I can have any boy I want, what do I want with him? I don't want anyone to even think he might be my boyfriend! Can you imagine my bringing him home? My life used to be so . . . so copacetic. Who wants to have to go through this? I don't have to. I like having pretty things around me, I always did. Doesn't everyone want pretty things?"

She was working herself up into an even bigger state.

"Let's get you something to eat and washed up, okay?" Wanda said.

"No, no thanks. I'm not hungry. What the fuck is wrong here? I know he wants me but he doesn't say it. You know we never ever held hands, let alone kissed or held each other— I mean not really. What does that tell you? Not even once. He never tried. Why is that? Don't answer. I know why. He needs to know I want it first. I have to make the first move. Otherwise he thinks I'll reject him or he'd make me feel repulsed by his face. No, that's not it. What is it? I've let other boys kiss me and touch me. Yeah, he says he doesn't want anything from me if it's out of pity. What does he want from me? Do you know what he wants from me? I don't know what he wants from me. Is he gay? Is this a game for him? No, I know it's not. He's good. But he's so strange and he's hiding something. Have you seen the things he can do? With Amanda, Mama Lou, Samantha? How about with Black Jack? No, of course you haven't. You don't even know who they are. Well, I have and they're fantastic! Where is he? Why doesn't he call me? Well, maybe because he doesn't have my number. But he can get it if he wanted. Maybe he doesn't want to get it, maybe he doesn't want to talk to me anymore. But then that wouldn't stop him from going to class last week, would it? Of course not. Would you go down to his suite and ask if he's there and okay? I did it a couple of hours ago and he wasn't there. Okay? Yes, do that and then at least I'll know something. I don't know what, something. Tell them down there I was asking about him. No, maybe I shouldn't do that. I don't know. I don't know."

"What will you know?" Erika asked.

"I don't know. That he doesn't want to deal with me anymore. Go on, would you find out for me if he is there? Maybe he was really there but not for me and he'll be there for you."

"I'm on my way, back in a sec," Wanda agreed to go downstairs.

Adrianna got up from the couch and started pacing. She went to the refrigerator and took out a green apple and put it on the counter. "I don't even like Granny Smith apples. He does, I like red ones. Why did I buy this one?" She paced some more and then took some mint chocolate chip ice cream from the freezer and put it next to the apple and went back to the couch leaving the green apple and ice cream on the counter.

Wanda came back. "Well, there's good news and there's bad news. Both are that he isn't in his room and one of his suitemates said he hasn't seen or heard from him for about a week, but if he comes in, he'll tell him you asked about him."

"Thanks. Maybe that explains why he didn't go to class. He left. What if he left school completely and I never see him again? I don't know how to reach him. I'm not even sure of his last name or real name. He says I should call him René, not Teo. I don't know what his real name is. I can't stand this! I don't want this! What's going on in me? Can you tell me? Should I see a doctor? Maybe I ate something hallucinogenic."

Erika and Wanda agreed she's a bit hysterical and they ought to stick around, besides, they wanted to see Samantha when she came back later.

Adrianna ignored them while she talked to herself, her face expressing what she was mumbling like a homeless woman on the streets.

"Boy, she's crazy," Erika said. "I wouldn't get so worked up over any guy, let alone that guy who undressed Samantha because he didn't happen to call me for a few days. I've been there, done that and never got worked up over it. Have you?"

"No, not with any guys I can remember, no way," Wanda replied.

"Absolutely!" Erika chimed in with a high five.

A knock at the door broke into the conversation and Wanda found Teo there.

"I got a message Adrianna was asking for me. Can you please tell her I'm here," he said. "I can wait here in the hall if you like." He looked bedraggled and tired and had a small carry-on suitcase.

"No, I think you'd better come in. Adrianna, s-o-m-e-o-n-e here to see you," Wanda said with a "let's see what happens now" lilt to her voice.

He walked over to the couch and Adrianna got up and wiped her nose and eyes on her sleeve. They looked at each other.

"Can we please have some privacy?" Teo asked.

Wanda and Erika looked at each other for an answer, and each said "Damn!", shrugged and went into Erika's room.

"You don't look so good. Having a hard time it seems. Have you been fighting with yourself?" and then he continued, "Who's winning?"

"Where were you? Why didn't you tell me you were gone, or going, or leaving, or whatever? You left after the play and didn't say anything. That wasn't very nice. I started to worry. Why didn't you call me? René, René? Is that your real name? Where were you, it's been almost a week? You missed classes. Did you stay at the hospital? I didn't think to check there. Did you know Samantha was released and is coming back tonight? Is that why you're here, to see her? What are you up to? I thought maybe you quit school, or me. René, you know me better than I know myself. You know what's going on in me, don't you? You knew this would happen. You told me so. I didn't listen. How do you know so much? You tricked me. You got inside me when I wasn't looking. René, you're inside me. How did you get through? I can't get you out. I thought I had managed to keep you out. I don't. I really don't. I don't. What is this René? Help me, please. I feel like my bubble is bursting and I'm breaking up with it. I don't know anything anymore. René . . . ."

She took a step towards him and her legs gave way and buckled. He caught her when she fell and had one arm crooked under her knees and the other around the small of her back and waist holding her. She put her head on his chest and sobbed.

"René, talk to me. I don't want to feel this way." She wiped her face on his shirt and stayed in his arms.

"Okay, well first help me. Put your arm around my neck so I can hold you better. That's it, right. I've got you. Comfortable?"

"Yes. René, I'm drowning, help me, please."

"Everything secure in that regard?"

"Yes. I'm not falling down if that's what you mean."

"Good. Okay, keep your head on my chest. Feel me breathing?"

"Yes."

"Now, you breathe too. In, out, in, out. Okay?" Adrianna took deliberate breaths in and out.

"Good. Feel that little bit of warmth on my chest where your head is?"

"Yeah, it's warm there."

"And it's getting warmer, right?"

"Yup."

"Okay. Now that we're comfy—and you feel safe, right?"

"Yeah," she took a deep breath and spoke more slowly, in control of herself.

"Good again. Let's start with something easy, okay? Ready?" He was talking her down from incoherent to calmer.

"Ready," she said with more control. She wasn't frenetic anymore.

"Do you like me?" was his first question, calm and matter of fact.

"Yes . . . I like you," she said slowly and deliberately.

"Good, we already knew that and I like you too. You know that, right?"

"Yes," and she nodded her head in his chest.

"Do you care for me?"

"Yes, I care."

"What do you think of me?" he continued.

"I think you're wonderful," she muffled it into his shirt but he heard it anyway.

"Good, I think you're very special too. Do you like doing things with me?"

"If you mean like sketching, and the hospital and Lorinda's and stuff like that, yes, I like that."

"Me too, I like being with you too. Now it's going to be a little tougher and rougher. Let's see, do you have any feelings for me, maybe more than just a friend?"

She didn't answer at first but knew where he was taking her. "Yes. I have feelings for you. René, why is this so hard for me? You know why it's hard for me don't you?"

"I know why. Let me tell you this. By tomorrow, you're going to feel a whole lot better. I promise. Let's just get through right now. You know I have feelings for you too, good strong feelings. You know that right? But I'll say it anyway. I have very strong feelings for you, Aimée."

She tightened her hold on him.

"Here's another question, have you felt this way about anyone else before, maybe Julian?"

"No. Just you."

Her body relaxed in his arms as she took another deep breath.

"I'll say it. I'm not afraid to. Aimée, I love you. I like saying it. I love you Aimée and you don't have to say anything back."

They kept still, waiting and feeling each other breathing in and out.

After being held by him for a while, she said, "René, how can I be in love with you when we haven't even kissed? And what kind of love can it be if I can't kiss you, if I don't want to kiss you?" She started to sob again.

"Let's go into your room. I think we used up our allotment of private time in the livingroom. Okay? I'll carry you there, okay?"

"Yeah, you know, or maybe you don't, it's the second door on the right."

He carried her to her room and with his foot closed the door. "I'm going to put you down on the bed, okay? You like fashion magazines I see. Oh, and you've gone from sketching dresses to someone's eyes."

He put her down and moved her onto her left side so she wasn't facing him. He sat on the edge of the bed with her back toward him.

"I guess it's okay if I sit on the edge of the bed, after all, we already shared a bed once," he said with a smile. "How about we do an experiment okay? Close your eyes and keep them closed. Are they closed?"

"Yes."

He put his hand on her arm and bent over her neck and kissed her gently on the nape of her neck. "How was that, was that okay?"

"Yes, it was okay," she spoke softly.

He bent down again and kissed the back of her neck again, still gently but more firmly and longer. "How was that?"

"Okay."

"So far so good, now keep your eyes closed and your head on the pillow just like you have it." He leaned over and kissed her on the cheek, a small kiss but more than a peck. "And?" he asked.

"Fine, nice."

"Nice is nice to hear." He moved to kiss her forehead. "And?"

"So far so good, keep it up," she said playfully.

"Okay, now we have to move into enemy territory. Keep your eyes closed while I sit on your other side but keep your eyes closed." He got up and sat on the other side of the bed. He put his hand on her cheek and kissed her very lightly on the lips. "How was that?"

"Not so bad. But I'm nervous."

"Shall I stop?" he moved away so he wasn't touching her at all.

"No, let's keep going. I know what you're doing, let's do it."

"Do you want to kiss me back a little when I kiss you, with your eyes closed? I'm going to kiss you again and it's up to you if you want to kiss me back or not."

He kissed her on the lips and lingered there. She almost kissed him back when she opened her eyes slowly. They were face to face, very close. He waited for her to speak or kiss him, or turn away. She looked at him. She wasn't repulsed or shocked but she didn't move.

"René, I can't, I just can't," she blurted out. "I want to, but I just can't. It wouldn't be real. I couldn't like it. You'd sense it, you'd know. I'm so sorry, I can't. You told me not to pretend. It's too hard for me. I'm sorry." She closed her eyes and grabbed him so her face was in his arm. "René, oh René. This is a curse. I wasn't prepared for this. I hate myself! Hate myself! I'm the beast, not you! Why did I have to be so pretty? Look what it's done to me! I want you and I'll work on it. I can. I promise. You can help me, slowly. We can get there, I promise. I love you René, I love you. I want you. I want to be with you. Don't leave me. Give me time, I can do it, give me time. René, please help me, please...! Please! Please!" she begged into his sleeve. "Help me!" she sobbed in an ebbing voice of exhaustion and defeat.

"Do you want me to help you?"

"Yes. You know I do," she cried.

"Maybe you could move your headbands down to cover your eyes and then you could be blindfolded?"

"How can you joke about this?" she sobbed.

"Okay, will you let me help you?" he asked and he put his hand on hers.

"Yes. Yes, I don't know what you can do, but you can do something, can't you?" She implored him against all hope.

He squeezed her hand, got up and took her by the hand to help her up. "Where's the bathroom?"

They went in and he closed the door; she sat on the commode cover while he let hot water fill the sink which steamed up the mirror.

"Stay here."

He went out and came back with a small black case from his carry-on. He took her hands and turned them palms up and then from his case, he took out a tube which he opened and squeezed out a cream that he put in her hands. He stood in front of her. He spoke to her slowly, mechanically, intensely.

"Aimée, look in my eyes. See only my eyes.... Don't look anywhere else... only my eyes.... Look at their color... their shape. Stare at them... memorize them... see only my eyes and nothing else... only my eyes. Study them... my eyes... my eyes...." He droned on and on.

"Now, and be careful, keep looking at my eyes... my eyes... and at the same time, spread the cream over my face but not my eyes.... Keep looking at my eyes... spread the cream over my face. That's it.... That's right. Use all the cream and keep looking at my eyes... only my eyes."

He took control of her and put her into a fog; she had no choice but to do what he said. She looked into his eyes and spread the cream over his face. When she was through, she kept looking at his eyes but could see the cream had covered his face. He handed her a towel.

"Okay, now when I take off the cream, you'll see my eyes and when you look at my face, you won't see anything unnatural or hideous, just a nice face, a natural face. Keep looking at my eyes so you'll know it's still me no matter what else you see.

You'll recognize my eyes and you won't see anything ugly. Close your eyes now, close them. Visualize my eyes. You can see my eyes in your mind, right? Okay, now ... open them slowly."

His back was to her and the mirror was steamed over. He bent over the sink and washed off the cream with hot water. He reached for a towel and began to dry his face. It was only then, when he turned around, she saw him.

"I ... don't ... understand," she said softly, dreamily. "What did you do? Your face, it's all gone. I mean I see a clear face, a nice face. What happened? Did you hypnotize me? Is that what you did? You hypnotized me, didn't you? Will everyone but me see you like you were before?"

He turned around toward the sink, took the tube of cream and put it into its case. While he was cleaning the sink and drying off, he spoke to her.

"A while ago it seemed to me people relate to each other in different ways, which is not so astounding. I noticed a good looker like you, had a different experience from someone who looked like me. People don't act themselves around a beautiful looking person. They want to impress them or they may feel awkward or insecure. They just can't be natural. The beautiful people get used to that and they don't act normally either. Knowingly or not, they get used to being on a pedestal. Even if they didn't put themselves there, there they are. It's the way it is. I'm sure you've noticed it. But talk to someone who looks like me, and it's very different. Haven't you ever noticed that the invisible people are the ones who don't particularly care what other people think so they say whatever they feel like whether people want to hear it or not? Well anyway, I thought it was the case and I wanted to see for myself. I did what lots of women do. I put on makeup. Except they put on makeup to look better and I put it on to look worse, to look ugly. I got this makeup they use in making movies, and put it on. It's very realistic and takes a pro to know it's only makeup. It fools almost everyone. I was mostly right. People no longer paid me any attention which was fine cause I didn't want those people around me anyway. It was easier for me to keep to myself and not have to deal with so many people. I told you that once—do you remember?—when you asked about plastic surgery, and I said I liked the privacy my face gave me. Only the few people who didn't care what I looked like paid attention. You paid attention. I wasn't ready to stop using the makeup until tonight. I think it's time for me to stop hiding from everyone, especially you. I want to start. No, you weren't hypnotized, at least not tonight you weren't .... Do you like what you see?"

She looked at him bewildered and confused. She got closer and slowly ran her finger over his forehead, and cheeks and scrutinized every part of his face. She put her hand to his face in a caress. He was as stunningly beautiful as she was pretty, maybe more so.

"You missed a spot here, on the side of your neck." She put her finger there.

"No, that's really me, it's a tattoo, and it's a long story," he answered.

"Oh? When are you going to tell me about those long stories? It's off putting to always hear you run away from an explanation by saying it's a long story."

"As soon as you ask."

"You mean all I have to do is ask for more, and you'd tell me?"

"Pretty much, more or less."

"What about the tattoo then? I'm asking now."

"That's on the less side," but he immediately realized he no longer had to be nor wanted to be so entirely opaque with her. "Sorry, no, I went into my automatic 'long story' mode.

The tattoo? It's really simple. When I was fifteen I decided on a whim to have a tattoo right there. I had no reason and I don't know why I did it. Do you like it?"

"It's small and hardly noticeable. It's okay."

Adrianna hesitated, she was a blank but slowly began to think on her feet.

"You made me suffer and I think I won't forgive you for a long time! How could you have done that to me? You knew what it was doing to me and you let me suffer. That was cruel and selfish. Selfish! If you loved me, how could you do it? I didn't think you were capable of that! You said we had to be brutally honest with each other, always. You weren't! You lied to me! You made me tell the truth and you lied to me! You betrayed me! You used me! You lied! All this time! You lied to me! You're nothing but a phony!"

"I'm who I am, and not as strong as you think. I had my reasons for hiding and fooling you and everyone else. I was pretty good at it too. Sure I fooled you, and yes, I was something of a phony, but I wanted to be sure you yourself were sure about how you felt, and I needed to be very, very sure. Call it insecurity, call it what you want. Tonight I was sure, and so were you. You'll always know you fell in love with me—me, not a face, pretty or not. Besides, didn't you hide behind your pretty mask? Didn't you keep yourself from me when you say you love me too? Not much of a consolation, but there it is."

"But you purposely hid behind your mask, and could have stopped at any time," Adrianna said. "I didn't and didn't even know I was trapped in one until a little while ago. Maybe I would have been able to stop using it too if I had more time." And then she added softly, "Not the same thing."

"Who says I could have stopped so easily? Why do you think it would have been easy for me but not for you? Which one of us suffered more? I needed my mask and didn't want to take it off. You didn't need yours but didn't even think to take it off," he said.

He paused and then said, "Don't you think it's about time we held hands or perhaps, do more? We waited long enough."

He reached over and interlaced his fingers with hers. She finally could admit to herself she loved him, and now to suddenly see him romantically and be physical with him was new and deeply strange. She needed a moment to understand and allow herself to want him that way. It was odd. He tightened and loosened his grip. She hesitantly did too so their hands were talking, getting used to this new way of connecting. He let go and brushed her hair from her forehead. She put her arms around his neck and looked into those eyes. He moved closer, his closed mouth moved over her forehead and brushed along it. His fingers glided downward on her cheek. He moistened his lips and gave her a sliding kiss as tender as a butterfly on a petal, from one side of her mouth to the other but not resting on her lips. She breathed deeply as this new feeling spread through her. He pulled back and looked at her, and when he saw she was ready, he brought his lips to hers and gently brought her whole body close to his.

She was transported into a state of being she never experienced—a state of being of no being at all—a mystical clear ether without color, sound, or motion, a bottomless and weightless other worldliness, wondrous and serene and supernatural, out of body. She sensed him enveloping her and he was with her, embraced in that unknowable. She was in a dream state barely conscious, and didn't want it to end. They both touched something endless.

They had no idea how long they were like that when they parted.

"Where did you learn to kiss like that?" she whispered.

"It's a long story. Sorry, I know, but I can't help myself. I'll get over it."

"René, I want to make love. I want you to be my only one. When you learned how to kiss, did you also learn how to make love?"

"You'll see. When we're ready and the time is right, you'll see."

"René, I want to see now."

"I know, but we're not quite ready and the time isn't right. We'll know when the time is right."

"Killjoy. I don't think we should wait. I don't feel good about that. What if something happens before you know the time is right? What about what I want?"

He started to move and they went back to her room. She was in a trance, no words in her mind. It was a long day after a very long week. They had each been through a lot and they both needed to catch up on lack of sleep. He said he'd meet her for breakfast in the dining hall at about nine. They enjoyed another long kiss, and after he left, Adrianna fell into a deep, dead sleep.

CHAPTER TWENTY SIX

The next morning, Erika and Wanda waited in the livingroom for Samantha and Adrianna to get up and go down for breakfast. Samantha came back late, after everyone had gone to sleep, and was eager to tell them everything she'd been through. When she walked into the livingroom, Wanda hugged her, Erika gave her a little kiss, and Samantha started telling them everything that happened including the IUD and her heart stopping and starting, and the miscarriage and ectopic pregnancy. Wanda and Erika were amazed, thinking they were the first ones to hear it. She was so happy to be back and feel close to normal again. She had heard what Teo did and wanted to thank him. Wasn't it scary for them? He really took off my clothes and did all that? And his face was really so hideous close up? She filled them in and they told her what they saw and asked her about the IUD and pregnancy.

Adrianna came in looking fresh and cheerful after taking a shower, and as soon as she did, Samantha jumped up and gave her a big hug.

"Oh, Sis!" Samantha exclaimed, brimming over with joy. "I always wanted a sister! And now I find out it's you! I heard you said we were sisters in the hospital. From now on, I'm calling you Sis! You're getting quite a few names!" she giggled. "I heard you and Teo rushed me to the hospital in an ambulance and of course what you told my mom and dad."

When Samantha finished, Erika and Wanda grabbed Adrianna to sit her down and make her tell all. What happened last night with Teo? They explained quickly to Samantha what Adrianna had gone through for the past week, nearly having had a nervous breakdown because Teo was AWOL and hadn't called.

Adrianna told them she didn't know why he had gone and not called but all was forgiven and she finally told him she loved him, and he said he loved her, that he actually said it first. They ooed and aahed about apparently good news and asked for more details but couldn't hide their astonishment though they had enough sense not to question her about falling in love with that face. Anyway, he was going to meet her, or, she guessed, all of them, at breakfast so they needed to save a seat for him.

The dining hall holds up to three hundred diners at a time. The decorations were institutional: floors covered in tan and rust squares of carpet, beige drapes on large windows overlooking a small copse of trees near the spring and a footbridge, and fifty identical rectangular tables with matching chairs.

They sat at a table for six and leaned two chairs against the table to reserve those two seats. They had a lot to catch up on. Samantha's awful time was replayed again, and has she seen Kendall yet? What did he know? Does Teo know Samantha is back? And then there was Adrianna. Whatever happened to Julian? How come no one ever saw Teo in the dining hall? Did she kiss him finally? How did she get past his face? Adrianna didn't say anything about Teo's makeup but admitted they kissed. In the meanwhile Samantha kept looking for Teo, she wanted to thank him. He saved her life and she was burning to thank him.

Wanda noticed him first. Holding a tray coming out of the buffet was this well groomed, poised, gorgeous young man dressed smartly and looking for a place to sit. He walked slowly, looking up and down the dining hall at the tables. More than one pair of eyes stared at him, he was good looking to say the least.

"Who is that, over there? That's one I'd like to know in the biblical sense!" Wanda said.

The others turned to see and agreed. He meandered through the aisles until he saw their table and its two empty seats and then headed straight for it. They all thought he looked familiar, very familiar, that they had seen him before but couldn't place it and wouldn't they remember if they had met someone like that!

"Good morning," he said, "may I please join you?"

"We're saving one seat for someone but there's still another," Erika said moving the chair for him to sit down. As he sat down, Samantha said they needed to be sure to save the last chair for Teo.

"Are you new here?" asked Wanda.

"Yes and no, depends," he answered but looked at Adrianna.

"Mystery man, huh?" said Erika.

He and Adrianna were looking at each other. He spoke to her as if the others didn't exist. He told her she was lovely, like a flower that finally decided to bloom after a cold winter, and without disrespect, and granted he had just sat down, he would die if he couldn't have one kiss. He proposed a wager. If his kiss wasn't at least as good as any she ever had, she could ask him for something, and if it was within his ability, he would give it to her. He would trust her about the kiss, and in turn, she would have to trust him to honor the bet. Samantha giggled while she kept looking at the buffet for Teo. Erika said go for it; Teo wasn't here yet and besides, all's fair in love and war. Adrianna smiled, got up and stepped away from the table. Teo got up and moved over to her. She put her arms around him and they repeated their first sublime kiss. It went on so long everyone nearby and anyone who could see them from the other end of the dining hall, stopped and simply gawked at them. When it was finally over, they sat down to applause and clinking glasses.

"Dear lady, the truth to be told, was that not better than any kiss you ever had?" Teo asked.

"Well kind sir, in all honesty, as enjoyable as that was, it was truly not better than any kiss I've ever had. You see sir, the man I love kisses as good as that, and I am hopeful his will be even better in time."

"Ah," Teo lamented in a theatrical manner, "would it be so that I could be here now and be that man as well."

"Could you not sir?"

"Could I not, you say? I say I could and by my saying I could, I not only could, I can, and thus I not only could but would be the man you say you love and myself as well." Teo acted this out with a flourish. "And if it be so, is't not true then that you indeed love me as that man you say you love?"

"Sir, you have overcome me and forsooth, by loving you, have I not made that other a hapless soul, who forever would be bereft of life?"

"Ah, dearest maiden, anyone would be bereft of all life if your love for him were to be nipped. But dear maiden, and surely you are the most lovely of all maidens that ever graced this mortal earth, since I am now the one you love and myself as well, there is no condition where he would be so bereft. So let me kiss your hand to seal this and kindly introduce me to your friends who look upon us agape."

He kissed her extended hand and looked at Samantha while Adrianna sat back amused to see what was coming next.

"Let me guess. You are Samantha. And how well you look Miss Samantha after such an ordeal. It is indeed a great pleasure to see you up and around. I believe the last time we met face to face you weren't feeling so well, were you?"

It took Samantha a moment to absorb this.

"Teo?" she asked.

"The very same. Perhaps there is something you want to say?" he said.

"I . . . I didn't recognize you! Oh my God, Adrianna, is this Teo?"

"The man you speak of, is the man I love and who verily is the one who sits beside us, and yes, he is known to some as Teo," she answered still playing out the scene.

"Teo? Teo!" Samantha jumped up and Teo got up anticipating her next move. Samantha hugged him and thanked him over and over for EVERYTHING! She would be forever in his debt and she solemnly swore if he ever, ever needed anything, she would do anything for him. She began to repeatedly kiss him on the cheeks and mouth when Adrianna loudly but good naturedly told her that was enough.

They sat down and the questions started cannoning out. The face, when? Why? And from Adrianna, where were you all week? And from Samantha, how did he know what was wrong with her?

The face was easy and he told them what he had told Adrianna about the makeup. They were spellbound as they listened and couldn't fathom why he would do that to himself—why anyone would—particularly since he was so handsome.

"Why not use a makeup of only scars? Wouldn't that have been easier?" Adrianna asked.

"It would have been easier to put on," he said, "but people have an easier time to relate to someone with scars rather than downright hideous. Scars elicit more sympathy and involvement, and questions, asked or not, like how did it happen? You can see more of a normal face behind scars and relate to the person there. Not so with a face abnormally repulsive which you shy away from."

"And what about your twitching lip? It isn't twitching now. That wasn't makeup," Adrianna asked.

"Right. I forgot about that. I can make that happen myself. I can start the muscle twitching, you know, like some people can move their ears when others can't. I'll show you." He contracted a muscle which raised his upper lip and it began to twitch on its own.

"How do you stop it from twitching?" Samantha asked.

"Wait, I'll show you," Adrianna said. She got up and kissed him on the mouth, and indeed, it stopped its twitching.

"I should have done that a long time ago and could have cured you myself!" she said.

"Why didn't you?" he replied with a grin.

"And what about you're going AWOL on me?"

Well, about that, he had to leave in a hurry right after Beauty and the Beast. He got an urgent text that Samuel (his grandfather, he told them), was taken to the hospital with a heart attack and may be dying. His only thought was to get to Paris immediately and he needed to run out and make calls and plans if he was going to catch the last plane of the day. Fortunately, it was only a mild heart attack and he was back in the house in Paris. He didn't know Adrianna was so distressed and would have called her if he had known.

The last answer about how he knew what was wrong with Samantha was more involved. He connected the dots to draw himself a picture. It wasn't rocket science to figure out they had their monthly meetings when they had their periods. Teo saw the freckle on Adrianna's neck change color when she had her period and she missed a class the day after one of them so he knew approximately when each month. He also knew Samantha wasn't at the one in February because Adrianna mentioned it was a pajama party with only Wanda and said nothing about

Samantha. Couple that with Kendall confiding in Teo that Samantha got an IUD, and it was a good guess she was pregnant before February. Finally, when Adrianna called him to help, he could feel the warmth of the blood she was hemorrhaging and estimated the amount from the distention of her belly and what came out of her. He thought she might be having a miscarriage from her distress, and it might have been an ectopic pregnancy gone bad. Since she had gone untreated for so many hours there was a good chance she would go into hypovolemic shock. He left out what he did in the O.R. and didn't know if Samantha knew that part.

He ran through each explanation succinctly without boasting or embellishment, and cooly, but he knew he was impressing them. As he went on, they sat still, enthralled, and when he finished, they stayed that way waiting for more to follow even though they knew he had finished.

CHAPTER TWENTY SEVEN

In three weeks they were going on their first real date to see the visiting New York City Ballet perform a part of *Sleeping Beauty*, *Afternoon of a Faun* and *Morgen*. Since he washed off his makeup, they spent as much time as they could together. Most evenings were in her suite or room but despite her requests and enticements, he refused to sleep with her and they didn't do much else other than those incredible kisses before each went to their own rooms to sleep. She thought he was overly prudish but he kept repeating, when we're ready and the time is right, it will happen, they can abstain and wait. Adrianna wasn't sure why he still held himself back and his waiting unnerved her. It augured something bad loomed ahead.

Although he told her about the different things he had learned over the past ten years, he still didn't say much more. Apparently, she was his first girlfriend and had no experience with that. She figured he needed more time to understand and adapt to it which was strange she thought for someone so talented and good looking.

Even with his new face, Teo wasn't noticed any more than before. It was an effort on his part and he went out of his way to keep a low profile. He left the dorm before most went down for breakfast, kept his hoodie over his head on campus, and as before, continued to keep himself busy in his room with the door locked. She had never seen his room and he kept it that way. It bothered her but she had no choice other than to accept his keeping a part of his life knowingly secret from her. She decided to be patient and give him the time he needed to open up to her.

On the afternoon of their date, he delivered a zippered dress bag to her suite which had a plastic tie-wrap on the zipper so no one could open it and peek in. Adrianna found it on her bed when she came back from jogging and they all wanted to see it. She knew instantly what he must have been doing holed up in his room for so long. Well, they said, put it on, let's see it. Adrianna said no, sorry to disappoint all of you but it was special and private and she wanted to put it on alone; they can see it when she goes out in a few hours. In the meantime, she was going to bathe, rest and then get ready to go out for their first real date, dinner and her first ballet.

At about five thirty Adrianna came out of her room wearing a gown. It was as good or better than any she ever saw in her fashion magazines. Teo had put a card in the bag, "For my Aimée, the first original of the Princess Aimée line." On the reverse side of the card, "The first original Princess Aimée is a pale green and white, V neck, sleeveless gown of thin layers of silk chiffon with contrasting raw silk threaded along the slit sides and around the hem, and a hand-pleated chiffon overlay from the crossover bodice into the skirt. On the back, is sheer chiffon overlaying crossed over panels exposing the back."

She walked into the livingroom barefoot carrying a pair of shoes which came in the bag. She looked magnificent wearing no jewelry and her hair pinned up. They looked at her and stared. She was more beautiful, more adult, more sophisticated than ever they had seen her, or most anyone else for that matter. She exuded a modest confidence in the self knowledge of how beautiful she was and would be for him. She turned around so they could see the back of the gown. Samantha checked that the straps on her back were right and adjusted them.

"This material is beautiful! And the gown is beyond words!" Samantha exclaimed. "I'll help you on with the shoes," and knelt down to put them on Adrianna's bare feet.

"Did Teo actually design this?" Wanda asked.

"He designed it and probably sewed most, if not all of it. Talented guy, my guy, huh?"

"It fits you like it was custom made for you. How did he know your size?" Wanda asked.

"It is custom made for me, and he knows me, but just by looking at me. Even the shoes fit. How do they look?"

Erika said the shoes, the gown, her hair, everything was perfect and the green color was perfect for her green eyes. Adrianna put her hand on her neck and asked if she should wear a necklace whereupon they ran to their rooms to scrounge for one but nothing could be found to match the elegance of the gown so they decided nothing was best.

Teo knocked at the door. Erika opened it and let out a loud whistle. He strode in wearing a classic black tie formal suit of lustrous satins that clearly showed expensive character and good taste. He was as handsome as Adrianna was beautiful and together they were breathtaking.

"You look more beautiful than I can say. A Grecian goddess would be green with envy," he told her and kissed her hand.

"You're quite a dish yourself! Thank you for the gown, it's spectacular, really, it's fabulous!" and she took his hand and kissed it.

"Is that all I get?" he asked.

She put her hands on his chest and kissed him on the mouth.

"Okay, that was a little better. Shall we?" he said.

They held hands and walked out the door to the elevators. They went down to the lobby and waited. Everyone crowded around to get a better look at the regal couple; some wondered who they were. Two cars pulled up and Amanda came out of the second one carrying a Tiffany's blue bag, followed by her mother and Mr. and Mrs. Hata. Amanda ran up to Teo and Adrianna in the lobby.

"Oh, you look so, so beautiful! You are a princess, I knew you were a princess the very first time, and you finally kissed the Beast and he really did become a prince, your prince. I knew it! I knew it! Oh, you're both so beautiful, a real prince and princess better than any fairy tale. It's true, really it is! I knew it. I knew it." Amanda gushed out in delight.

"Amanda, as Princess Aimée's lady-in-waiting, don't you have something for her to wear?" Teo asked.

"Yes! Yes, I do!" She turned around and Mr. Hata gave her a jewelry case. "Here, Princess Aimée, is your necklace."

Adrianna opened it and took out a string of Japanese Akoya cultured, cream colored pearls. She fingered it and looked at Teo humbly. Amanda reached into the Tiffany's bag and took out the magic mirror which she held up for Adrianna while Teo put on the pearl necklace that fell just under her freckle. Adrianna looked and adjusted the pearls, and turned to Teo to kiss him on the cheek with a whispered thank you.

She knelt down pushing the gown up taking advantage of the full side slits on both sides of the gown, and held up the mirror so both she and Amanda were cheek to cheek looking at themselves in the mirror.

"You're a very pretty girl Amanda and one day you'll be a beautiful woman. See, the magic mirror shows you now and also what you will look like when you grow up."

They squeezed together like two little girls to look at each other in the mirror.

"Can I please kiss your head?" Adrianna asked and Amanda nodded. "You don't need this knitted cap, do you?" and Amanda shrugged a no.

Adrianna slowly pulled off Amanda's cap to reveal her bald scalp as they both continued to look in the mirror.

"You're beautiful just the way you are, and when you're older and better, you'll be even more beautiful with a prince of your own!" Adrianna kissed Amanda on her bare head and gave her the mirror.

Amanda put her cap and the mirror in the bag and gave Adrianna a big hug.

"I love you Princess Aimée!"

And she turned and then gave Teo a big hug too.

"And I love you too Teo! I love you both, I can do that, can't I? Love you both I mean?" she asked.

There were a few eyes with smeared makeup in the lobby. Mrs. Hata came forward and put a silk shawl over Adrianna's shoulders and ushered her out, bowing her head a little as she led her to the first shiny car which smelled of the simonize wax that must have just been put on. Amanda's father sat at the wheel wearing a black jacket and white shirt, the chauffeur for the evening. Adrianna fingered the pearls and asked Teo how did Mr. Hata get involved. He owns a jewelry store, he said, and was instrumental in finding the pearls.

They went to a Japanese restaurant run by Mr. Hata's cousin. The restaurant was upscale for the city but nonetheless they were oddities there. Teo explained what the sushis and sashimis were and showed her how to use the chopsticks which he told her are never to be used to point or to stab the food, both being ill-mannered in Japan. Adrianna tried them with a newfound daring and drank the warmed saki so by the end of dinner, she found a new cuisine she liked.

At a far table facing the entrance and Teo's table, sat the same couple who had been at the wrestling match and in the car at the airport parking lot just before Christmas.

Amanda's father waited for them outside and dropped them at the Opera House. He parked behind the shiny limousines that made a long black snake on the street where they stayed until their patrons came out later. It was Saturday night and many were dressed in formal attire or as close to it as they could manage. When Teo and Adrianna entered the large gilded, chandeliered entry hall, they were a focus of attention as many of the patrons stared at them.

She didn't want to come to the ballet unprepared so she read up on the evening's performances beforehand: the City Ballet's adaptation of the Sleeping Beauty fairytale of good and evil; the short Robbins' pas de deux of a faun and a nymph in *Afternoon of a Faun*; and finally *Morgen*, where three couples keep exchanging partners in search for romance in a series of romantic pas de deux.

In the car heading back to Anstace they talked about each ballet and clearly she was as knowledgeable as he was, if not more so. They both loved the music of *Afternoon of a Faun* and wanted to hear it again and both loved *Morgen* for its mystical quality and the constant changing of partners and daring-do of the dancers. They agreed *Sleeping Beauty* was more pageantry and the least favorite but still got high marks.

Teo answered her questions about the gown, how did he get the material, how long did it take to design, did he sew all of it, and so on. It was *Grand-Mère* Jeanne-Marie, he said, who helped a lot and he needed to go back to Paris to see her and Samuel. "Do you have a passport?" he asked Adrianna, "you'll be needing one."

It was nearly eleven o'clock when Amanda's father left them at Anstace. In the elevator Adrianna pressed the button for the fifth floor and Teo pressed one for the third.

"Why aren't you coming up?" she asked sounding very disappointed and quite surprised.

"No, tonight I think I'm not coming up. Do you mind?" And then he added, "Can you come down instead?"

She smiled and they went to his suite and his room which he unlocked. Inside, she saw a tatami mat in the center, a bed, and a wall unit filled with expensive looking equipment, books, folk art and sculpture from around the world, fabrics, a small hot plate, and there was a sewing machine on the opposite wall with a small work table nearby. It was very crowded but neat and pristine.

They went in. He took off his dress jacket, locked the door and poured some water into a kettle and put it on a low heat. Adrianna openly spied everything in site. She was looking at his inner sanctum for the first time, she was in his lair. She looked at the shelves, ran her finger along things, felt the fabrics.

He watched her patiently while she filled herself with this hidden treasure and then she turned to face him. He said to her softly, "Please take off my shirt," and he waited for her approach.

She undid his bow tie and gently laid it on the small table, and then faced him and methodically unbuttoned his shirt and cuff links, and laid them on the table. He took off his shoes and she unfastened his cummerbund and dress pants; he raised one leg and then the other as she guided his pants down and off and put them on top of the shirt. He removed his socks. She stood watching him in his clean white underwear and took off her own shoes, and with her foot pushed them under the bed.

He stepped behind her and unclasped the pearl necklace; she removed a pin to free her blond hair, and held it up for him to take from behind. Still standing behind her, he placed the necklace and pin on a shelf, and slid the silk chiffon crossed panels of her gown over her shoulders to fall upon her arms. He stepped in front and they looked at each other. Together they slid the rest of the gown from her and let it drop to the floor and she stepped out of it while he held it and laid it on top of the pile of their evening's wear. They gazed at each other, and Teo pulled his tee shirt and briefs off, totally unclothed at this point. He showed himself to her by making a complete, slow turn around and then faced her again. She removed her top and panties and made a complete turn for him to gaze upon her. They were both secure and serene, and shared themselves with each other without any self consciousness. They allowed themselves to simply look at each other, not nervous, not embarrassed.

He extended his left hand toward her which she clasped, and then his right. He pulled her into his arms and she put her head on his chest. Without words she instinctively recognized how right it was and sighed with utter contentment. They laid down on the bed and he began to kiss and caress every part of her. She opened herself to him and felt protected and cared for like no time before. There was no part of her that seemed private with him. When he positioned his face near hers, she kissed him lusciously until he broke off to move his lips over her neck and then turning her, her back and buttocks and thighs, and behind her knees. She was mesmerized and couldn't do anything but receive all that he was doing to her. Her enjoyment was so thorough and opiate, she was spellbound and she selfishly let him do it all. She never experienced physical contact like this.

He moved the pillows and helped position her. He held himself up so he didn't have his full weight on her, put on a condom, and she guided him into her as he gently began a rhythm.

Afterward she thought how marvelous this first time was, how great a lover he was, and put her arms around him and drew him down with his full weight upon her.

"Thank you," she said sweetly in his ear, "I couldn't have imagined it any better."

"Good," he said, "I thought it was special too, in fact, a whole dimension better than . . . well anything. But that was only the first course, this is a four course dessert."

He got up and brought her a small towel while he prepared a tea.

"Let's rest and have some tea. It'll make you, and me, more sensitive to the touch."

He drank some and gave her the rest to finish. They got under the covers and talked about the ballet until Teo began stroking her and she did the same to him. This time he was firmer, less cautious. She followed his expert lead, his knowing, confident, respectful orchestration which culminated in a powerful orgasm.

"Oh René, that was unbelievable! I don't think I can do it again, let alone twice! I think your lessons paid off. That was utterly fantastic! What about you? Did you come?"

"First you tonight. There'll be lots of other times. Tonight, it's for you. More tea?"

He made a fresh batch of tea and brought over a small jar.

"This tea will taste more bitter than the first one, it will help you. Drink it up, you'll need it!" he said with a knowing smile.

He took the cup when she finished and made her lie on her back looking up, and put his finger to his lips in the sign for her to stay still and quiet. He took cream from the jar and rubbed it in his hands to warm it, and put some on her. Adrianna quivered a moment but with blind faith, closed her eyes and let him.

"Okay, now for instructions. When you get to where you think you're at the top, I'm going to press in on some small areas to hold you back. Try to keep yourself going but without letting yourself finish."

He took his time putting the cup and the cream away before he started again, but when he did, he started in in ways different from the first two times. He brought her up to a heightened state slowly and then pressed firmly on certain small muscles inside her. When her orgasm was about to start, she did what he asked. Instead of letting it take its own course, she controlled it. She forced herself to relax her muscles enough to stop from climaxing, and kept her muscles in a heightened state of tension without letting them release it. She rode within the unrelenting tension like a surfer catching a mammoth wave, staying inside the curl of a vortex of powerful water encircling and crashing around her. And she kept surfing and pulsating and throbbing and arching her back to and fro.

"René, enough, it's enough," she said. He continued. After a few minutes of her writhing in ecstacy, she said, "René, please, I mean it, I don't think I can take any more, it's okay," and still no let up from him. She continued to be throttled and dragged along the curl of the wave. She was sweating and breathing rapidly. She could feel her legs and body tingle and begin to tire from the exertion of pulsating and muscles contracting. "René, I'm begging you, please, if you love me, let me finish, please I'm begging you! No more!"

"Okay," he said. He eased off gradually on his pressure as he gauged where she was in her control and orgasm. She gave up total control of her body and the waves took her even faster and stronger. She was flushed and breathing very fast and shallow, like a sprinter in a 100 meter dash. From a place deep within her, a muffled sound struggled to get up and out and she moaned out between her rapid breaths. Her muscles now uncontrollably convulsed and exploded all that tension that had built up and been held back in fifteen disorienting, body convulsing, euphoric sensations of the nth degree.

She lay back motionless, exhausted, sweaty, flushed, and awed for a few minutes, selfishly into her own world of what just happened to her. In the meanwhile, he made some more tea and got back into bed to drink it. When she finally recovered enough to speak, she opened her eyes, and spoke to him in a voice that reflected her awe. She never imagined it could ever be like that. She took his hand, kissed his palm, turned it over and sweetly kissed more of his hand, and pressed it into her breasts and brought her legs together. She lay there overwhelmed and exhausted. He put his leg over both of hers and they rested for a few minutes. After a while, he got up and put on music, *Afternoon of a Faun* by Debussy.

"Last dessert course about to be served," he said.

"René, I couldn't. I can't. I can't do that again. Really, really. I absolutely cannot do that again."

"Shh, a little more tea, a little more cream. This'll be different."

They rested and listened to the music. When it was over, he had her stand up, put a sheet around her and gave her some fresh tea. He straightened the bed and then held her in his arms as they stood on the tatami mat and he massaged her neck, back, and buttocks, and then her arms and legs and hands. While he took care of her, she looked at the bookshelves and all his personal things, luxuriating in his caring of her.

They got back into bed and he started to make love to her in a much different way. It was mature, like two long time lovers, familiar, unhurried, knowing. They kissed and floated into space. They melded and breathed in each other's personal aromas and total acceptance.

He moved into a position where they could look at each other. He went into her slowly. She felt it deep inside her, not painfully though uncomfortably. He sensed her discomfort and adjusted their positions and she nodded. She had to hold onto him to maintain the position and he began to move back and forth. With his free hand behind her, he pressed her into him to keep inside her. They began a long, slow rhythm. It was as if all of him were inside her, physically and emotionally. There was no difference between what was his and what was hers. They had melded, each feeling they were one of two parts and at the same time, there was just one single jointness of them, and it was right. They came together. She climaxed quietly and differently, more emotionally than physically. Different parts of her body gave her her pleasure this time. They separated themselves and let go their holding to fall asleep, side by side.

CHAPTER TWENTY EIGHT

The next morning he let himself sleep more than his usual five and a half hours. When he awoke, she was on her side studying his face, what a lovely face he kept hidden under that mask of hideousness, and to hide behind such a mask when his own was so beautiful!

She opened a drawer to look for a tee shirt to put on when Teo jumped up. He reached over and closed the drawer a little too quickly and went to another drawer to get a tee for her and one for him.

"I'm sorry, I thought it would be okay to look for a tee."

"No, no, it's okay. Good morning. Do you want something else?"

She shrugged her head no. There was a long silence which made them both uncomfortable until he spoke.

"Aimée, remember when we first met, I asked you to keep a secret? And we kept Samantha's condition a secret until she came back? I don't want to keep secrets from you, they can be destructive. Well, I have one to tell you but before I do, I need you to agree to keep it a secret beforehand. It's important. I can't explain it without revealing it, kind of a dilemma. What I can do is repeat what I once told you. If you fall in love with me, your life will never be the same, never what you might have imagined. It'll be worth it although you'll have to make sacrifices in ways you're not used to. I'll be by your side so you'll always be safe but you can't discuss this with anyone, only me. But you have to agree to keep the secret before I can tell it to you."

Once again he ripped out the rug from under her. Will it ever stop? She sat down on the bed, propped herself up against the pillows and the wall, brought up her knees and held them in her arms with a sheet she threw over them. She thought this might be the part he kept from her and would explain his living like a stranger. He sat on the one chair.

"This secret is not one I can take lightly, right?" and he nodded.

"And it's not illegal is it? Can you answer that?"

"Not illegal."

"And it's something that's already happened or going to happen?"

He nodded again.

"And I can never tell anyone, not even my sister?"

Another nod.

"But I'll like it but I have to make sacrifices?"

A nod.

"And if I don't agree to keep the secret?"

Teo shrugged.

"Well that doesn't help me, does it?"

He shrugged again.

"Right! Tell you what. Let's go out for dinner tonight, away from here, and I'll give you my answer tonight. In the meantime, I have to say last night was the most spectacular—on a scale of one to ten, it was a million—the most... the most everything, there aren't words to describe it. I love you, René. Thank you."

She got up, sat on his lap, put her arms around him and held him tightly.

"And I've loved you a long time." He heard those words emanate from his mouth in that faint, far off hollow whisper he'd heard before.

They went into the bathroom where they showered and washed each other. They talked about the gown, the ballet, the necklace, Amanda, and the silk shawl Mrs. Hata left for her. It was like they had showered together a hundred times before. They dried each other and she went up to her room to fetch clothes for herself while he boiled water for tea. Over tea, they agreed to meet in Adrianna's suite at six. In the meantime, each had homework or things to take care of (one of which was for Adrianna to tell Samantha, Wanda and Erika what her night was like!).

Teo arrived at six to envious and incredulous eyes and a couple of "Did she make any of that up?" and "You gotta be kidding!"

Teo shrugged and said, "Is there nothing private around here?"

They left, and in his car Teo suggested they go to Angelina's, an Italian restaurant.

"Is it expensive?" she asked, "I can't afford too much."

"No, your share shouldn't be more than a buck three eighty."

"How much?" she asked, "I don't understand."

"A buck three eighty. You can afford that. What's the big deal?"

"I need to know, that's all. Don't be like that," she said. "The dinner at Lorinda's was a freebee cause you knew her and played the piano. You said Samuel gave you the money for the dinner at the Japanese restaurant and the ballet tickets as a present for something. Is Angelina's going to be free too? There's a limit to what I can afford."

"Nope, only a buck three eighty. Trust me, okay?" he said with a smile.

"Can't you give me a straight answer and not be so controlling?" she demanded.

He thought for a moment, realized she was right and had called him squarely for what he had always done, and he no longer wanted to be that way.

"You're right. When you're right, I'll say so. Dinner shouldn't be more than about sixteen dollars apiece. You can afford that, right?"

"Thank you, and yes. Let's go!" she was happy to say.

The Italian restaurant was definitely a local, low cost affair. Their table was covered with a red and white checkered plastic table cloth and a bud vase with an artificial red carnation, paper napkins and plastic water glasses with an embossed see-through floral design. From the plastic coated menu they ordered pasta, a four dollar glass of red wine de la casa, and they split a salad for a first course.

"I thought about it," she said. "We just started together and you're asking me to make 'sacrifices' but you won't tell me what. I know you're private and I love you but it's a leap of faith you're asking of me. If I don't agree to keep some big secret of yours, it's going to be bad for us. There may not even be an 'us'. I want to trust you but you keep yourself hidden—on purpose. Why? I know you ran away from home, and Samuel, but you're holding something back. And this morning when I opened a drawer, you made me feel... well, like you were afraid to let me see things. How do you think that made me feel?"

She took a sip of wine and looked at a waiter who passed by while she thought of what to say next.

"I like how you know so much and do the things you do but I don't want to be just an admirer. I want to do it with you, and how can I? And what if this secret stops me from doing that? What then? I want to be a full part of your life. I want to help you. This secret has given you a reason to hold back on your emotions or something else, out of some fear. What are you afraid of? From what you told me about Samuel, he didn't teach you anything about your own emotions. What if this secret keeps you like that? I can help you if you'd only let me in. Can't you tell me any more?"

They both drank some wine.

"It's a leap of faith for me too," he said. "To love you is the same leap of faith for me as it was or is for you. In spite of what you see, I need your help. I no longer want to go this alone and all my learning didn't teach me everything."

"Would you like me to help you?" she asked.

"Yes, that's what I'm trying to tell you."

"Will you let me help you?" she asked with a smile.

"Right. I think I've heard that before. Couldn't you at least be original!" he answered.

"I still don't know why you always ask that twice before you help someone. Why do you?"

"I think I got that from Samuel and just made it a part of me. It comes out of me naturally, without thinking about it. I have to do it."

"It is strange you know."

"Well, and I can help you if you want," he said. "I've been a loner, never opened up to anyone before, never wanted to, never had to. This is new terrain. I've hid behind my mask on purpose. I think you hid behind your pretty mask too. We're both afraid and we both have demons—you see yours, I hear mine. I think I've been waiting for you. Samuel told me to find something but could never explain to me what it was. He didn't know himself. We belong together, we're connected. I know we share something other people don't, and you feel it too."

He drank more wine; they both ate some salad; they both waited. Finally, Adrianna broke the silence.

"René, I love you so I guess I have to trust you. That's hard for me. Nothing has been easy since I met you. Nothing has been what it seemed. You keep changing winds on me. First it's in one direction, then out of the blue, you blow me in another. I haven't been in control or even in balance with you since we first spoke in class. And when I thought that was over, you're doing it again. Will it ever stop? Will I ever know which way your wind is going to take me? Can't I make the winds go my way? Why do you have to make things so difficult? It's not fair."

"All's fair in love and war."

"Not so funny. Besides, I already know I have to do what you want. You didn't give me any choice, did you? But I'm reserving the right to get even, that's my condition. Do we have a deal? I have the right to get even."

"Deal!"

"Okay. I guess I'm as ready as I'll ever be. What are you hiding, what's the secret? What am I getting into?"

"Well, I was hoping we'd get this far so I arranged for someone to be here to explain it to you. Her name is Marta and she's been cleared to talk to you. Stay here. I'll be right back."

He got up and walked over to a dimly lit booth in a corner of the restaurant. It was hardly noticeable and neither was the couple dining there, the same couple that had been in the sports stadium, and in the car in the parking lot, and in the Japanese restaurant. They spoke for a while, nodded their heads, and then Teo came back with the woman. She was in her late thirties or early forties, Spanish looking, average but athletic build, dark short hair, plainly dressed, not stylish nor provincial, and carried a large purse.

"Adrianna, please meet Marta. She will explain everything to you. You can trust her completely, she's here to help you."

Teo left them and joined the other man sitting in the booth.

"May I please sit down?" Marta asked in an accent Adrianna didn't recognize.

"I'm sorry, of course."

She sat down and took out an envelope from her purse that covered her Smith & Wesson 380 pistol. "Where to begin?" she said. She began by telling Adrianna that Teo was brought up by Samuel since he was ten and given an unusual and extraordinary education of which Adrianna already knew a part. Samuel is a very successful businessman. He owns many enterprises and has government and military contracts and projects, and had the money to pay for Teo's unique education. Samuel has no family and Teo is the closest thing to a son Samuel ever had. Samuel is in his nineties and hasn't got much longer since his last heart attack. Teo was a runaway and so he had no family ties of his own to worry about.

She explained she worked for Samuel but with the transition, she now works for Teo. In fact, there are dozens of people who work on Teo's matters in New York, Paris and around the world. To maintain their safety, Samuel and Teo, and now Adrianna, each has a full time security team to protect them. Marta is prepared to help in that regard but that's not her function and she is not technically on the security team. The man in the booth sitting with Teo is Boris, the head of Adrianna's security team. She'll meet him afterward.

"But why do they . . . and I . . . need to be protected?" Adrianna asked nervously, afraid of what that answer was going to be.

Well, Marta explained, Samuel is a very, very wealthy man with many business enterprises and government contracts with the U. S. and other countries. In spite of so many relationships, he has managed to keep his true identity well under cover. All of that and all of his wealth, which is quite considerable, is in the process of being transferred to Teo. It's been in process for a year or more and will continue. *The transfer of power to a young Teo and the amount of the wealth and the fact of it, is the secret Teo needs her to keep.* She couldn't tell Adrianna how much, that would be up to Teo, but said if she and Teo each spent tens of millions of dollars each year, it wouldn't make a ripple. So much wealth and power comes with a price, you—and the people you care about—could be a target for extortion, kidnapping, or worse. Teo has been drilled in keeping a low profile and a very private life and all of them do the same not to let anyone see who Teo has become. This is one of the biggest sacrifices Teo had mentioned to her. She absolutely cannot tell her sister, her parents, her friends, or anyone, any of this. Adrianna will have to, at times, lie to them to conceal his wealth and what Teo does. It will be hard for her to lie but that's the secret and the sacrifice but it's not without its own rewards.

Marta passed the envelope over the table to Adrianna for her to open later, in private. Teo wanted Adrianna to be economically free and not feel beholden to him for everything, particularly considering the life style she's about to enter. Inside she'll find ten thousand dollars in cash, a credit card, a check book, and Marta's card showing all the ways Adrianna can reach her. The credit card has a limit of one hundred thousand dollars and the checks draw on a line of credit of one million dollars. If Adrianna needs more, she can call Marta or her private accountant and they will give her more. All the statements go to her private accountant who may ask her from time to time to verify a charge but never to question it. He will replenish her spending accounts to their maximum each time.

The only time Teo might be notified of an item, is if Marta or the accountant believe it would put Teo or Adrianna in danger, otherwise her use of the funds is totally in her own discretion. Marta cautioned Adrianna to be discreet, especially at first, that coming home with expensive jewelry or clothing or cars, would certainly raise questions. In fact, for a while, there's little she could buy which wouldn't cause suspicion. Another sacrifice to be made.

Marta went on to explain she was on duty 24/7 every day for Adrianna. No matter when, where or why, Marta was now Adrianna's personal and private 'you name it', assistant, shopper, travel agent, fixer, gopher, expert on everything, investigator, what have you. Anything at all Adrianna wanted to know, buy, learn about, arrange—just call Marta. If Adrianna wanted to build a villa in the Palmeraie in Marrakech or on Palm Island in Dubai, call Marta. And have it furnished in French Provincial with hand crafted furniture made by Grange in France, call Marta. Arrange an around the world itinerary on private jets, start a hospital in Senegal, learn to speak Swahili, pilot a Bombardier Global 7000 jet, call Marta. Marta gets paid handsomely for her work and that's what her job is, to be sure all of Adrianna's requests get taken care of, no matter the cost or time.

"If you want," she said to Adrianna, "I can be your confidant too, that's totally up to you. Whatever you tell me is between you and me and no one else, including Teo, unless I think you or he would be in danger. Here is a special cell phone good to use anywhere in the world. It's been programmed with numbers to reach me, your accountant, Teo, the New York and Paris apartments, and the other residences you will be going to. Now before I introduce you to Boris, I want to ask you something, something very personal and private, and of course, you can tell me I'm out of line. In fact, I am out of line to ask but I can't resist. If you tell Teo, I could possibly lose my job so I am trusting you. Anyway, I've worked for Samuel for eight years so I've seen Teo grow up from a teenager to quite an astonishing young man. He's had private lessons from the academics to massage and acu-manipulation, medical arts, music, martial arts, and more. He's had special lessons in Asia from an elderly couple with a large family, in, I don't know how to put this delicately, in the ways to please a woman. My question is—how do I put this?—can you tell me if he learned his lessons well?"

Marta obviously adored Teo and perhaps had her own fantasies or hopes of one day being in Adrianna's shoes but understood the age difference and circumstances made it impossible except vicariously. Adrianna picked up on that, put her hand on Marta's, and said, as one confidant to another, he had learned his lessons well, very, very well, and that as Adrianna's confidant, she told Marta the details of the après ballet night. Adrianna then gave Marta her first assignment, to arrange for private lessons from that Asian couple for Adrianna to learn how to please a man. They became friends at that moment.

Marta introduced Adrianna to Boris, her security team captain, a bald Eastern European. He explained the security procedures they suggested for her and how she can help them to help her with the least amount of interference in her life. When she was on campus, they would most likely remain off campus nearby and Teo was more than capable of protecting her given his own training. He gave her a brooch to wear or keep handy and showed her how to work the hidden buttons to call for immediate help. He demonstrated it by pressing the panic button and heard the small click to acknowledge it worked. Two men came briskly into the restaurant, walked through the room in a hurry and surveyed it quickly, caught the captain's eye who nodded to them that it was okay. He called them over and introduced Adrianna to them. They were polite and all business, barely friendly; they were not there to be friends or chat but to do their job to protect Adrianna. They left as quickly as they came in.

Teo joined the captain, Marta and Adrianna. He thanked them and they went back to the booth to finish their cold meal.

"I see Marta filled you in," he said.

"I'll say. You're full of surprises. René, why me? That's what I want to know, why me?"

"Cause I love you and then some."

"You can have anyone in the world. There's not a single girl who wouldn't want you. Why me? I don't know if I qualify for all this."

"I told you. You're the one I must have been waiting for without even knowing it. That means you qualify."

Adrianna looked down at the envelope and held it up. She hadn't the foggiest idea of what to do with it. "I'll need your help on how I handle this, to keep it a secret, and everything. René, is this for real? Is everything Marta told me on the level, this isn't an elaborate trick? You're giving me all this? I feel intimidated by what Marta said, about you, about who you are. I don't think I belong here in this world of yours. I'm the girl next door from Bellevue. You have to remember that."

"You're with me and you belong. And the answers are yes, yes, no and yes. Start thinking about what you want to do, what we should do, keep in mind we can do almost anything we want to. It's daunting but I've had lots of time to think about it and you haven't. After you think it through a little, we'll start going over it, and I don't think we'll ever finish that conversation. But you can't tell anyone or even let on about all this. That's really important for your safety, mine, and your family's as well. Remember that and think big. In the meantime, I'm not hungry anymore, and if you're ready to go, let's get into that jalopy of mine and go back home."

"Home?"

"From now on, wherever you sleep, I sleep. Home. Is that okay?"

"I wouldn't have it any other way."

CHAPTER TWENTY NINE

It was Spring break. Samantha and Kendall went home to her family where he was not particularly welcomed since her parents blamed him for nearly killing Samantha. They abandoned that when they realized he was just too simple to be blamed. Of course, Samantha and Kendall still had to deal with the problem of perhaps not having children, but they were too young to be scarred or feel that psychic pain. Kendall blamed himself despite Samantha's insistence it was an unlucky accident. They had been as careful as anyone could be and it was bad karma that first the IUD didn't do its job, and then the pregnancy was ectopic. Regardless, he became more attentive, forced himself to be more outgoing and came away from her ordeal a better man, for himself and for her.

Wanda and Erika were hardly affected in their own microcosm and continued to fall back on each other for company. They went to Cancun on a college package deal after Wanda tortured Erika by vacillating between Cancun and two other choices, or going to Brazil to Erika's family.

Teo and Adrianna slept most nights in Teo's room. A door with good locks gave them privacy and Teo's suitemates showed no interest in them unlike Samantha, Wanda and Erika who would have been too interested.

They went to Paris for Spring break to visit Samuel, the first time for Adrianna and the last for Teo. Adrianna wasn't sure what clothes to bring that would fit into one carry-on but packed enough to get by for a short stay. Her mind was spinning. René, all that money, what to do after graduation, and now her first trip to see Paris, and his family!

When they arrived at Charles de Gaulle, their French bodyguards picked them up in an ordinary looking car. He took her on a winding scenic route through the grand boulevards and small twisted streets of Paris to Park Monceau. Every outdoor café was busy in late Spring: Parisians and tourists from France and elsewhere, chatted, read their paper, or looked at everyone else as they leisurely sipped an espresso at small bistro tables covering the sidewalks. Adrianna was wide-eyed and thrilled looking out the window holding Teo's hand as they went by the Marais, Place Vendôme, the Île de la Cité, the Trocadéro, the bridges called *ponts* over the Seine, and several other well known areas.

"You really know these places pretty well, don't you?" she asked.

"Even though I spent more time in New York, I know this place better, it's more a part of me and I feel quite at home here."

"But let's find new places so they'll be new for both of us and we can have fun learning about them together, for the first time," she said. "I hope there are still places you haven't seen yet," she teased.

"Absolutely, but until we graduate, we should stay in school and live the way we are now, it's only a couple of months away. After that, well, I don't know what to do. Let's go around the world and look for exotic places to buy and then we can live there too. Samuel says a home is primarily an investment that has the added benefit of being able to live in it as well."

"Samuel would say that," she said.

"I've never been to Nice here in the south of France. How about that?" he asked.

"What about in the U S of A?"

"That too! A ski chalet in Deer Valley in Park City, Utah! We can ski together. That would be great! And, I've never been there . . . yet."

"Sorry, but I don't ski."

"I'll teach you. You've got great posture and you're athletic. You'd pick it up easily."

"No, I don't think so."

"Why not? What's the big deal?"

"Well for one, I don't know how to ski. I could fail, I could fall. I'd hold you back. You wouldn't have any fun."

"You'll have to start doing new things if you're going to keep up and if we're going to conquer the world."

"Well," Adrianna said, "if I have to learn to give up my old ways then you have to learn to give up some of yours too. Deal? If I fall, you have to stick around to pick me up! And you have to promise to stay with me the whole time. There really is a lot we can do, isn't there? Can we open a clinic for kids like Amanda?"

"We can do practically anything we can dream of," he said.

"But are we a 'we'? What if I put off graduate school and then we aren't 'we' anymore? It'd be late for me to start over."

"Look, no matter what happens to us, I promise you you'll always be financially secure. I hope you know that."

Adrianna knew she couldn't share this with her family and hadn't figured out how to live this new life in secret. She wished she could have brought Teo home before he took off his makeup, then her mother would have seen that Adrianna finally broke out of her mother's straight jacket. Now her mother will say she was right all along and claim victory on seeing a gorgeous Teo. Adrianna could live with that but not with her father's blind spot and distance from her. If only she understood it, she could work on it and make him feel close to her too like he does with Charlotte.

It was a lovely spring day at Park Monceau. *Grand-Mère* Jeanne-Marie greeted them with her arms outstretched in an exuberant overflowing welcome. They hugged and Teo introduced Adrianna who approached *Grand-Mère* Jeanne-Marie as if she were meeting her mother-in-law for the first time.

Jeanne-Marie looked wizened yet trim, compact and full of energy in a full length dress pulled tight at the waist. She put Adrianna at ease with a warm, loving acceptance like they had known each other for years and she was happy to see her after a long trip away. They kissed on the cheeks and went into the sitting room. She urged them to say hello to Samuel, he would fall asleep soon and she warned them he was failing fast, his eyesight, memory, cognition, worse than ever, especially after the last heart attack.

Samuel sat engulfed and swallowed up in his big leather chair. A half finished glass of absinthe was on the table by his side. Teo came in and kissed him and introduced Adrianna.

"This is Adrianna I told you about, but I call her Aimée and you can too. Aimée, this is Samuel."

Samuel struggled to push himself off the back of the chair to sit up and get a better look as Adrianna bent over and kissed him four times on the cheeks. Samuel stiffened and looked at Adrianna surprised.

"You are Aimée? Can that be? Why does René say 'Aimée'? You look so young and beautiful." He touched her freckle, perplexed, as if he were examining something familiar that had changed.

Samuel shook his head in disbelief and fell back into his big chair. *Grand-Mère* Jeanne-Marie said they can talk over dinner but René and Aimée needed to settle in and besides, Samuel has to take his nap now. In the meantime, she can show Adrianna the rooms of the magnificent old mansion on their way upstairs.

The mansion retained the Belle Époque sense of the comfortable and well off life that existed leading up to the Great War. The wooden floors were worn down by their age with a pleasing patina, fifteen foot ceilings and elegant chandeliers offered up a nostalgia of what was or might have been. The main rooms contained large hanging tapestries with oriental, medieval or nautical scenes, museum-quality carved desks and end tables, ornate chairs and sofas with curved backs covered in toile, brocades or silk, and pieces with inlaid marquetry, veneers of tortoiseshell and ivory—it was more a tour of a museum, not someone's home.

There were two main floors. From the entrance hall and its separate small cloakroom, was the sitting room, and opening to the left beyond that was the very large formal dining room which had an enormous table that could seat twenty four guests at least. Behind that was the oversized kitchen as big as a small studio apartment, with hanging copper pots and pans. To the right, after passing a graceful broad, curved mahogany staircase, was the living room with a stone fireplace, and the library which was now used as Samuel's bedroom since it had the only bathroom on the ground floor. Upstairs were eight bedrooms off of a long hallway (one was Jeanne-Marie's sewing room), bathrooms, dressing rooms, and side closets. On the walls hung paintings of known and unknown artists with ornate wood frames but those on the second floor were predominantly Impressionist which gave it a gayer and more colorful feeling than the ones on the entrance level.

Adrianna mentioned how unusual it was to see a caduceus in one of the paintings in the dining room mistakenly thinking it was related to medicine and she knew that Samuel wasn't a doctor. She was particularly interested in one tapestry which was different from the other tapestries. It was vibrant and colorful in strong blues, reds and greens, showing a shtetl with a surrealistically elongated bride holding a bouquet of vivid flowers. A strange, unreal animal that had horns but a human body, played a violin while the bride and groom celebrated among the angels. Imaginary birds and people hovered with them over the rooftops of the village. Teo explained it was a rare tapestry made by des Gobelins in France along with Marc Chagall, the famous Jewish artist who created it. Samuel bought it a few years after Didier had died.

Jeanne-Marie led them to Teo's bedroom upstairs. Unlike the rest of the mansion, it was decorated in a Restoration Hardware motif of monochromatic soft browns and wheat colors, all greyed out, with modern or contemporary furniture including an oversized bed and oversized pillows, a mohair throw across it, a large cracked brown leather club chair, a wooden trunk at the foot of the bed, small metal side pieces, a sisal rug and contemporary sconces and art.

Jeanne-Marie looked at Teo and arched an eyebrow to ask if it was correct to bring her to his bedroom. He smiled, hugged her and said *mais oui*. She then took Adrianna to one of the guest bedrooms, much more feminine than Teo's, where she had arranged the drawers and closet with clothes in case Adrianna needed them. There were stockings, pants, dresses, lingerie, various perfumes, toiletries, scarves, blouses, sweaters, and hats—a complete trousseau. Adrianna touched the dresses and opened the drawers, and then embraced Jeanne-Marie. "*Merci beaucoup, Grand-Mère!* This is so special, what you did for me, and you don't even know me! I can call you *Grand-Mère*, can't I?"

"Of course, my child, I would like that very much. You remind me of my daughter Mimi when she was your age. This was her room. If she hadn't died so young, so tragically, you could have been her daughter. You have green eyes too and look so alike. I think René has found a special person, *n'est-ce pas*? And may I also call you Aimée, like René does?" Adrianna answered of course she could.

Aside from Adrianna, Jeanne-Marie and Samuel were the only ones to call Teo by the name René. It made Adrianna feel like she had been invited into a secret society and she was a special guest of honor, but she wasn't given the secret code; she still didn't understand why they all wanted to call her Aimée and not Adrianna. She let it pass. She had just been adopted by a loving grandmother in a beautiful mansion who gave her an entire wardrobe, and René to show her Paris. There were way too many fabulous and exciting things happening all around her to get bogged down with names—after all, what's in a name?

Teo walked in and Adrianna showed him what *Grand-Mère* Jeanne-Marie had done for her. He put his arm around his grey haired *Grand-Mère* and they walked to the closet where he examined each dress, critiquing and denigrating them playfully as they laughed at the badinage. She took them into the sewing room to show them her latest works. The room was filled with rolls of colored and white cottons, silks and chiffon fabrics and ribbons, all lying helter-skelter, and buttons, threads, zippers, pins, notions, and a cutting table, several big scissors, the heavy duty sewing machine which Samuel bought long ago, half finished garments, sketch pads, and cut remnants littering the old wooden floors.

On a mannequin, under a sheet, was an unfinished work in a white material which reminded Teo of sketches Mimi had done. One sketch was partially hidden under a pair of fabric scissors. Teo picked it up for Adrianna to look at when she became faint and sat down. She had another déjà vu experience like she had had before with those old sketches, a powerful one.

Maybe she was allergic to the dust in the old paper and suffered from jet lag, she thought. She also had the vision of the dead woman standing very close by, closer than ever, but this time, strangely enough, she didn't feel afraid of it. She had enough of the house tour and needed to settle in. She absent-mindedly rubbed her freckle and they went into Teo's bedroom.

They showered, unpacked, and Adrianna decided to put her things in Mimi's bedroom. She liked that room better than Teo's and would have preferred to sleep with him there; she was at home in Mimi's room, but didn't make it an issue. She tried on the dresses and though her preferred style was less conservative, she was comfortable in them. She chose one to wear with a headband but forgot to pack some. Instinctively, she went directly to the second draw of the smaller chest of drawers by the bed where she found headbands hidden under other garments that must have been left for her too.

Grand-Mère Jeanne-Marie made *Lapin à la cocotte* (French rabbit stew), they drank a Châteauneuf-du-Pape, and finished with a small portion of Chaubier and Saint-Paulin cheese and crackers.

Adrianna was right at home and barely needed any direction from Jeanne-Marie to find the plates and put things away. She chatted with Jeanne-Marie the whole time in French who kept forgetting that Adrianna's French was limited, as she constantly spoke too quickly. Adrianna had to ask her to repeat what she said but Jeanne-Marie said it wasn't important, she was mumbling aloud like she often does. Adrianna was actually surprised at how much she did understand and marveled at how her accent got so much better when she spoke to Jeanne-Marie.

CHAPTER THIRTY

Over the next few days, Teo took Adrianna to see the popular sights: the former Gare d'Orsay Beaux-Arts railway station converted to the Musée D'Orsay on the left bank of the Seine; the Place des Vosges in the Marais, a prototype of residential squares built in 1612; the elevated Highline; the Opéra de Paris Garnier; the Musée Marmottan in the Sixteeenth Arrondissment to see the large Monets and the nearby museum designed by Frank Gehry in the Bois de Boulogne which looked like twelve large glass sails; and the Pont des Arts by the Pont Neuf Métro where lovers used to add their own love locks, but today they just took a selfie standing on the bridge over the Seine. He also took her to the lesser known attractions like the beautiful old Bibliothèque National de France and the Sainte-Geneviève Library which are off the beaten tourist tracks and Teo's favorites. With her headband in place, they walked or took the Métro which she wanted to see, rested at cafés, and had endless energy for the adventure. At the end of a day of sightseeing, he said they had to go to the canal lock over the Canal Saint-Martin where Samuel first met Didier.

They began to walk there from the Place de La République which was being set up for an outdoor rock concert. They approached an intersection whose street light was out of order—all its lights were flashing green. Adrianna had another of her strong déjà vu experiences but this time coupled with the vision of the barefoot woman running toward her, frightened herself, her arms outstretched ready to embrace Adrianna, frantic and silently screaming at Adrianna. Adrianna was terrified and became hysterical.

"We can't go this way! Let's go back!" she screamed. "That woman is here! She's running toward me. She's about to grab me! René, help me!" she screamed.

"What's the matter?"

"I don't know. Something isn't right. Please, let's turn around. Something is wrong, very, very wrong. That dead woman is over there and she's running toward me. She's almost here!"

"Come on, we're almost there. You know it's not real," Teo said.

"No! No! No! We can't go there! I don't know but... but René, René... we have to leave. Now! We have to get out of here now! I've been here before. We shouldn't be here!" At that, she grabbed her security alarm brooch and pressed the panic button.

"I don't know what you mean, but sure. We can come back here another time. Let's go back to the house. Okay?"

"Yes. I want to go back now. I've had enough for now. Something's not right here. Please, call for one of the cars to come get us. It's not safe here!"

In the meantime, the security team rushed toward them and looked around for a source of danger while they kept Teo and Adrianna in a tight circle within them. A car screeched to a halt half way up on the sidewalk and they speedily got Teo and Adrianna into the car which then sped away.

They went back to the mansion and didn't talk any more about it. Adrianna had been overwhelmed with fright by something she saw and didn't understand. She didn't want to talk about it and Teo let it be. He didn't want her to re-live her frightening experience and thought it would pass like it always did.

In the evening, after resting up and donning one of *Grand-Mère's* dresses, they dined at Chez Les Anges in the Seventh Arrondissement and walked home to Park Monceau in the neighboring Eighth. Adrianna recovered enough from that earlier episode to suppress it and she tried to keep it from ruining the evening. A French couple on their security team stayed behind them and another stayed in front, and they kept a closer than usual distance as an extra precaution after the strange incident earlier at the traffic light. Boris insisted on the extra protection.

Back at the mansion, more relaxed now, Adrianna and Teo examined the dresses in Mimi's room.

"You know," she said, "these are as good and maybe better than lots of dresses I see in my magazines. *Grand-Mère* is really very good."

"What about me? Don't I get credit for any of it?"

"Of course! You know, I think they could hold their own on a fashion runway, even a Paris fashion show," she said.

"Sure, why not," he said, simply paying an honest compliment that wasn't going anywhere.

"Really, you think so?" she said disingenuously.

"They're really good. She is truly a marvel at this."

"I don't know," she lied, "let me try one on and see how it looks when I actually wear it." She took a dress hanging on the rack and changed into it.

"I don't have the right shoes, you'll have to imagine it with shoes."

The dress fit her well and needed only minor adjustments, and the length was perfect for her in her bare feet. As she modeled it, she curled her toes.

"Seems good to me," he said.

"Absolutely, a sure knockout!" she joked and did a three hundred sixty degree turn with a big grin on her face.

Teo smelled a rat. "Wait a minute, just wait a minute. You're not thinking you're going to model these on a fashion runway, here in Paris, or anywhere else for that matter? No way! Aimée, I thought you don't like new things like that, and in front of so many people. No. Boris and his security teams would have a fit! I hope Marta didn't encourage this!"

"Oh, come on! Can't you see it? Princess Aimée models the first show of her Princess Aimée line in this year's Spring Fashion Runway in Paris! You always said I have the body and stature of a supermodel, the perfect shape. It would be great. You can use those contacts and resources of yours to get a spot, can't you? Come on. The hell with the security team. Didn't you enter the wrestling competition where there were hundreds of spectators? We both agreed to change our old ways, didn't we?"

"Yeah, and they gave me grief over it for quite a while."

"René, if I can come out of my chrysalis, so can you!" she said.

"Using big words now, are we?"

"Look, you know how hard this would have been for me only a short time ago. I'll still be anxious but there's something about being here in Paris, in this mansion, this room, that is giving me a courage I never had. Don't stop me, please. I want to do it, for once in my life I want to do it and not let some old fear stop me. I need your support. Don't fight me. And you can tell Boris and Marta it was all my doing."

"I've never done anything quite like that, and I think it's only the beginning with you," he said. "Okay Ms. Fashion World, how do you see this happening?"

"I'm going to be me. No shoes, barefoot. No eye makeup either. I don't want to compete with the other models. I am the girl next door, what women want, a beautiful young woman without artifice."

"What about your freckle? It's gotten bigger and redder since you came here?"

"Stop making excuses!" She theatrically fluttered the dress from her hips, walked a few steps and turned around, practicing.

"I guess you could do it. You think you can do it, really? Don't push yourself into something we'll regret."

She stepped toward him and she took him into her arms. He stayed in her embrace while she collected her thoughts, and then kissed him quickly and said, "Let's do it!"

She got Teo to use his contacts (and money!) to finagle a last minute, new comer entry for the Princess Aimée line in the fashion show a few days away. The three of them went to work choosing which designs to use, in which order to show them and making adjustments for a better fit on Adrianna. *Grand-Mère* Jeanne-Marie was thrilled and she worked day and night to get everything ready. She added a logo to each garment, a P interlocked with an A in bright green.

They decided Adrianna would not wear any makeup nor jewelry, only a fine golden ankle bracelet Teo just gave her (which she wore from then on). Her hair would be kept simple, and down, not up. She practiced walking but Teo urged her not to over practice, she should walk like herself, she didn't need any practice to do that. They ran through and fine tuned the quick changes she would need to make since she was the only model. Teo prepped her on the cameras and lights that would be in her face and how she needed to keep her eyes focused on a spot on the back wall. Their security team was told and neither Boris nor Marta were happy to provide security in that setting.

When the day came, they were ready and a little nervous. They took their positions behind the curtains and waited anxiously for their turn at the very end. They had rehearsed what to do and when the time came, they went into action. Adrianna walked out onto the runway in the middle of a long exhibition room which had ten rows of onlookers on both sides of the runway. Cameras clicked, lights flashed, and the security team scrambled to look everywhere for any sign of trouble. There was a hush for a moment as the reviewers realized this was a new look—barefoot, young, wholesome, the girl next door—and then they applauded.

Adrianna tried to keep her eyes on a spot on the back wall as Teo told her to do but she saw the audience and froze. She looked down at her bare feet and curled her toes. She couldn't take a step, couldn't move, and kept looking down. Teo whispered loudly, "You can do it. Go for it. Now walk!" A fog suddenly came over her. Unrecognizable hazy images and feelings that weren't hers, swept through her. She heard the music from *Afternoon of a Faun* and went into a total out-of-body experience. The applause stopped and people stared at her as she stood motionless, expressionless, looking down at her curled toes which didn't seem like hers in that fog. Clearly, she was in some other world and saw what they couldn't. When the music which only she could hear slowly faded, she began to recognize where she was, in front of an audience sitting and waiting for her, staring at her.

She rubbed her freckle slowly, took a breath, recovered and went on. Teo also took in a breath of relief. She resumed her novice demeanor and innocent look, stopped at the end of the runway and pretended to fix her hair as if to get ready for a date, turned around, and walked back to meet him. They quickly got her into the next dress while she kept her toes curled and then she repeated her insouciant barefoot walk.

The designs were well received and when they finished, the announcer brought them out, Adrianna in the last dress she modeled, Teo in jeans and a black tee, and Jeanne-Marie holding sewing items and a backup dress in case one was needed. They held hands, took their bows and made a prompt exit with the discreet help of their relieved bodyguards and a waiting car.

Back at the mansion, she helped Jeanne-Marie put things away in the sewing room. Jeanne-Marie remarked how strange it was that Aimée looked so much like Mimi, and also liked to model dresses like Mimi loved to do, and even curled her toes the way Mimi did. She never saw anyone other than Mimi curl their toes like that.

Samuel was too frail to join them but that night, over a simple supper at home, he heard them tell all about it as they relived each moment and near catastrophe. Adrianna decided not to tell Teo what really happened to her on the runway and let him think she froze because she was standing in front of so many people.

In the meantime, Samuel took Teo aside to ask him if Aimée was his other half. It seemed she might be, that he recognized something about her, or maybe it was the way René and Aimée fit so well together, particularly in so short a time. It was familiar. As always, Teo was noncommital. He still didn't know whether this idea was a crazy figment of an old man's mind or not. Fortunately, Samuel nodded off before Teo had to answer.

It was time for them to return to the States. They packed their bags and Adrianna managed to squeeze in one of the dresses from the fashion show. They cleaned up the breakfast dishes and moved into the formal living room. Jeanne-Marie hugged and kissed them and said, "Aimée, you be sure René brings you here again, and soon. And René, you take care of Aimée, I think Aimée is very special and belongs here."

Adrianna kissed Jeanne-Marie and then bent down and gave Samuel a French cheek kiss, four times. Samuel leaned back on the couch and looked up dreamily at Adrianna through rheumy eyes.

"Aimée... Mimi, is that you? It's been so long but now it seems like only yesterday. I missed you. Can I buy you some more rolls of silk? Do you need more note paper? You are my Mimi, aren't you?"

Teo, Adrianna and Jeanne-Marie looked at each other and nodded. Adrianna bent down and kissed Samuel gingerly on the cheek, hugged him and said softly in a perfect French and Parisian accent, yes, I am your Mimi. I miss you too: *"Oui, c'est ta Mimi. Tu me manques aussi."*

Samuel struggled to sit up and prepare himself to speak but fell back. He closed his eyes and sighed. He just heard from his Mimi.

CHAPTER THIRTY ONE

Adrianna told her parents Teo would help pack and move her things by the time she had to vacate her dorm room after graduation. Explaining where she was going next was a small problem and began the white lies; she knew she had no choice but that didn't make it any easier. The cover story was Teo knew of a place in New York City they could crash in during the summer until they figured out what to do next; they might travel around from there before they started on a career path. That ought to buy them time until they needed another story. And so off to Bellevue to meet her family.

Predictably, Mrs. Bittfield was overjoyed when she saw Teo, a vindication of her dogma, and someone she would proudly introduce as her daughter's boyfriend at her niece's wedding that weekend. Their future plans could be uncertain as long as he was so handsome. Teo was cordial to her parents, and they to him, but no chemistry took place. Charlotte couldn't be as welcoming as she would have liked with the beginnings of a migraine and had to stay quiet in her darkened room with the curtains drawn but told Adrianna to bring Teo up anyway so they could get to know each other a little.

"I'm sorry you're getting a migraine, they can be pretty awful. Hopefully you'll be better for your cousin's wedding tomorrow," Teo said.

"Thanks, I think so. Sorry to have to meet you this way. We'll get to know each other better tomorrow, I'm sure," Charlotte said, her eyes showing the pain of the migraine.

"Would you like me to help you feel better, if I can, with your migraine I mean?" Teo asked.

"Let him, he's good at this, I've seen him help a lot of people," Adrianna said confidently.

"Would you like me to help you?" he asked again.

"Sure, yes, why not," looking to Adrianna for approval.

"Will you let me help you?" he asked and Adrianna smiled.

"Okay."

Teo sat next to her on the bed and looked into her eyes and told her to close them. He gently touched the sides of her face to the right and left of her eyes, manipulated the area at the base of her neck, felt her pulse at her neck and wrists, and massaged her calves. After a few minutes he got up.

"Well, I think I actually feel a little better, thanks."

"The relief will be short lived, migraines are not my specialty. I can't do much with them. I'll give Adrianna some teas for you which might reduce the number of attacks."

"Thanks. Adrianna, you're lucky not to have them."

Sleeping arrangements had been skirted when they first arrived but the moment of truth was upon them as they needed to finally put their bags somewhere. Adrianna told her mother they would be sleeping in her room, that they hadn't slept apart for a couple of months and had no intention otherwise. That was a real dilemma for Mrs. Bittfield. She didn't want to offend the good looking young man but she wasn't comfortable condoning such cohabitation, and what would Dad and the neighbors say? It's such a small parochial town. Adrianna clinched it when she announced if it was a problem, they would go to a motel and come back in the mornings which only made it more visible to the town and their neighbors. Mrs. Bittfield thought it through and decided, as long as they didn't tell anyone, it would be alright and she'll tell Mr. Bittfield what's happening, though he won't be pleased. They could handle this little secret.

Teo settled into Adrianna's childhood bedroom, answered emails and took care of some business matters while Adrianna visited Charlotte. She beamed over how Adrianna fought through their mother's sick dogma and fell in love with an ugly duckling who became prince charming, and went with her to Paris! Adrianna avoided details about that and lied that they went on a cheap package deal for Spring break. Charlotte dreamed she could travel, find a new job that wasn't dead-ended, and get out of the house, but economics kept her stuck. The thought of ending up like her father scared her. To be born, live your entire life, and then die in Bellevue was an unexciting, predictable, and conforming life she did not want to copy.

With her newfound resources, Adrianna could wave her magic wand and change Charlotte's life, but not without exposing Teo's wealth. Some sacrifices he said were harder than others, and this one was hard.

That evening, at the dinner table, Mr. Bittfield asked Teo about his family, where he lived, his future plans, etc. Teo used a lot of words to say very little which amused Adrianna by his totally unrevealing and long-sounding answers from which all they could glean was he had no brothers or sisters, went to private schools they hadn't heard of, and his family started in the fur business. As for the future, after they traveled around to get that out of their systems, he might consider a career in business or dress designing. The Bittfields didn't want to pursue that last career choice and changed the subject.

Mr. Bittfield described the plumbing supply business he inherited from his father who couldn't work it anymore because of his hypertension and heart condition. Mr. Bittfield took it over and continued its fine reputation which in a small place like Bellevue, was not just important, but essential: a bad reputation in Bellevue would ostracize you from the rest of that small town. After dinner, the photos were taken out and Teo learned about this aunt, and that uncle, and the cousin whose wedding was tomorrow.

He borrowed the photos to look at upstairs before he went to sleep. Teo's sleep regime was a problem they hadn't sorted out yet. They both wanted to fall asleep and wake up together but she needed to sleep more than five and half hours a night. They usually started off together but after love making, he stayed up. Tonight she made quiet love in the room she grew up in. Familiar shadows moved across the walls cast by the street light which shone on the black maple tree outside her window—the same shadows made by the sway of the tree when she fell asleep growing up. It brought together emotions and memories, of her father's blind spot toward her, her mother's neurotic emphasis on being pretty and her outgrowing that and leaving her family home. It was then she told Teo she wanted to make love to him one time with his makeup back on. She didn't know why, but she wanted to do it that way once and wished when they did, it would be like she was before her unnecessary nose job.

The cousin's wedding was a formal afternoon affair at a local reception hall complete with hors d'oeuvres, a sit down dinner and a very loud band. Adrianna was overdressed in the gown she wore to the ballet. She had wanted to wear the dress she had taken from Mimi's room in Paris but Teo insisted she wear the one she wore at the ballet. She and Teo made such a royal couple it was embarrassing how they took the spotlight from the bride and groom. Fortunately for Teo, conversation with anyone was impossible over the band's blaring, and gratefully while seated at the ubiquitous dining tables too.

"Shall we dance?" he extended his hand and asked Adrianna.

"Can you dance?" But in an instant, realized, of course he could.

While on the dance floor, a woman in her fifties approached them and reached into her purse as she drew near. Adrianna's security team, who had managed to gain entrance under the ruse of being in-house security, moved in fast until Adrianna waved them off discreetly. The woman jabbered away in French as she pulled out her business card. She saw them at the Paris fashion show and was beside herself with delight to find them, here of all places! She owned a small but exclusive shop in the Faubourg Saint-Honoré district and had wanted to sell the Princess Aimée line there but no one knew how to reach them, and now she found them! She urged them to contact her so she could see their full line and then market them. Would she let her be their exclusive outlet in Paris?

A younger woman interrupted and explained her great aunt was from Paris, didn't speak much English, and apologized if there had been any misunderstanding. The woman didn't quite know what was happening but told Teo and Adrianna, in French, to take her card and call her when they were back in Paris. She was beaming and chattered away in French as she went back to her table. Teo explained to Charlotte who had seen this, that the French woman mistook them for someone else, or wanted them to model clothes for her, he wasn't quite sure what she actually said. Charlotte didn't believe him; she'll talk to Adrianna after the wedding.

Back home, everyone gathered in the livingroom before they changed out of their good clothes, where they dissected the wedding, the music, the guests, and such. Charlotte thought it was nice, predictable and nothing special; her parents didn't want to voice anything negative; and to Adrianna, it was staged and lacked any display of the commitment it was meant to memorialize.

Teo said nothing but moved closer to Adrianna. He stood in front of her, faced her and took her hands in his. The others stopped talking and looked at Teo wondering what this was about.

"I agree," he said looking directly at Adrianna in that serious mood she recalled when he once or twice knocked the wind out of her, and oh my God, he's about to do it again! Not pinned immobilized to a screen, opened and vulnerable like once before, she waited for him to do the something he always does to her. What now?

"Aimée, I want to say something and I want to say it to you in front of your family so later there can be no mistake about what was said." He continued to hold her hands.

"When you first saw me, I hid under a mask to keep everyone out. But you didn't stay out and I'm glad you didn't. Together, we found ourselves and each other. Now, I don't want to spend a single day without knowing you are safe and I want to be with you and take care of you, forever. So, I make these vows without expectation of anything in return. You can leave me tomorrow, and these vows are still yours. I will love and care for you, watch over and provide for you, and if earthly possible, be there for you if ever you want or need me, no matter what will happen to us, no matter what time or distance or the fates may do to us. I reaffirm my immortal love for you. I love you Adrianna, my Aimée. You are my other half, I cannot imagine my life ever complete without you. That's all except I have a ring to give you to remind you of my vows. You've been keeping it close to your heart so you'll have to help me get it."

He reached over and eased down the left side of her gown from her shoulder so it fell on her arm. She made room for him to reach into the top inside of her bodice and feel for a secret compartment in the panels of silk and chiffon that held a ring. He pushed the gown back and presented her with a simple gold ring which she put on her ring finger.

"When did you put that there?"

"You've had that by your heart from the night at the ballet," he answered.

"That's why you wanted me to wear this today, and not the one I took from . . . you know."

Adrianna stood there, moist eyed, and remembered what Brenda once said about wearing eye makeup.

"You'll keep doing that, won't you? Change my life every day. Make me be, make me see, and grow, and feel, and do things I never knew were in me. Make me love you more and more each day. And I love you with every living part of me. I must have always loved you. I know now you have always been in me even when I was blind to see you standing there. I am yours, all of me. I couldn't live without you, and if I had to, I would . . . I don't know, I would miss a part of me too. Okay then, my vows. I will be there for you whenever you need or want me. I vow to be the woman you said I am and to stand by you, side by side, to support and help you. I will devote my life to you as a woman to a man, and as your life's partner on that journey we're taking. I don't think I covered it all but I have the rest of my life to show you."

They embraced and kissed one of their long, dimensionless kisses while Charlotte looked on in sweet amazement, and her parents speechless.

"I'm sorry, I didn't anticipate this so I don't have a ring for you but let's get one right away, one to match, okay?"

She was choked up. Teo hushed her with his finger to his mouth and then to hers and he eased her gown down again while he searched for and found the other gold ring. Silently, he gave it to her, and she put it on his ring finger and they hugged again.

Adrianna showed her family the ring and they all said how sweet and romantic that was, and how they seemed to be a match made in heaven.

Teo then said to Adrianna, "Will you please marry me? I love you and I'm selfish and I need you. Please don't say no."

She looked at him and down at her ring, and then her family. She was in a fog drifting off somewhere while she shook her head no. She had a new déjà vu experience she couldn't place but it was of something pleasantly familiar, not fearful.

"Yes, I would marry you in any time and in any place, and over and over. Yes. Yes. Yes."

Teo reached into his pocket, opened a jewelry case and took out a diamond ring and slid it onto her finger.

"Can't have an engagement without a ring, can we now?"

The ring was a three carat, emerald shaped solitaire in a platinum setting, a perfectly clear and flawless diamond.

Her family was now standing, somewhat shocked. She showed Charlotte and her mother the ring. They all hugged and wanted to see the ring over and over, and give congratulations and say how exciting that was.

When it calmed down, Mrs. Bittfield spoke.

"When do you think you'll get married?"

"Mom, they just got engaged, give them a break!" Charlotte said.

"Well," Teo said, "I don't want to wait and I don't think we should. There is no reason to put it off and every reason not to. It's meant to be. If it's okay with Adrianna, I'd like to get married right here and right now, and Charlotte, you can officiate and ask the questions traditionally asked at a wedding."

Adrianna shrugged again and marveled at how he can keep doing what he does.

"Fine by me. And Charlotte, this is not a shotgun wedding, if that's what you're thinking! René, how are you going to orchestrate this one, or did you already?"

"Well, I managed to get Charlotte a thirty day license to perform marriage ceremonies in this county so it'd be totally legal, you only have to sign some forms I happen to have with me. Bet you didn't know that was possible!"

"I'm glad I have this dress to wear, otherwise I'd be getting married in my jeans!" Adrianna said.

"No way," Teo said. "Aimée, if you would be so kind to go up to your room, you'll find a more suitable gown to wear. Jeanne-Marie started to make it a long time ago for her daughter's wedding but there was no wedding so she never finished it. She said now that a wedding is taking place, she could finish it. Charlotte, if you could please sign these papers and then help your sister get into her wedding gown. Mrs. Bittfield, you should go up and help them too. Mr. Bittfield, can you please put the champagne you'll find in the refrigerator, in an ice bucket and find your champagne glasses, and then rearrange some furniture to make an aisle."

While everyone carried out their respective duties, Teo made a phone call and within minutes, flowers arrived at the front door along with a technician who quickly set up a video camera, speaker and a satellite feed, checked the connection to the other end, and left as quickly and quietly as she came in.

Upstairs, Charlotte told Adrianna they had serious talking to do after the wedding ceremony and she and her mother ooed and aahed at the beautiful, classic wedding gown that happened to fit Adrianna perfectly. Charlotte asked where were the shoes to which Adrianna replied, no shoes, just the gold ankle bracelet.

They heard Teo play a piece by Debussy on the piano and when Mrs. Bittfield came down to say they were ready, Teo played the traditional wedding march. Mr. Bittfield took Adrianna's arm when she got to the bottom of the stairs and walked her down the short makeshift aisle he made. Teo was waiting and looked at the video camera to be sure the light was on and working. Jeanne-Marie was in Paris watching even though it was in the middle of the night there and Samuel was sleeping.

Charlotte asked them the questions. "Do you, Adrianna Bittfield, take this man, to be your lawfully wedded husband, to love and care, comfort and aid, in sickness and in health, till death do you part?"

"I do, forever."

"And do you Teo René, take my sister, to be your lawfully wedded wife, to love and care, comfort and aid, in sickness and in health, till death do you part?"

"I do as well, and will, forever."

"Well, then, by some rule or other, I'm not sure what, I pronounce you husband and wife. You may kiss the bride."

Adrianna looked into his eyes and remembered when he made her look into his eyes and memorize them while she put a cream all over his face, and he hypnotized her forever.

Adrianna turned to the camera and in fluent French, thanked *Grand-Mère* Jeanne-Marie for the gown and told her how happy she was she could be there, and she'll try to be a daughter to her as much as her Mimi was. She couldn't see Jeanne-Marie cry tears of joy and the video was turned off.

Charlotte closed in on Adrianna and whispered where did you learn to speak French like a native? Who is *Grand-*

Mère Jeanne-Marie? What gives with the wedding gown and the French woman at the wedding earlier?

Adrianna smiled at her sister and said, "It's a long story. We'll talk later."

They opened the champagne and toasted. Teo and Adrianna went up to her bedroom which was miraculously filled with flowers and rose petals strewn on the floor; the window was open and the curtain shimmering in the early summer evening breeze.

"I know what I want for a wedding present," she said. "It's a wedding present and also something you owe me when I agreed to keep your secret, my right to get even."

"Let's have it."

"I want to tell Charlotte. I want you to give her a job in New York and Paris, so she can travel, and meet people, and learn more sophisticated bookkeeping and accounting. She knows the rudiments of them already. You can have her trained and she can become my personal accountant, someone I can trust and then I can tell her everything without lying. And she can come with me or us, when we go places, not all the time but sometimes. You know what I want. Please, it would mean so much to me, and to her. I know why we have to be private but I know her. I can trust her and so can you. Please, René, please, do this for me."

"But not your parents, right?"

"No, certainly not my parents."

"Okay, but Aimée, come tomorrow, I want you to remember this and how happy you are for it. Don't forget. Deal?"

"I'm not sure I like that, but deal! Can I tell her right now?"

"On our wedding night?"

"I'll make it up to you. I forgot to tell you I've been taking lessons from the same couple you did when you were in Asia! Don't fall asleep on me and make us some teas, okay?"

Charlotte was surprised to see Adrianna tonight of all nights.

"You got a new fashion magazine. Look at this on page eleven, is this you on a fashion runway in Paris modeling a 'Princess Aimée' line? And Teo calls you Aimée? Okay, what is this all about? And how come you've started to dress in such an old fashioned way? And you're speaking more . . . I don't know . . . more slowly, carefully. And your freckle is bigger and redder. And you're speaking French like I've never heard before. What's going on?"

"Well, before I explain, you have to promise me something. You have to keep what I tell you a secret, not an ordinary secret but a sacred one. It will mean sacrifices on your part. I can tell you you'll be glad you agreed but you have to take a leap of faith to agree even if you don't know what it is. For what it's worth, I took the same vow and I did and still do make sacrifices which, at times, you won't like either, but it will be worth it and I really want you to agree. I'll be sharing it with you, more or less. Tell me you don't need time to think about this because if you do, I think I'll explode!"

"I don't know what's gotten into you. Since Christmas you're different, in a good way I think, but different. It's Teo, isn't it? He's done a number on you but I think I like it. This must have something to do with him, something about him. He doesn't add up to me, and I know numbers! Is he mafia or something? Like the French Connection? CIA? And his face? He goes from beast to beauty?"

"He's not illegal or anything like that. I cannot tell you any more unless you solemnly swear you'll keep my secret."

"And this is a secret you keep too, so we'd both be keeping the exact same secret, right?"

"That is correct."

"Well, we've always kept each other's secrets, one more can't hurt even if you are melodramatic about it, and you sure have been melodramatic!"

"Is that a yes?"

"Yes, it's a yes, I solemnly swear to keep your secret."

Adrianna kept it to a bare minimum. Teo inherited a fortune and that's most of the secret. No one can know he, and she, are super wealthy, control many businesses, that they have bodyguards and several homes, which even Adrianna hasn't seen yet. And best of all, they want to hire Charlotte to be trained as Adrianna's personal accountant to be based in New York and Paris, with an expense account, and a great salary, and a start up bonus so she can move into a nice apartment. It didn't take Charlotte more than ten seconds to realize Adrianna was on the level and gave her the opportunity of a lifetime. Until they worked out a cover story, Charlotte should continue to do what she has been doing but in a few weeks they'll sort it out and she can start packing, but not until then. She must remember not to break the low profile they work hard at keeping.

"And what about this fashion magazine?"

"Oh that," she feigned nonchalance. "The short version is *Grand-Mère* Jeanne-Marie takes care of Samuel in Paris. He's Teo's guardian—sort of—and he's very, very old and dying. It's up to Teo to tell you about that part of his life. *Grand-Mère* Jeanne-Marie helped Samuel raise Teo and became like a mother to him though she ain't so young either. She taught him to design and sew and she's quite fabulous. I couldn't have asked for a nicer mother-in-law. Anyway, she and Teo designed a line of dresses and gowns which I wanted to model at the fashion show and I was their model. Teo was really against it but I kind of insisted. The woman at the wedding had seen us there and wanted to buy the dresses for her shop in Paris."

"You wanted to model them in front of all those people? This is not the you I know. It's Teo, isn't it?"

"Maybe. He told me once I had an internal compass which I should follow. He didn't know exactly what he meant when he said it, but I've learned something from that . . . from him, from I don't where. He thought my internal compass pointed to the core of who I must really be inside which I didn't see, and I should follow where it pointed. But I can change where it points and change who I am inside! You can too. What was me, whether I recognized it or not, doesn't have to be, or it can be. I can steal and make mine whatever I see around me. It doesn't matter if I was born with it or not. It doesn't matter where it came from or who I copy it from. And if I'm not comfortable with something, I can chuck it and try something else, or nothing else. When I was in Paris, I had the urge to model the dresses, and I went for it. I don't know where that urge came from, and it didn't matter. I did it. I no longer doubt or mistrust myself like I used to. I don't have to be pretty, or I can be if I want. It's all up to me!"

"Easy for you to say. It's too late for me."

"Never! It's never too late to realize you can change, or to actually change." Adrianna took a deep breath. "Look, this is my wedding night and I would like to get back to my husband and wedding bed, if that's okay with you. You have plenty to think about, and we'll try to be quiet! Charlotte, I am so happy, for me and for you. It's going to be great, just great! We're both getting out of Bellevue!"

CHAPTER THIRTY TWO

The next morning after breakfast, Teo found an opportunity to speak to Mrs. Bittfield alone.

"Mrs. Bittfield, can we have a little chat please, outside on the back porch?" They went out and sat down.

"I have a problem. It's my problem and it's your problem. I know something I can't and won't keep secret. I wish I didn't know it but I do, and I have no choice but to tell Adrianna. I wish it were otherwise because I love her and don't want to hurt her but I can't start our marriage by keeping this from her. You already know secrets can be destructive. Either way, I'll end up hurting her."

Mrs. Bittfield hadn't a clue what he was talking about and maintained her usual naive look and wondered when she could get back to clean up the kitchen.

"So here it is. I have to tell Adrianna Mr. Bittfield is not her biological father."

Mrs. Bittfield squirmed and furrowed her brows.

"Don't be silly, young man. Of course he's her father. Why would you ever say such a thing? That isn't nice."

"I know too much about these things. I studied the old photos. There is no resemblance between Adrianna and Mr. Bittfield: not body type, not hair color, not eye color. Charlotte inherited hypertension from Mr. Bittfield's side of the family; she has migraines as a result, Mr. Bittfield's father died of it. Adrianna does not have that. The photos show Mr. Bittfield always keeping Adrianna at arms length distance, not like Charlotte. You dote on Adrianna. He favors Charlotte. I have other indications as well. I don't think I'm wrong but I know it'd be wrong if I don't tell her what I think in case I am right. Which means then you would have to either deny it or admit it. If I am wrong, DNA tests can help establish that. If I am right, then it would be better if you made the announcement, not me. You can blame it on the weddings yesterday, that they made you realize it was time to come clean."

Mrs. Bittfield's countenance went from bewilderment to terror to shame. She stared at Teo and suddenly the tears came gushing out nonstop. She covered her face in her hands as she sobbed. Fortunately, no one was around to hear it.

"Mrs. Bittfield, it's going to be painful all around, but I have no choice which means you don't either. If you do nothing, I will. You'll have to muster up the courage to face this and get it over with, and the sooner the better. Even now. Either I go up and tell Adrianna or you do, or probably better yet, do it at one time, and tell them all at once. It affects each one. Shall I call them into the living room, you can come in after everyone is there? If you don't do it, they will find out anyway. Shall I get them?"

She kept crying and nodded. Teo left her outside sobbing and went in to get Charlotte. He told her to get Mr. Bittfield and bring him into the living room. Charlotte thought Teo might be telling them about giving her a job and her moving out. He then went upstairs to the bedroom and told Adrianna everyone was going into the living room but said no more. Adrianna suspected something ominous was about to happen.

"This isn't good, is it?"

He took her in his arms, "We're together now, everything will work out," which only intensified her dread. He wasn't about to make light of it and needed to give her an emotional warning.

Mr. Bittfield sat in his chair, Teo on the piano bench behind him, and the girls on the couch wondering what this was about when Mrs. Bittfield came in. She had red puffy eyes and a tissue in her hand. They all waited for her to speak.

"I don't know how to start. This is very painful for me, to tell you something I'm so ashamed of and kept secret all these years. I'm sorry. Maybe seeing Adrianna get married yesterday moved me so much it got me thinking. Thinking about how you two are so much in love!" She started to cry but got control enough to continue. "Your father and I were in love like that once. Remember dear? We were. We made such a nice couple. Your father wasn't so heavy then and I was good looking. Well, you know children, sometimes marriages have rocky spots, that's no surprise to anyone, you know that. We had ours too. There was a period when we weren't getting along very well. Charlotte, you were a little girl so you wouldn't remember. Anyway, it was during that rough patch that your father said he had to visit his aunt who wasn't feeling well and he stayed with her for three weeks. I was so angry for leaving me at that time and I thought he might be seeing another woman."

She cried more loudly and forced herself to speak while she continued to cry. "I did something bad, very, very bad, and foolish, and I wish I could take it back but I can't." She looked at the table; she couldn't look at anyone. Tears rolled out and she had trouble speaking. "I'm not going to give you any details, not now, but . . . but I slept with another man, a good looking Jewish businessman who was traveling through, and that man is Adrianna's father. Oh dear, oh God, please forgive me, forgive me! I'm so ashamed but this is such a small town and there was the plumbing business and our reputation, and all," she said looking at Mr. Bittfield. She became inconsolable and buried her head in her hands.

"What?" Adrianna said. She was stunned and stared at her mother who didn't answer.

Mr. Bittfield looked down. Everyone was lost in their own thoughts and had no ability to reach out to anyone else. There was silence except for Mrs. Bittfield's crying. After a minute, Teo approached Mr. Bittfield from behind and whispered into his ear.

Mr. Bittfield straightened up and stiffened while Teo kept his hand on Mr. Bittfield's shoulder and kept whispering to him. After a moment, Mr. Bitfield spoke up.

"Dear, I know. I've always known. I may be simple, but I knew I wasn't the one to make you pregnant back then. At first I figured you needed time to get the courage to tell me, that you wanted to tell to me. And when you did, I could forgive you and we would handle it. I waited until you told me, when you were ready to tell me. I figured I should let you be the one first so you wouldn't think I found out and forced you into a confession, shaming you more. So I waited. I waited so long I started to live it and pretended it the way you wanted. If you wanted it to be that way, then I let it be that way. It was too late for me to say anything. I knew your secret hurt you. All these years I saw it hurt you, but it was too late for me, for the girls. It hurt me too all this time, that each of us had the same secret but couldn't share it. I'm afraid now I was wrong, not strong enough or just stupid for doing that. I watched you suffer, I suffered, and I don't think it was good for the girls either, especially Adrianna. So you're not the only one to be sorry. I am too and I apologize to all of you for my stupidity, and Adrianna, I hope one day you forgive me for this. I always loved you and do now, you're so beautiful and I am so proud of you, and you found yourself a smart young man. You are my daughter as much as Charlotte and I hope and pray you know that. Maybe from now on I can learn to be better for you. I love you, and I love Charlotte, and your mother. I was stupid for not speaking up years ago."

He was crying too and the Norman Rockwell painting of your picture perfect family peeled off yet another layer.

CHAPTER THIRTY THREE

They walked from the black limousine to the grave site. Marta and the French security team were in a second car and Marta walked by herself to the open grave at a respectful distance away. Teo, Adrianna and Jeanne-Marie were the only ones there except for two cemetery workmen in overalls with shovels who stood on both sides of the hole that was dug to receive the coffin and who would lower it in. They had decided Samuel was not a religious man, that in fact he had a very low opinion of religion and its protagonists, and he certainly would not have wanted a man of the cloth to attend. They were somber but shed no tears. Now that his René and Aimée were married, he let himself die, fulfilled, in peace at last.

One of the workmen moved away from the opening in the ground to give the mourners more space and privacy. He had been standing in front of Mimi's footstone which now could be seen as he backed away. Jeanne-Marie had ordered all the footstones be reset and the grass cut so the graves were neat and the stones were clearly visible.

Adrianna looked at Mimi's footstone. On it she read "Aimée Durand, Born May 8, 1962, Died January 31, 1995." Adrianna was confused. Who was Aimée Durand and where is Mimi? She thought that was Mimi's grave. Oh, Jeanne-Marie explained, Mimi was her nickname, her birth name was Aimée. When she was a baby she had trouble saying "Aimée" but could say "Mimi" so they called her Mimi too. Adrianna also noted she died the day after Adrianna was born which was awfully coincidental. Teo corrected her. Because of the time zone difference between Paris and Bellevue, Adrianna was born the day Mimi died.

As they stood silently over the coffin, the workmen waited for the signal to lower it. Jeanne-Marie spoke up from behind her black veil and said this was as good a time as any to reveal a secret she had been keeping. She didn't think Samuel knew and she never brought it up because she was told not to.

On her mother's deathbed, Camille confessed to Jeanne-Marie that Camille and Didier had been lovers while she was married. That was no surprise to Jeanne-Marie, but what did surprise her was the revelation that Jeanne-Marie's father was Didier, making him Mimi's grandfather. Didier had feared such knowledge would affect his special relationship with Samuel, and both Camille and Didier agreed Jeanne-Marie should never be told because it might hurt her in some way. So the secret was born along with Jeanne-Marie, to be kept from everyone especially Samuel and Jeanne-Marie.

When Jeanne-Marie was finally told, she was already thirty four years old with a child of her own, had lost her own husband, and the shocking news of her own parentage was not so shocking. She had loved Didier growing up even when she didn't know he was her father. He was a good man, loved her and her mother, and was good to them both. It all made sense to her. Of course, by then Didier, and her so-called father and mother, were gone or about to be gone, and Jeanne-Marie would never have to confront any of them face to face to deal with it.

Adrianna marveled at how blasé Jeanne-Marie was about something so significant. At least Jeanne-Marie found out who her real father was when Camille finally told her about it. Adrianna had wanted the same thing—to know who was her biological father. She was frustrated that her mother refused to discuss it. Her father wouldn't be of any help, and Charlotte, who was normally supportive, discouraged Adrianna from looking for him. Teo was no help either. He never wanted to find out whether or not his father was his real father, and he couldn't understand Adrianna's insistence to know.

Thoughts raced through her mind on overload: she was born the day Mimi died; she had green eyes and curled her toes like Mimi; Samuel, Jeanne-Marie and Teo called her "Aimée", Mimi's real name; she looked like Mimi and even had a freckle where Mimi's birthmark was; her déjà vu episodes were getting stronger; and the ever present dead woman. These all came tumbling together as if they meant for her to see something. Any one of these would have given Adrianna cause for concern at the least, and fright otherwise, except there was no time. Before she had a chance to think more about it, Teo told the workmen to lower the coffin into the freshly dug up ground, and as they did, Adrianna collapsed.

In a split second, she suffered déjà vu and frightening hallucinations. Her legs gave out, she fainted and fell face up onto the pile of freshly dug up earth, spread out and facing Mimi's footstone. Her shoes fell off and disappeared into the dark hole under Samuel's coffin.

In a flash of consciousness before all turned black, she saw herself on a path in an old country cemetery where there was freshly dug up earth and men lowering a coffin into a grave. A young woman in her wedding dress lay in the coffin staring up at Adrianna with her green eyes.

Dr. Letum pushed Adrianna and she tumbled down through the void to the Père Lachaise cemetery into Samuel's open coffin where he was sitting up with the barefoot dead woman and green eyed Mimi who was kissing Samuel four times on the cheeks, over and over.

The Chagall tapestry came to life and Didier floated over the shtetl rooftops holding a bouquet of flowers in handcuffed hands. The craggy faced woman behind him smiled and toasted him with a glass of absinthe as she unlocked the handcuffs and licked his hand.

Two snakes entwined around the staff of a caduceus changed into Mimi and Adrianna while the staff itself turned into the young girl in her wedding dress, and then they all morphed into a winged Adrianna who flew up to the craggy faced woman.

The dead woman lying on the street got up and took Mimi's hand and they coalesced into one. Didier and Samuel held hands and emptied a bottle of absinthe as they sat in an old wooden cart; René sat in the back on a bicycle with Phi Beta Kappa in his lap, its dog tag flickered between one side worn away and another shiny and bright.

She was falling and falling into a dark space and the craggy faced woman, Didier, Samuel, Jeanne-Marie, Mimi, the dead woman and an old hag of a fortune teller made a human chain to reach down to her. All these phantasms reached out their hands and their impossibly elongated rubberized arms and put them under Adrianna and lifted her up as she drifted down into an abyss.

EPILOGUE

Aimée sat in their Bombardier jet on its way to a chateau they bought in Fayence near the Côte D'Azur in France. She was sketching a design of a nurse's uniform Jeanne-Marie was going to make for Brenda in a size for a woman like Brenda. She also confirmed a text to set up a program to get Mary out of Lorinda's bar for a chance at a brighter future. In spite of days overstocked with businesses, foundation work, private lessons, and traveling around the world to see it all firsthand, she keeps up a daily correspondence with Amanda who is getting better, slowly by slowly.

René, with three books in his lap, sits across from her, Phi Beta Kappa nuzzled at his feet. He still tries to keep a low profile and fights with Aimée who thinks he's being overly cautious about his ideas on their privacy and needs to stop using it as a crutch. He was now teaching himself how to care for animals like a veterinarian while Aimée took on the laboring oar in administering the businesses and affairs they inherited from Samuel. She is slowly educating René about his stunted emotional side, and wonders as she copes with not knowing who her birth father is: do she and René have the same father? Shouldn't she persevere and look for her biological father, or should she just let it be?

In her mind, she's seen Death and came away with her own understanding of what happened to her. Both Aimeé and René were principal actors although they didn't know it.

Recognizing something is much easier if you know what to look for, and if you don't know what to look for, you won't find it—usually. Samantha knew what to look for and now she and Kendall are engaged and planning their futures, helping each other and caring for and protecting each other.

And sometimes you find what you're looking for by chance without having any idea of what you were seeking, like Wanda who went with Erika to São Paulo to face her family and announce their love.

But on rare occasions, without knowing what you are looking for and without realizing you actually found it, it comes to you unbeknownst where it remains found but unrecognized.

After Adrianna collapsed at Samuel's burial, she recovered enough for them to take her back to the mansion. Jeanne-Marie put her in Mimi's room to sleep off the sedative the doctor had given her. It was a restful and comforting sleep. When she awoke, she knew where she was immediately, got up and rummaged around the room in private. She opened the closet and drawers being nosy or maybe looking for something she misplaced. She opened one drawer too far and it fell out of the chest. As she put it back, she saw an envelope stuck in the back which must have been lying under the drawer. It was addressed to "Aimée" and inside was a photograph and a letter. The letter, dated the day she died, was written on pale green paper in French but she understood it.

"Dear Aimée,

I feel compelled to write this, something inside me is telling me I must write this today, it must be today. I want it to be another romantic love poem but only these words can I write. This is not one of my made-up love stories, I believe all this to be true, so very true. I don't understand but it is easier to write it than to fight it, and I feel a sense of having helped someone—me, or you, I think—to have written it. I don't know if ever, I—or you dear reader—will read this again, or if it will make more sense to you than it does to me.

I remember Samuel's stories about Didier. He told me they both didn't know what they were looking for but were compelled to search for something. Didier said he never found it. Samuel thought that he, Samuel, did and he said it was me, his Mimi. Yes, I think so, but not exactly as he imagined. I think they both unknowingly found what they had been forced to look for—and to do.

Didier was cursed—or would it be better for me to say "sentenced"?—by the craggy faced woman he met as a young salesman in a country village, the black veiled woman who just buried a green eyed, young girl in her wedding dress, the woman who made him sip the absinthe, licked the back of his hand and pressed her green spot there. With that sip of absinthe and touch of green, she mystically passed something indelibly on to him. She sentenced him to a lifelong, unrequited, inexorable and relentless search to find "it". But though he never found it himself, he unknowingly sentenced Samuel to carry on the same search.

He enlisted Samuel, unbeknownst to either of them, to find the "it" which they mistakenly called their other half or missing part, the top half of a glass they could never fill. Didier first thought he was looking for his soul mate, but later realized it was something else since his loves for Camille and others—including Samuel—did not end his urge to keep searching, and so it wasn't just a search for love. Samuel said after a lifetime of looking, he realized he was meant to find me, but didn't know why. The truth as I now know, and strange as it seems, is that they were sentenced to find not just me, but me and Philippe, and to reunite us because we were that young bride and groom who died on their wedding day in that small village so many years ago—to bring together those two soul mates who had been separated by death, two young lovers now lost in time and blindly looking for each other but unable to recognize each other now.

Didier looked but never found them during his own lifetime, so he unwittingly but fatefully passed on his occult mission to Samuel to find them and bring them back together again, here and now, in this time. Alas, I was the unfortunate bride who died and was buried on that day in that village cemetery and the one for whom the old woman mourned and bemoaned her inability—her lack of power—to bring us . . . them, together again. It was to reunite those young lovers who died back then—now embodied in me and Philippe—that she set Didier on his servitude who then impressed Samuel to continue after his death. Neither one ever knew this.

Here I am now, again, about to finally marry my beloved Philippe. I don't understand how this is possible but it feels right to me. Samuel reunited us—my beloved Philippe, my soul mate, and me. I pray Samuel nurture him until we finally marry. Philippe is a good man, one look at his eyes can tell you that. He and I love each other, have always loved each other, and will love each other for all eternity, and when we no longer walk this earth, we will find each other again, if others continue to help us along the way.

We have been blessed that Samuel found us and brought us together again now. I have always felt protected, guided, and even when alone, I never thought I was really alone, but rather watched over by others. While there are things we cannot know, I know this to be true.

January 31, 1995

Aimée."

Perhaps Samuel had a sense of this because before he died he changed his Last Will and Testament. He left half of whatever had not already been transferred to René, to Adrianna, his

Aimée—his Mimi—roughly equivalent to what would have been Didier's share.

Aimée keeps in her sketch pad, along with some of Mimi's sketches, the photograph she found. She looks at it as she touches her freckle and wonders. Were the demons she saw, and the ones René heard, actually fragments of their past come to help them find each other? Can she really be both Mimi and the young woman who died long ago? And René was Philippe and the other young man who died on his wedding day? Did Death get even with René back then for René's fight with Death now, as Brenda would believe? So many connections, so many similarities. Why were we chosen? Who decides? What was the "gift to see" Mama Lou saw in her and is that what her father was afraid of? So many questions which would continue to haunt her.

In the photograph, Mimi stands barefoot in a field around a tablecloth laid over some hay on the ground, donning a pink headband and a green dress. An old cart pulled by a mule is behind her. She is eating a mint chocolate chip ice cream cone and rubbing her birthmark on the side of her neck. Next to her is Philippe, a small tattoo on the side of his neck eating a green apple and looking strikingly like René, especially his eyes. He is petting a puppy nuzzled against Philippe's legs wearing a chain collar. There is a barely discernible logo of a P interlocked with an A on the shiny stainless steel dog tag. Both look straight ahead at the camera with Mona Lisa smiles _____

ABOUT THE AUTHOR

T. F. Feldman lives on the Upper West Side of Manhattan in New York City as well as in Columbia County in upstate New York and in the south of France.